Classics of Modern Science Fiction

THE CLASSIC
PHILIP JOSÉ FARMER
1952–1964

Volume 4

Books by Philip José Farmer,
published from 1952—1964:

The Green Odyssey, 1957
Flesh, 1960
A *Woman A Day,* 1960 (revised 1968 as *The Day of Timestop;*
revised again as *Timestop!,* 1974)
The Lovers, 1961 (revised 1979)
Cache from Outer Space, 1962
Inside Outside, 1964
Tongues of the Moon, 1964

Classics of Modern Science Fiction

THE CLASSIC
PHILIP JOSÉ FARMER
1952–1964

Volume 4

**Edited and Introduction by
Martin H. Greenberg
Foreword by Isaac Asimov**

Series Editor: George Zebrowski

CROWN PUBLISHERS, INC.
NEW YORK

Contents

Retrieving the Lost
by Isaac Asimov

The history of contemporary science fiction begins with the spring of 1926, when the first magazine ever to be devoted entirely to science fiction made its appearance. For a quarter-century thereafter science fiction continued to appear in magazines—and only in magazines.

They were wonderful days for those of us who lived through them, but there was a flaw. Magazines are, by their very nature, ephemeral. They are on the newsstands a month or two and are gone. A very few readers may save their issues, but they are fragile and do not stand much handling.

Beginning in 1950, science fiction in book form began to make its appearance, and some of the books retrieved the magazine short stories and serials in the form of collections, anthologies and novels. As time went on, however, it became clear that the vast majority of science-fiction books were in paperback form, and these, too, were ephemeral. Their stay on the newsstands is not entirely calendar-bound, and they can withstand a bit more handling than periodicals can—but paperbacks tend to be, like magazines, throwaway items.

That leaves the hardback book, which finds its way into public libraries as well as private homes, and which is durable. Even there, we have deficiencies. The relatively few science-fiction books which appear in hardback usually appear in small printings and few, if any, reprintings. Out-of-print is the usual fate, and often a not very long delayed one, at that.

Some science-fiction books have endured, remaining available in hardcover form for years, even decades, and appearing in repeated paperback reincarnations. We all know which these are because, by enduring, they have come to be read by millions, including you and me.

It is, of course, easy to argue that the test of time and popularity has succeeded in separating the gold from the dross, and that we have with us all the science-fiction books that have deserved to endure.

That, however, is too easy a dismissal. It is an interesting and convenient theory, but the world of human affairs is far too complex to fit into theories, especially convenient ones. It sometimes takes time to recognize quality, and the time required is sometimes longer than the visible existence of a particular book. That the quality of a book is not recognizable at once need not be a sign of deficiency, but rather a sign of subtlety. It is not being particularly paradoxical to point out that a book may be, in some cases, too good to be immediately popular. And then, thanks to the mechanics of literary ephemerality, realization of the fact may come too late.

Or must it?

Suppose there are dedicated and thoughtful writers and scholars like George Zebrowski and Martin H. Greenberg, who have been reading science fiction intensively, and with educated taste, for decades. And suppose there is a publisher such as Crown Publishers, Inc. which is interested in providing a second chance for quality science fiction which was undervalued the first time round.

In that case we end up with Crown's *Classics of Modern Science Fiction* in which the lost is retrieved, the unjustly forgotten is remembered, and the undervalued is resurrected. And you are holding a sample in your hand.

Naturally, the revival of these classics will benefit the publisher, the editors, and the writers, but that is almost by the way. The real beneficiaries will be the readers, among whom the older are likely to taste again delicacies they had all but forgotten, while the younger will encounter delights of whose existence they were unaware.

Read—

And enjoy.

Introduction
by Martin H. Greenberg

un/con/ven/tion/al. Not adhering to convention
con/ven/tion. General usage or custom

Philip José Farmer certainly did not and does not adhere to the thematic and stylistic conventions of science fiction; in fact, he was personally responsible for changing several of the most important and long-lasting conventions in the field. Science fiction had ignored one of the most important of all human concerns—sexuality—partly because pulp science fiction's audience was considered to be adolescent boys (a strange reason on the face of it), and partly because the men who controlled the field didn't think the readership wanted strong doses of it mixed in with the adventure and the technology.

Farmer proved them wrong with his first published work, "The Lovers," which appeared in the August 1952 issue of *Startling Stories.* It's gripping depiction of love and sex between a man and an alien insectlike creature had a tremendous impact on the field, broadening what was "acceptable" and opening up the market for others to explore. Largely because of this single story, he was voted a Hugo Award for 1953 as New Writer of 1952." It was the first of what to date constitutes a body of work totaling more than forty novels and collections, characterized by originality, inventiveness, and a use of symbolism that has yet to be equalled.

Philip José Farmer was born in Terre Haute, Indiana, in 1918 but was raised in Peoria, Illinois, where he spent the bulk of his life. He enrolled at Bradley University in 1941 but had to drop out due to lack of funds. He later returned to school as an evening student, earning a degree in 1950; he also worked in a steel mill for many years. Farmer began to write in the mid-1940s, and "The Lovers" was published when he was thirty-four, an advanced age by the standards of the science-fiction community. However, he quickly made up for lost time by an astounding prolificity, although he did not write for considerable portions of time during the first decade of his career.

His major literary themes and obsessions were clear from early on and have been noted by all who have written on him—a concern with sexuality and reproduction in all its variety; the good and evil that he seems to believe resides in all of us; an interest in religious beliefs and imagery, especially with matriarchal religions; parasitology, frequently coupled with sexuality; and a deep love of American popular culture and the books he read and adored as a child and as a young man, especially Burroughs, Baum, and Twain but also including the characters and magazines of the pulp era. Indeed, he has reworked these stories and characters in his own writing to the extent that he has produced a whole body of work about parallel universes, parallel places, and parallel people, books where Samuel Clemens, Tarzan, Odysseus, and Doc Savage all interact, and most are even related to one another.

His writing is characterized by rapid pacing, some weakness of plot, a wonderful use of puns, protagonists who are deeply flawed—a quality especially true in his "heroic" figures—and a deep cynicism that pervades even his humorous work.

But most of all, Farmer (like the late Philip K. Dick) writes of the real, the unreal, and the maybe real, combining and integrating them into the same story in ways that have revolutionized one corner of modern science fiction. Few writers have been as daring so early as Farmer, few so willing to shock, in his case usually to good effect. One of his most important critics, Mary T. Brizzi, has commented that "He is certainly among the brightest stars in the science fiction sky," and that "His early works were beautifully crafted, exploring unconventional themes in a sensitive way." His work has also been called "nauseating," "filthy," and "obscene." John W. Campbell, Jr., said that one of his stories (which he didn't buy) made him "want to throw up." He notes that other, more admiring critics have noted the powerful influence of Freud and Jung in his work, but he rejects these references saying that "The term Farmerian should be good enough." Indeed it is.

This volume collects what I consider to be representative selections of his best work from the years 1952 to 1964, years that saw the publication of several important longer works and collections, including *The Green Odyssey* (1957), *Flesh* (1960, revised 1968; a novel which gives new meaning to the term *father-figure*), *A Woman A Day* (1960, also revised 1968), *The Lovers* (expanded and published in 1961 and revised again in 1979), *Cache from Outer Space* (1962), *Inside Outside* (1964, a major work), and *Tongues of the Moon* (1964).

Outstanding examples of his best work since 1964 will be included in a future volume in this series. For now, we offer you such stunning stories as "Sail On! Sail On!," based on a recurring dream Farmer had in which he says "I saw the tiny galleon of the Portuguese Prince Henry the Navigator (A.D. 1394-1460). It was sailing along in a heavy sea and on a dark night. A small building was on the poopdeck; in it sat a very fat monk. He had earphones on and was tapping out a coded message, in Latin, on a spark-gap transmitter. . . ."

"Mother" contains many of the themes and obsessions mentioned earlier, including some of the underground passages that are partially responsible for his reputation as a Freudian, and the family relationships that were so important in all his early work. The story later became the centerpiece of his collection *Strange Relations* (1960).

"My Sister's Brother" (originally published as "Open to Me, My Sister") is especially important to Farmer, and he considers it one of his two favorites—the other is "Riders of the Purple Wage," included in the following volume in this series. Like "The Lovers," this story had a difficult time finding a publisher, being rejected by the major magazines because of its sexual content. Robert P. Mills took it for *The Magazine of Fantasy and Science Fiction* after having rejected it when first submitted to him—times had changed, and Farmer had changed them, a rare example of a writer developing a market for his own work. Farmer says that this powerful story is "a hardcore science-fiction tale. But it is also about an Earthman's hangups, extraterrestrial ecosystems, sexobiological structures, and religion."

The remarkable "The Alley Man" is one of the best prehistoric-man-in-modern-times stories ever written. It finished a close second to Daniel Keyes' "Flowers for Algernon" in the voting for the Hugo Award in 1960. One of the many amazing features of Farmer's career is the incredible number of series he has sustained—his ideas are simply too big for even very large novels.

"The King of Beasts" is a gem of a short-short, while "The God Business" is one of those stories that is much better read than discussed.

If you have not encountered Farmer or these stories before you are in for a treat. In the words of Leslie Fiedler, "Thanks for the feast."

Sail On! Sail On!
1952

F RIAR SPARKS SAT wedged between the wall and the realizer. He was motionless except for his forefinger and his eyes. From time to time his finger tapped rapidly on the key upon the desk, and now and then his irises, gray-blue as his native Irish sky, swiveled to look through the open door of the *toldilla* in which he crouched, the little shanty on the poop deck. Visibility was low.

Outside was dusk and a lantern by the railing. Two sailors leaned on it. Beyond them bobbed the bright lights and dark shapes of the *Niña* and the *Pinta*. And beyond them was the smooth horizon-brow of the Atlantic, edged in black and blood by the red dome of the rising moon.

The single carbon filament bulb above the monk's tonsure showed a face lost in fat—and in concentration.

The luminiferous ether crackled and hissed tonight, but the phones clamped over his ears carried, along with them, the steady dots and dashes sent by the operator at the Las Palmas station on the Grand Canary.

"*Zzisss!* So you are out of sherry already. . . . *Pop!* . . . Too bad . . . *Crackle* . . . you hardened old winebutt . . . *Zzz* . . . May God have mercy on your sins. . . .

"Lots of gossip, news, et cetera. . . . *Hisses!* . . . Bend your ear instead of your neck, impious one. . . . The turks are said to be gathering . . . *crackle* . . . an army to march on Austria. It is rumored that the flying sausages, said by so many to have been seen over the capitals of the Christian world, are of Turkish origin. The rumor goes they have been invented by a renegade Rogerian who was converted to the Muslim religion. . . . I say . . . *zziss* . . . to that. No one of us would do that. It is a falsity spread by our enemies in the Church to discredit us. But many people believe that. . . .

"How close does the Admiral calculate he is to Cipangu now?

"Flash! Savonarola today denounced the Pope, the wealthy of Florence, Greek art and literature, and the experiments of the disciples of Saint Roger Bacon. . . . *Zzz!* . . . The man is sincere but misguided and dangerous. . . . I predict he'll end up at the stake he's always prescribing for us. . . .

"*Pop.* . . . This will kill you. . . . Two Irish mercenaries by the name of Pat and Mike were walking down the street of Granada when a beautiful Saracen lady leaned out of a balcony and emptied a pot of . . . *hiss!* . . . and Pat looked up and . . . *Crackle.* . . . Good, hah? Brother Juan told that last night. . . .

"PV . . . PV . . . Are you coming in? . . . PV . . . PV . . . Yes, I know it's dangerous to bandy such jests about, but nobody is monitoring us tonight. . . . *Zzz.* . . . I think they're not, anyway. . . ."

And so the ether bent and warped with their messages. And presently Friar Sparks tapped out the PV that ended their talk—the "*Pax vobiscum.*" Then he pulled the plug out that connected his earphones to the set and, lifting them from his ears, clamped them down forward over his temples in the regulation manner.

After sidling bent-kneed from the *toldilla*, punishing his belly against the desk's hard edge as he did so, he walked over to the railing. De Salcedo and de Torres were leaning there and talking in low tones. The big bulb above gleamed on the page's red-gold hair and on the interpreter's full black beard. It also bounced pinkishly off the priest's smooth-shaven jowls and the light scarlet robe of the Rogerian order. His cowl, thrown back, served as a bag for scratch paper, pens, an ink bottle, tiny wrenches and screwdrivers, a book of cryptography, a slide rule, and a manual of angelic principles.

"Well, old rind," said young de Salcedo familiarly, "what do you hear from Las Palmas?"

"Nothing now. Too much interference from that." He pointed to the moon riding the horizon ahead of them. "What an orb!" bellowed the priest. "It's as big and red as my revered nose!"

The two sailors laughed, and de Salcedo said, "But it will get smaller and paler as the night grows, Father. And your proboscis will, on the contrary, become larger and more sparkling in inverse proportion according to the square of the ascent—"

He stopped and grinned, for the monk had suddenly dipped his nose, like a porpoise diving into the sea, raised it again, like the same animal jumping from a wave, and then once more plunged it into the heavy currents of their breath. Nose to nose, he faced them, his twinkling little eyes seeming to emit sparks like the realizer in his *toldilla*.

Again, porpoiselike, he sniffed and snuffed several times, quite loudly. Then satisfied with what he had gleaned from their breaths, he winked at them. He did not, however, mention his findings at once, preferring to sidle toward the subject.

He said, "This Father Sparks on the Grand Canary is so entertaining. He stimulates me with all sorts of philosophical notions, both valid and fantastic. For instance, tonight, just before we were cut off by that"—he gestured at the huge bloodshot eye in the sky—"he was discussing what he called worlds of parallel time tracks, an idea originated by Dysphagius of Gotham. It's his idea there may be other worlds in coincident but not contacting universes, that God, being infinite and of unlimited creative talent and ability, the Master Alchemist, in other words, has possibly—perhaps necessarily—created a plurality of continua in which every probable event has happened."

"Huh?" grunted de Salcedo.

"Exactly. Thus, Columbus was turned down by Queen Isabella, so this attempt to reach the Indies across the Atlantic was never made. So we could not now be standing here plunging ever deeper into Oceanus in our three cockle-shells, there would be no booster buoys strung out between us and the Canaries, and Father Sparks at Las Palmas and I on the *Santa Maria* would not be carrying on our fascinating conversations across the ether.

"Or, say, Roger Bacon was persecuted by the Church, instead of being encouraged and giving rise to the order whose inventions have done so much to insure the monopoly of the Church on alchemy and its divinely inspired guidance of that formerly pagan and hellish practice."

De Torres opened his mouth, but the priest silenced him with a magnificient and imperious gesture and continued.

"Or, even more ridiculous, but thought-provoking, he speculated just this evening on universes with different physical laws. One, in particular, I thought very droll. As you probably don't know, Angelo Angelei has proved, by dropping objects from the Leaning Tower of Pisa, that different weights fall at different speeds. My delightful colleague on the Grand Canary is writing a satire which takes place in a universe where Aristotle is made out to be a liar, where all things drop with equal velocities, no matter what their size. Silly stuff, but it helps to pass the time. We keep the ether busy with our little angels."

De Salcedo said, "Uh, I don't want to seem too curious about the secrets of your holy and cryptic order, Friar Sparks. But these little angels your machine realizes intrigue me. Is it a sin to presume to ask about them?"

The monk's bull roar slid to a dove cooing. "Whether it's a sin or not depends. Let me illustrate, young fellows. If you were concealing a bottle of, say, very scarce sherry on you, and you did not offer to share it with a very thirsty old gentleman, that would be a sin. A sin of omission. But if you were to give that desert-dry, that pilgrim-weary, that devout, humble, and decrepit old soul a long, soothing, refreshing, and stimulating draught of lifegiving fluid, daughter of the vine, I would find it in my heart to pray for you for that deed of loving-kindness, of encompassing charity. And it would please me so much I might tell you a little of our realizer.

Not enough to hurt you, just enough so you might gain more respect for the intelligence and glory of my order."

De Salcedo grinned conspiratorially and passed the monk the bottle he'd hidden under his jacket. As the friar tilted it, and the chug-chug-chug of vanishing sherry became louder, the two sailors glanced meaningfully at each other. No wonder the priest, reputed to be so brilliant in his branch of the alchemical mysteries, had yet been sent off on this halfbaked voyage to devil-knew-where. The Church had calculated that if he survived, well and good. If he didn't, then he would sin no more.

The monk wiped his lips on his sleeve, belched loudly as a horse, and said, "*Gracias*, boys. From my heart, so deeply buried in this fat, I thank you. An old Irishman, dry as a camel's hoof, choking to death with the dust of abstinence, thanks you. You have saved my life."

"Thank rather that magic nose of yours," replied de Salcedo. "Now, old rind, now that you're well greased again, would you mind explaining as much as you are allowed about that machine of yours?"

Friar Sparks took fifteen minutes. At the end of that time, his listeners asked a few permitted questions.

". . . and you say you broadcast on a frequency of eighteen hundred k.c.?" the page asked. "What does 'k.c.' mean?"

"K stands for the French *kilo*, from a Greek word meaning thousand. And c stands for the Hebrew *cherubim*, the 'little angels.' Angel comes from the Greek *angelos*, meaning messenger. It is our concept that the ether is crammed with these cherubim, these little messengers. Thus, when we Friar Sparkses depress the key of our machine, we are able to realize some of the infinity of 'messengers' waiting for just such a demand for service.

"So, eighteen hundred k.c. means that in a given unit of time one million, eight hundred thousand cherubim line up and hurl themselves across the ether, the nose of one being brushed by the feathertips of the cherub's wings ahead. The height of the wing crests of each little creature is even, so that if you were to draw an outline of the whole train, there would be nothing to distinguish one cherub from the next, the whole column forming that grade of little angels known as C.W."

"C.W.?"

"Continuous wingheight. My machine is a C.W. realizer."

Young de Salcedo said, "My mind reels. Such a concept! Such a revelation! It almost passes comprehension. Imagine, the aerial of your realizer is cut just so long, so that the evil cherubim surging back and forth on it demand a predetermined and equal number of good angels to combat them. And this seduction coil on the realizer crowds 'bad' angels into the left-hand, the sinister, side. And when the bad little cherubim are crowded so closely and numerously that they can't bear each other's evil company, they jump the spark gap and speed around the wire to the 'good' plate. And in this racing back and forth they call themselves to the attention of the 'little messengers,' the yea-saying cherubim. And you, Friar Sparks, by manipulating your machine thus and so, and by lifting and lowering your key, you bring these invisible and friendly lines of carriers, your etheric and winged postmen, into reality. And you are able, thus, to communicate at great distances with your brothers of the order."

"Great God!" said de Torres.

It was not a vain oath but a pious exclamation of wonder. His eyes bulged; it was evident that he suddenly saw that man was not alone, that on every side, piled on top of each other, flanked on every angle, stood a host. Black and white, they presented a solid chessboard of the seemingly empty cosmos, black for the nay-sayers, white for the yea-sayers, maintained by a Hand in delicate balance and subject as the fowls of the air and the fish of the sea to exploitation by man.

Yet de Torres, having seen such a vision as has made a saint of many a man, could only ask, "Perhaps you could tell me how many angels may stand on the point of a pin?"

Obviously, de Torres would never wear a halo. He was destined, if he lived, to cover his bony head with the mortar-board of a university teacher.

De Salcedo snorted. "I'll tell you. Philosophically speaking, you may put as many angels on a pinhead as you want to. Actually speaking, you may put only as many as there is room for. Enough of that. I'm interested in facts, not fancies. Tell me, how could the moon's rising interrupt your reception of the cherubim sent by the Sparks at Las Palmas?"

"Great Caesar, how would I know? Am I a repository of universal knowledge? No, not I! A humble and ignorant friar, I! All I can tell you is that last night it rose like a bloody tumor on the horizon, and that when it was up I had to quit marshaling my little messengers in their short and long columns. The Canary station was quite overpowered, so that both of us gave up. And the same thing happened tonight."

"The moon sends messages?" asked de Torres.

"Not in a code I can decipher. But it sends, yes."

"Santa Maria!"

"Perhaps," suggested de Salcedo, "there are people on that moon, and they are sending."

Friar Sparks blew derision through his nose. Enormous as were his nostrils, his derision was not smallbore. Artillery of contempt laid down a barrage that would have silenced any but the strongest of souls.

"Maybe"—de Torres spoke in a low tone— "maybe, if the stars are windows in heaven, as I've heard said, the angels of the higher hierarchy, the big ones, are realizing—uh—the smaller? And they only do it when the moon is up so we may know it is a celestial phenomenon?"

He crossed himself and looked around the vessel.

"You need not fear," said the monk gently. "There is no Inquisitor leaning over your shoulder. Remember, I am the only priest on this expedition. Moreover, your conjecture has nothing to do with dogma. However, that's unimportant. Here's what I don't understand: how can a heavenly body broadcast? Why does it have the same frequency as the one I'm restricted to? Why—"

"I could explain," interrupted de Salcedo with all the brashness and impatience of youth. "I could say that the Admiral and the Rogerians are wrong about the earth's shape. I could say the earth is not round but is flat. I could say the horizon exists, not because we live upon a globe, but because the earth is curved only a little ways, like a greatly flattened-out hemisphere. I could also say that the cherubim are coming, not from Luna, but from a ship such as ours, a vessel which is hanging in the void off the edge of the earth."

"What?" gasped the other two.

"Haven't you heard," said de Salcedo, "that the King of Portugal secretly sent out a ship after he turned down Columbus' proposal? How do we know he did not, that the messages are from our predecessor, that he sailed off the world's rim and is now suspended in the air and becomes exposed at night because it follows the moon around Terra—is, in fact, a much smaller and unseen satellite?"

The monk's laughter woke many men on the ship. "I'll have to tell the Las Palmas operator your tale. He can put it in that novel of his. Next you'll be telling me those messages are from one of those fire-shooting sausages so many credulous laymen have been seeing flying around. No, my dear de Salcedo, let's not be ridiculous. Even the ancient Greeks knew the earth was round. Every university in Europe teaches that. And we Rogerians have measured the circumference. We know for sure that the Indies lie just across the Atlantic. Just as we know for sure, through mathematics, that heavier-than-air machines are impossible. Our Friar Ripskulls, our mind doctors, have assured us these flying creations are mass hallucinations or else the tricks of heretics or Turks who want to panic the populace.

"That moon radio is no delusion, I'll grant you. What it is, I don't know. But it's not a Spanish or Portuguese ship. What about its different code? Even if it came from Lisbon, that ship would still have a Rogerian operator. And he would, according to our policy, be of a different nationality from the crew so he might the easier stay out of political embroilments. He wouldn't break our laws by using a different code in order to communicate with Lisbon. We disciples of Saint Roger do not stoop to petty boundary intrigues. Moreover, that realizer would not be powerful enough to reach Europe, and must, therefore, be directed at us."

"How can you be sure?" said de Salcedo. "Distressing though the thought may be to you, a priest could be subverted. Or a layman could learn your secrets and invent a code. I think that a Portuguese ship is sending to another, a ship perhaps not too distant from us."

De Torres shivered and crossed himself again. "Perhaps the angels are warning us of approaching death? Perhaps?"

"Perhaps? Then why don't they use our code? Angels would know it as well as I. No, there is no perhaps. The order does not permit perhaps. It experiments and finds out; nor does it pass judgment until it knows."

"I doubt we'll ever know," said de Salcedo gloomily. "Columbus has promised the crew that if we come across no sign of land by evening tomorrow, we shall turn back. Otherwise"—he drew a finger across his throat— "*kkk!* Another day, and we'll be pointed east and getting away from that evil and bloody-looking moon and its incomprehensible messages."

"It would be a great loss to the order and to the Church," sighed the friar. "But I leave such things in the hands of God and inspect only what He hands me to look at."

With which pious statement Friar Sparks lifted the bottle to ascertain the liquid level. Having determined in a scientific manner its existence, he next measured its quantity and tested its quality by putting all of it in that best of all chemistry tubes, his enormous belly.

Afterward, smacking his lips and ignoring the pained and disappointed looks on the faces of the sailors, he went on to speak enthusiastically of the water screw and the engine which turned it, both of which had been built recently at the St. Jonas College at Genoa. If Isabella's three ships had been equipped with those, he declared, they would not have to depend upon the wind. However, so far, the fathers had forbidden its extended use because it was feared the engine's fumes might poison the air and the terrible speeds it made possible might be fatal to the human body. After which he plunged into a tedious description of the life of his patron saint, the inventor of the first cherubim realizer and receiver, Jonas of Carcassonne, who had been martyred when he grabbed a wire he thought was insulated.

The two sailors found excuses to walk off. The monk was a good fellow, but hagiography bored them. Besides, they wanted to talk of women. . . .

If Columbus had not succeeded in persuading his crews to sail one more day, events would have been different.

At dawn the sailors were very much cheered by the sight of several large birds circling their ships. Land could not be far off; perhaps these winged creatures came from the coast of fabled Cipangu itself, the country whose houses were roofed with gold.

The birds swooped down. Closer, they were enormous and very strange. Their bodies were flattish and almost saucer-shaped and small in proportion to the wings, which had a spread of at least thirty feet. Nor did they have legs. Only a few sailors saw the significance of that fact. These birds dwelt in the air and never rested upon land or sea.

While they were meditating upon that, they heard a slight sound as of a man clearing his throat. So gentle and far off was the noise that nobody paid any attention to it, for each thought his neighbor had made it.

A few minutes later, the sound had become louder and deeper, like a lute string being twanged.

Everybody looked up. Heads were turned west.

Even yet they did not understand that the noise like a finger plucking a wire came from the line that held the earth together, and that the line was stretched to its utmost, and that the violent finger of the sea was what had plucked the line.

It was some time before they understood. They had run out of horizon.

When they saw that, they were too late.

The dawn had not only come up *like* thunder, it *was* thunder. And though the three ships heeled over at once and tried to sail close-hauled on the port tack, the suddenly speeded-up and relentless current made beating hopeless.

Then it was the Rogerian wished for the Genoese screw and

the wood-burning engine that would have made them able to resist the terrible muscles of the charging and bull-like sea. Then it was that some men prayed, some raved, some tried to attack the Admiral, some jumped overboard, and some sank into a stupor.

Only the fearless Columbus and the courageous Friar Sparks stuck to their duties. All that day the fat monk crouched wedged in his little shanty, dot-dashing to his fellow on the Grand Canary. He ceased only when the moon rose like a huge red bubble from the throat of a dying giant. Then he listened intently all night and worked desperately, scribbling and swearing impiously and checking cipher books.

When the dawn came up again in a roar and a rush, he ran from the *toldilla*, a piece of paper clutched in his hand. His eyes were wild, and his lips were moving fast, but nobody could understand that he had cracked the code. They could not hear him shouting, "It is the Portuguese! It is the Portuguese!"

Their ears were too overwhelmed to hear a mere human voice. The throat clearing and the twanging of a string had been the noises preliminary to the concert itself. Now came the mighty overture; as compelling as the blast of Gabriel's horn was the topple of Oceanus into space.

1

"LOOK, MOTHER. THE clock is running backwards."

Eddie Fetts pointed to the hands on the pilot room dial.

Dr. Paula Fetts said, "The crash must have reversed it."

"How could it do that?"

"I can't tell you. I don't know everything, son."

"Oh!"

"Well, don't look at me so disappointedly. I'm a pathologist, not an electronician."

"Don't be so cross, mother. I can't stand it. Not now."

He walked out of the pilot room. Anxiously, she followed him. The burial of the crew and her fellow scientists had been very trying for him. Spilled blood had always made him dizzy and sick; he could scarcely control his hands enough to help her sack the scattered bones and entrails.

He had wanted to put the corpses in the nuclear furnace, but she had forbidden that. The Geigers amidships were ticking loudly, warning that there was invisible death in the stern.

The meteor that struck the moment the ship came out of Translation into normal space had probably wrecked the engine-room. So she had understood from the incoherent highpitched phrases of a colleague before he fled to the pilot room. She had hurried to find Eddie. She feared his cabin door would still be

12

locked, as he had been making a tape of the aria "Heavy Hangs the Albatross" from Gianelli's *Ancient Mariner.*

Fortunately, the emergency system had automatically thrown out the locking circuits. Entering, she had called out his name in fear he'd been hurt. He was lying half-unconscious on the floor, but it was not the accident that had thrown him there. The reason lay in the corner, released from his lax hand; a quart free-fall thermos, rubber-nippled. From Eddie's open mouth charged a breath of rye that not even Nodor pills had been able to conceal.

Sharply she had commanded him to get up and onto the bed. Her voice, the first he had ever heard, pierced through the phalanx of Old Red Star. He struggled up, and she, though smaller, had thrown every ounce of her weight into getting him up and onto the bed.

There she had lain down with him and strapped them both in. She understood that the lifeboat had been wrecked also, and that it was up to the captain to bring the yacht down safely to the surface of this charted but unexplored planet, Baudelaire. Everybody else had gone to sit behind the captain, strapped in crashchairs, unable to help except with their silent backing.

Moral support had not been enough. The ship had come in on a shallow slant. Too fast. The wounded motors had not been able to hold her up. The prow had taken the brunt of the punishment. So had those seated in the nose.

Dr. Fetts had held her son's head on her bosom and prayed out loud to her God. Eddie had snored and muttered. Then there was a sound like the clashing of the gates of doom—a tremendous bong as if the ship were a clapper in a gargantuan bell tolling the most frightening message human ears may hear—a blinding blast of light—and darkness and silence.

A few moments later Eddie began crying out in a childish voice, "Don't leave me to die, mother! Come back! Come back!"

Mother was unconscious by his side, but he did not know that. He wept for a while, then he lapsed back into his rye-fogged stupor—if he had ever been out of it—and slept. Again, darkness and silence.

❖   ❖   ❖

It was the second day since the crash, if "day" could describe that twilight state on Baudelaire. Dr. Fetts followed her son wherever he went. She knew he was very sensitive and easily upset. All his life she had known it and had tried to get between him and anything that would cause trouble. She had succeeded, she thought, fairly well until three months ago when Eddie had eloped.

The girl was Polina Fameux, the ash-blonde long-legged actress whose tridi image, taped, had been shipped to frontier stars where a small acting talent meant little and a large and shapely bosom much. Since Eddie was a well-known Metro tenor, the marriage made a big splash whose ripples ran around the civilized Galaxy.

Dr. Fetts had felt very bad about the elopement, but she had, she hoped, hidden her grief very well beneath a smiling mask. She didn't regret having to give him up; after all, he was a full-grown man, no longer her little boy. But, really, aside from the seasons at the Met and his tours, he had not been parted from her since he was eight.

That was when she went on a honeymoon with her second husband. And then she and Eddie had not been separated long, for Eddie had gotten very sick, and she'd had to hurry back and take care of him, as he had insisted she was the only one who could make him well.

Moreover, you couldn't count his days at the opera as a total loss, for he vised her every noon and they had a long talk—no matter how high the vise bills ran.

The ripples caused by her son's marriage were scarcely a week old before they were followed by even bigger ones. They bore the news of the separation of Eddie and his wife. A fortnight later, Polina applied for divorce on grounds of incompatibility. Eddie was handed the papers in his mother's apartment. He had come back to her the day he and Polina had agreed they "couldn't make a go of it," or, as he phrased it to his mother, "couldn't get together."

Dr. Fetts was, of course, very curious about the reason for their parting, but, as she explained to her friends, she "respected" his silence. What she didn't say was that she had told herself the time would come when he would tell her all.

Eddie's "nervous breakdown" started shortly afterward. He had been very irritable, moody, and depressed, but he got worse the day a so-called friend told Eddie that whenever Polina heard his name mentioned, she laughed loud and long. The friend added that Polina had promised to tell someday the true story of their brief merger.

That night his mother had to call in a doctor.

In the days that followed, she thought of giving up her position as research pathologist at De Kruif and taking all her time to help him "get back on his feet." It was a sign of the struggle going on in her mind that she had not been able to decide within a week's time. Ordinarily given to swift consideration and resolution of a problem, she could not agree to surrender her beloved quest into tissue regeneration.

Just as she was on the verge of doing what was for her the incredible and the shameful, tossing a coin, she had been vised by her superior. He told her she had been chosen to go with a group of biologists on a research cruise to ten preselected planetary systems.

Joyfully, she had thrown away the papers that would turn Eddie over to a sanatorium. And, since he was quite famous, she had used her influence to get the government to allow him to go along. Ostensibly, he was to make a survey of the development of opera on planets colonized by Terrans. That the yacht was not visiting any colonized globes seemed to have been missed by the bureaus concerned. But it was not the first time in the history of a government that its left hand knew not what its right was doing.

Actually, he was to be "rebuilt" by his mother, who thought herself much more capable of curing him than any of the prevalent A, F, J, R, S, K, or H therapies. True, some of her friends reported amazing results with some of the symbol-chasing techniques. On the other hand, two of her close companions had tried them all and had gotten no benefits from any of them. She was his mother; she could do more for him than any of those "alphabatties"; he was flesh of her flesh, blood of her blood. Besides, he wasn't so sick. He just got awfully blue sometimes and made theatrical but insincere threats of suicide or else just sat and stared into space. But she could handle him.

2

So now it was that she followed him from the backward-running clock to his room. And saw him step inside, look for a second, and then turn to her with a twisted face.

"Neddie is ruined, mother. Absolutely ruined."

She glanced at the piano. It had torn loose from the wallracks at the moment of impact and smashed itself against the opposite wall. To Eddie it wasn't just a piano; it was Neddie. He had a pet name for everything he contacted for more than a brief time. It was as if he hopped from one appellation to the next, like an ancient sailor who felt lost unless he was close to the familiar and designated points of the shoreline. Otherwise, Eddie seemed to be drifting helplessly in a chaotic ocean, one that was anonymous and amorphous.

Or, analogy more typical of him, he was like the nightclubber who feels submerged, drowning, unless he hops from table to table, going from one well-known group of faces to the next, avoiding the featureless and unnamed dummies at the strangers' tables.

He did not cry over Neddie. She wished he would. He had been so apathetic during the voyage. Nothing, not even the unparalleled splendor of the naked stars nor the inexpressible alienness of strange planets had seemed to lift him very long. If he would only weep or laugh loudly or display some sign that he was reacting violently to what was happening. She would even have welcomed his striking her in anger or calling her "bad" names.

But no, not even during the gathering of the mangled corpses, when he looked for a while as if he were going to vomit, would he give way to his body's demand for expression. She understood that if he were to throw up, he would be much better for it, would have gotten rid of much of the psychic disturbance along with the physical.

He would not. He had kept on raking flesh and bones into the large plastic bags and kept a fixed look of resentment and sullenness.

She hoped now that the loss of his piano would bring tears and shaking shoulders. Then she could take him in her arms and give him sympathy. He would be her little boy again, afraid of the dark, afraid of the dog killed by a car, seeking her arms for the sure safety, the sure love.

"Never mind, baby," she said. "When we're rescued, we'll get you a new one."

"When—!"

He lifted his eyebrows and sat down on the bed's edge.

"What do we do now?"

She became very brisk and efficient.

"The ultrad automatically started working the moment the meteor struck. If it's survived the crash, it's still sending SOS's. If not, then there's nothing we can do about it. Neither of us knows how to repair it.

"However, it's possible that in the last five years since this planet was located, other expeditions may have landed here. Not from Earth but from some of the colonies. Or from nonhuman globes. Who knows? It's worth taking a chance. Let's see."

A single glance was enough to wreck their hopes. The ultrad had been twisted and broken until it was no longer recognizable as the machine that sent swifter-than-light waves through the no-ether.

Dr. Fetts said with false cheeriness, "Well, that's that! So what? It makes things too easy. Let's go into the storeroom and see what we can see."

Eddie shrugged and followed her. There she insisted that each take a panrad. If they had to separate for any reason, they could always communicate and also, using the DF's—the built-in direction finders—locate each other. Having used them before, they knew the instruments' capabilities and how essential they were on scouting or camping trips.

The panrads were lightweight cylinders about two feet high and eight inches in diameter. Crampacked, they held the mechanisms of two dozen different utilities. Their batteries lasted a year without recharging, they were practically indestructible and worked under almost any conditions.

Keeping away from the side of the ship that had the huge hole in it, they took the panrads outside. The long wave bands were searched by Eddie while his mother moved the dial that ranged up and down the shortwaves. Neither really expected to hear anything, but to search was better than doing nothing.

Finding the modulated wave-frequencies empty of any significant noises, he switched to the continuous waves. He was startled by a dot-dashing.

"Hey, mom! Something in the 1000 kilocycles! Unmodulated!"

"Naturally, son," she said with some exasperation in the midst of her elation. "What would you expect from a radio-telegraphic signal?"

She found the band on her own cylinder. He looked blankly at her. "I know nothing about radio, but that's not Morse."

"What? You must be mistaken!"

"I—I don't think so."

"Is it or isn't it? Good god, son, can't you be certain of *anything*!"

She turned the amplifier up. As both of them had learned Galacto-Morse through sleeplearn techniques, she checked him at once.

"You're right. What do you make of it?"

His quick ear sorted out the pulses.

"No simple dot and dash. Four different time-lengths."

He listened some more.

"They've got a certain rhythm, all right. I can make out definite groupings. Ah! That's the sixth time I've caught that particular one. And there's another. And another."

Dr. Fetts shook her ash-blonde head. She could make out nothing but a series of zzt-zzt-zzt's.

Eddie glanced at the DF needle.

"Coming from NE by E. Should we try to locate?"

"Naturally," she replied. "But we'd better eat first. We don't know how far away it is, or what we'll find there. While I fix a hot meal, you get your field trip stuff ready."

"O.K.," he said with more enthusiasm than he had shown for a long time.

When he came back he ate everything in the large dish his mother had prepared on the unwrecked galley stove.

"You always did make the best stew," he said.

"Thank you. I'm glad you're eating again, son. I am surprised. I thought you'd be sick about all this."

He waved vaguely but energetically.

"The challenge of the unknown. I have a sort of feeling this is going to turn out much better than we thought. Much better."

She came close and sniffed his breath. It was clean, innocent even of stew. That meant he'd taken Nodor, which probably meant he'd been sampling some hidden rye. Otherwise, how explain his reckless disregard of the possible dangers? It wasn't like him.

She said nothing, for she knew that if he tried to hide a bottle in his clothes or field sack while they were tracking down the radio signals, she would soon find it. And take it away. He wouldn't even protest, merely let her lift it from his limp hand while his lips swelled with resentment.

3

They set out. Both wore knapsacks and carried the panrads. He carried a gun over his shoulder, and she had snapped onto her sack her small black bag of medical and lab supplies.

High noon of late autumn was topped by a weak red sun that barely managed to make itself seen through the eternal double layer of clouds. Its companion, an even smaller blob of lilac, was setting on the northwestern horizon. They walked in a sort of bright twilight, the best that Baudelaire ever achieved. Yet, despite the lack of light, the air was warm. It was a phenomenon common to certain planets behind the Horsehead Nebula, one being investigated but as yet unexplained.

The country was hilly, with many deep ravines. Here and there were prominences high enough and steep-sided enough to be called embryo mountains. Considering the roughness of the land, however, there was a surprising amount of vegetation. Pale green, red, and yellow bushes, vines, and little trees clung to every bit of ground, horizontal or vertical. All had comparatively broad leaves that turned with the sun to catch the light.

From time to time, as the two Terrans strode noisily through the forest, small multicolored insect-like and mammal-like creatures scuttled from hiding place to hiding place. Eddie decided to carry his gun in the crook of his arm. Then, after they were forced to scramble up and down ravines and hills and fight their way through thickets that became unexpectedly tangled, he put it back over his shoulder, where it hung from a strap.

Despite their exertions, they did not tire quickly. They weighed about twenty pounds less than they would have on Earth and, though the air was thinner, it was richer in oxygen.

Dr. Fetts kept up with Eddie. Thirty years the senior of the twenty-three-year-old, she passed even at close inspection for his older sister. Longevity pills took care of that. However, he treated her with all the courtesy and chivalry that one gave one's mother and helped her up the steep inclines, even though the climbs did not appreciably cause her deep chest to demand more air.

They paused once by a creek bank to get their bearings.

"The signals have stopped," he said.

"Obviously," she replied.

At that moment the radar-detector built into the panrad began to ping. Both of them automatically looked upward.

"There's no ship in the air."

"It can't be coming from either of those hills," she pointed out. "There's nothing but a boulder on top of each one. Tremendous rocks."

"Nevertheless, it's coming from there, I think. Oh! Oh! Did

you see what I saw? Looked like a tall stalk of some kind being pulled down behind that big rock."

She peered through the dim light. "I think you were imagining things, son. I saw nothing."

Then, even as the pinging kept up, the zzting started again. But after a burst of noise, both stopped.

"Let's go up and see what we shall see," she said.

"Something screwy," he commented. She did not answer.

They forded the creek and began the ascent. Halfway up, they stopped to sniff in puzzlement at a gust of some heavy odor coming downwind.

"Smells like a cageful of monkeys," he said.

"In heat," she added. If his was the keener ear, hers was the sharper nose.

They went on up. The RD began sounding its tiny hysterical gonging. Nonplussed, Eddie stopped. The DF indicated the radar pulses were not coming from the top of the hill they were climbing, as formerly, but from the other hill across the valley. Abruptly, the panrad fell silent.

"What do we do now?"

"Finish what we started. This hill. Then we go to the other one."

He shrugged and then hastened after her tall slim body in its long-legged coveralls. She was hot on the scent, literally, and nothing could stop her. Just before she reached the bungalow-sized boulder topping the hill, he caught up with her. She had stopped to gaze intently at the DF needle, which swung wildly before it stopped at neutral. The monkey-cage odor was very strong.

"Do you suppose it could be some sort of radio-generating mineral?" she asked, disappointedly.

"No. Those groupings were semantic. And that smell. . . ."

"Then what—?"

He didn't know whether to feel pleased or not that she had so obviously and suddenly thrust the burden of responsibility and action on him. Both pride and a curious shrinking affected him.

But he did feel exhilarated. Almost, he thought, he felt as if he were on the verge of discovering what he had been looking for for a long time. What the object of his search had been, he could not say. But he was excited and not very much afraid.

He unslung his weapon, a two-barreled combination shotgun and rifle. The panrad was still quiet.

"Maybe the boulder is camouflage for a spy outfit," he said. He sounded silly, even to himself.

Behind him, his mother gasped and screamed. He whirled and raised his gun, but there was nothing to shoot. She was pointing at the hilltop across the valley, shaking, and saying something incoherent.

He could make out a long slim antenna seemingly projecting from the monstrous boulder crouched there. At the same time, two thoughts struggled for first place in his mind: one, that it was more than a coincidence that both hills had almost identical stone structures on their brows, and, two, that the antenna must have been recently stuck out, for he was sure he had not seen it the last time he looked.

He never got to tell her his conclusions, for something thin and flexible and irresistible seized him from behind. Lifted into the air, he was borne backwards. He dropped the gun and tried to grab the bands or tentacles around him and tear them off with his bare hands. No use.

He caught one last glimpse of his mother running off down the hillside. Then a curtain snapped down, and he was in total darkness.

4

Eddie sensed himself, still suspended, twirled around. He could not know for sure, of course, but he thought he was facing in exactly the opposite direction. Simultaneously, the tentacles binding his legs and arms were released. Only his waist was still gripped. It was pressed so tightly that he cried out with pain.

Then, boot-toes bumping on some resilient substance, he was carried forward. Halted, facing he knew not what horrible monster, he was suddenly assailed—not by a sharp beak or tooth or knife or some other cutting or mangling instrument—but by a dense cloud of that same monkey perfume.

In other circumstances, he might have vomited. Now his stomach was not given the time to consider whether it should clean house or not. The tentacle lifted him higher and thrust him against something soft and yielding—something fleshlike and womanly—almost breastlike in texture and smoothness and warmth and in its hint of gentle curving.

He put his hands and feet out to brace himself, for he thought for a moment he was going to sink in and be covered up—enfolded—ingested. The idea of a gargantuan amoeba-thing hiding within a hollow rock—or a rocklike shell—made him writhe and yell and shove at the protoplasmic substance.

But nothing of the kind happened. He was not plunged into a smothering and slimy jelly that would strip him of his skin and then his flesh and then dissolve his bones. He was merely shoved repeatedly against the soft swelling. Each time, he pushed or kicked or struck at it. After a dozen of these seemingly purposeless acts, he was held away, as if whatever was doing it was puzzled by his behavior.

He had quit screaming. The only sounds were his harsh breathing and the zzzts and pings from the panrad. Even as he became aware of them, the zzzts changed tempo and settled into a recognizable pattern of bursts—three units that crackled out again and again.

"Who are you? Who are you?"

Of course, it could just as easily have been, "What are you?" or "What the hell!" or "Nov smoz ka pop?"

Or nothing—semantically speaking.

But he didn't think the latter. And when he was gently lowered to the floor, and the tentacle went off to only-God-knew-where in the dark, he was sure that the creature was communicating—or trying to—with him.

It was this thought that kept him from screaming and running around in the lightless and fetid chamber, brainlessly seeking an outlet. He mastered his panic and snapped open a little shutter in the panrad's side and thrust in his right-hand index finger. There he poised it above the key and in a moment, when the thing paused in transmitting, he sent back, as best he could, the pulses he had received. It was not necessary for him to turn on the light and spin the dial that would put him on the 1000 kc. band. The instrument would automatically key that frequency in with the one he had just received.

The oddest part of the whole procedure was that his whole body was trembling almost uncontrollably—one part excepted. That was his index finger, his one unit that seemed to him to have a definite function in this otherwise meaningless situation. It was the section of him that was helping him to survive—the only part that knew how—at that moment. Even his brain seemed to have no connection with his finger. That digit was himself, and the rest just happened to be linked to it.

When he paused, the transmitter began again. This time the units were unrecognizable. There was a certain rhythm to them, but he could not know what they meant. Meanwhile, the RD was pinging. Something somewhere in the dark hole had a beam held tightly on him.

He pressed a button on the panrad's top, and the built-in flashlight illuminated the area just in front of him. He saw a wall of reddish-gray rubbery substance. On the wall was a roughly circular, light gray swelling about four feet in diameter. Around it, giving it a Medusa appearance, were coiled twelve very long, very thin tentacles.

Though he was afraid that if he turned his back to them the tentacles would seize him once more, his curiosity forced him to wheel about and examine his surroundings with the bright beam. He was in an egg-shaped chamber about thirty feet long, twelve wide, and eight to ten high in the middle. It was formed of a reddish-gray material, smooth except for irregular intervals of blue or red pipes. Veins and arteries?

A door-sized portion of the wall had a vertical slit running down it. Tentacles fringed it. He guessed it was a sort of iris and that it had opened to drag him inside. Starfish-shaped groupings of tentacles were scattered on the walls or hung from the ceiling. On the wall opposite the iris was a long and flexible stalk with a cartilaginous ruff around its free end. When Eddie moved, it moved, its blind point following him as a radar antenna tracks the thing it is locating. That was what it was. And unless he was wrong, the stalk was also a C.W. transmitter-receiver.

He shot the light around. When it reached the end farthest from him, he gasped. Ten creatures were huddled together facing him! About the size of half-grown pigs, they looked like nothing so much as unshelled snails; they were eyeless, and the stalk growing from the forehead of each was a tiny duplicate of that on the wall. They didn't look dangerous. Their open mouths were little and toothless, and their rate of locomotion must be slow, for they moved like snails, on a large pedestal of flesh—a foot-muscle.

Nevertheless, if he were to fall asleep they could overcome him by force of numbers, and those mouths might drip an acid to digest him, or they might carry a concealed poisonous sting.

His speculations were interrupted violently. He was seized, lifted, and passed on to another group of tentacles. He was carried beyond the antenna-stalk and toward the snail-beings. Just before he reached them, he was halted, facing the wall. An iris, hitherto invisible, opened. His light shone into it, but he could see nothing but convolutions of flesh.

His panrad gave off a new pattern of dit-dot-deet-dats. The iris widened until it was large enough to admit his body, if he were shoved in head first. Or feet first. It didn't matter. The convolutions straightened out and became a tunnel. Or a throat. From thousands of little pits emerged thousands of tiny, razor sharp teeth. They flashed out and sank back in, and before they had disappeared thousands of other wicked little spears darted out and past the receding fangs.

Meat-grinder.

Beyond the murderous array, at the end of the throat, was a huge pouch of water. Steam came from it, and with it an odor like that of his mother's stew. Dark bits, presumably meat, and pieces of vegetables floated on the seething surface.

Then the iris closed, and he was turned around to face the slugs. Gently, but unmistakably, a tentacle spanked his buttocks. And the panrad zzzted a warning.

Eddie was not stupid. He knew now that the ten creatures were not dangerous unless he molested them. In which case he had just seen where he would go if he did not behave.

Again he was lifted and carried along the wall until he was shoved against the light gray spot. The monkey-cage odor, which had died out, became strong again. Eddie identified its source with a very small hole which appeared in the wall.

When he did not respond—he had no idea yet how he was supposed to act—the tentacles dropped him so unexpectedly that he fell on his back. Unhurt by the yielding flesh, he rose.

What was the next step? Exploration of his resources. Itemization: The panrad. A sleeping-bag, which he wouldn't need as long as the present too-warm temperature kept up. A bottle of Old Red Star capsules. A free-fall thermos with attached nipple. A box of A-2-Z rations. A Foldstove. Cartridges for his double-barrel, now lying outside the creature's boulderish shell. A roll of toilet paper. Toothbrush. Paste. Soap. Towel. Pills: Nodor, hormone, vitamin, longevity, reflex, and sleeping. And a thread-thin wire, a hundred feet long when uncoiled, that held prisoner in its molecular structure a hundred symphonies, eighty operas, a thousand different types of musical pieces, and two thousand great books ranging from Sophocles and Dostoyevsky to the latest bestseller. It could be played inside the panrad.

He inserted it, pushed a button, and spoke, "Eddie Fetts's recording of Puccini's *Che gelida manina*, please."

And while he listened approvingly to his own magnificent voice, he zipped open a can he had found in the bottom of the sack. His mother had put into it the stew left over from their last meal in the ship.

Not knowing what was happening, yet for some reason sure he was for the present safe, he munched meat and vegetables with a contented jaw. Transition from abhorrence to appetite sometimes came easily for Eddie.

He cleaned out the can and finished with some crackers and a chocolate bar. Rationing was out. As long as the food lasted, he would eat well. Then, if nothing turned up, he would . . . But then, he reassured himself as he licked his fingers, his mother, who was free, would find some way to get him out of his trouble.

She always had.

5

The panrad, silent for a while, began signaling. Eddie spotlighted the antenna and saw it was pointing at the snail-beings, which he had, in accordance with his custom, dubbed familiarly. Sluggos he called them.

The Sluggos crept toward the wall and stopped close to it. Their mouths, placed on the tops of their heads, gaped like so many hungry young birds. The iris opened, and two lips formed into a spout. Out of it streamed steaming-hot water and chunks of meat and vegetables. Stew! Stew that fell exactly into each waiting mouth.

That was how Eddie learned the second phrase of Mother Polyphema's language. The first message had been, "What are you?" This was, "Come and get it!"

He experimented. He tapped out a repetition of what he'd last heard. As one, the Sluggos—except the one then being fed—turned to him and crept a few feet before halting, puzzled.

Inasmuch as Eddie was broadcasting, the Sluggos must have had some sort of built-in DF. Otherwise they wouldn't have been able to distinguish between his pulses and their Mother's.

Immediately after, a tentacle smote Eddie across the shoulders and knocked him down. The panrad zzzted its third intelligible message: "Don't ever do that!"

And then a fourth, to which the ten young obeyed by wheeling and resuming their former positions.

"This way, children."

Yes, they were the offspring, living, eating, sleeping, playing, and learning to communicate in the womb of their mother—the Mother. They were the mobile brood of this vast immobile entity that had scooped up Eddie as a frog scoops up a fly. This Mother. She who had once been just such a Sluggo until she had grown hog-size and had been pushed out of her Mother's womb. And who, rolled into a tight ball, had free-wheeled down her natal hill, straightened out at the bottom, inched her way up the next hill, rolled down, and so on. Until she found the empty shell of an adult who had died. Or, if she wanted to be a first class citizen in her society and not a prestigeless *occupée*, she found the bare top of a tall hill—or any eminence that commanded a big sweep of territory—and there squatted.

And there she put out many thread-thin tendrils into the soil and into the cracks in the rocks, tendrils that drew sustenance from the fat of her body and grew and extended downwards and ramified into other tendrils. Deep underground the rootlets worked their instinctive chemistry; searched for and found the water, the calcium, the iron, the copper, the nitrogen, the carbons, fondled earthworms and grubs and larvae, teasing them for the secrets of their fats and proteins; broke down the wanted substance into shadowy colloidal particles; sucked them up the thready pipes of the tendrils and back to the pale and slimming body crouching on a flat space atop a ridge, a hill, a peak.

There, using the blueprints stored in the molecules of the cerebellum, her body took the building blocks of elements and fashioned them into a very thin shell of the most available material, a shield large enough so she could expand to fit it while her natural enemies—the keen and hungry predators that prowled twilighted Baudelaire—nosed and clawed it in vain.

Then, her evergrowing bulk cramped, she would resorb the hard covering. And if no sharp tooth found her during that process of a few days, she would cast another and a larger. And so on through a dozen or more.

Until she had become the monstrous and much reformed body of an adult and virgin female. Outside would be the stuff that so much resembled a boulder, that was, actually, rock: either granite, diorite, marble, basalt, or maybe just plain limestone. Or sometimes iron, glass, or cellulose.

Within was the centrally located brain, probably as large as a man's. Surrounding it, the tons of organs: the nervous system, the mighty heart, or hearts, the four stomachs, the microwave and longwave generators, the kidneys, bowels, tracheae, scent and taste organs, the perfume factory which made odors to attract animals and birds close enough to be seized, and the huge womb. And the antennae—the small one inside for teaching and scanning the young, and a long and powerful stalk on the outside, projecting from the shelltop, retractable if danger came.

The next step was from virgin to Mother, lowercase to uppercase as designated in her pulse-language by a longer pause before a word. Not until she was deflowered could she take a high place in her society. Immodest, unblushing, she herself made the advances, the proposals, and the surrender.

After which, she ate her mate.

The clock in the panrad told Eddie he was in his thirtieth day of imprisonment when he found out that little bit of information. He was shocked, not because it offended his ethics, but because he himself had been intended to be the mate. And the dinner.

His finger tapped, "Tell me, Mother, what you mean."

He had not wondered before how a species that lacked males could reproduce. Now he found that, to the Mothers, all creatures except themselves were male. Mothers were immobile and female. Mobiles were male. Eddie had been mobile. He was, therefore, a male.

He had approached this particular Mother during the mating season, that is, midway through raising a litter of young. She had scanned him as he came along the creekbanks at the valley bottom. When he was at the foot of the hill, she had detected his odor. It was new to her. The closest she could come to it in her memory-banks was that of a beast similar to him. From her description, he guessed it to be an ape. So she had released from her repertoire its rut stench. When he seemingly fell into the trap, she had caught him.

He was supposed to attack the conception-spot, that light gray swelling on the wall. After he had ripped and torn it enough to begin the mysterious workings of pregnancy, he would have been popped into her stomach-iris.

Fortunately, he had lacked the sharp beak, the fang, the claw. And she had received her own signals back from the panrad.

Eddie did not understand why it was necessary to use a mobile for mating. A Mother was intelligent enough to pick up a sharp stone and mangle the spot herself.

He was given to understand that conception would not start unless it was accompanied by a certain titillation of the nerves—a frenzy and its satisfaction. Why this emotional state was needed, Mother did not know.

Eddie tried to explain about such things as genes and chromosomes and why they had to be present in highly-developed species.

Mother did not understand.

Eddie wondered if the number of slashes and rips in the spot corresponded to the number of young. Or if there were a large number of potentialities in the heredity-ribbons spread out under the conception-skin. And if the haphazard irritation and consequent stimulation of the genes paralleled the chance combining of genes in human male-female mating. Thus resulting in offspring with traits that were combinations of their parents.

Or did the inevitable devouring of the mobile after the act indicate more than an emotional and nutritional reflex? Did it hint that the mobile caught up scattered gene-nodes, like hard seeds, along with the torn skin, in its claws and tusks, that these genes survived the boiling in the stew-stomach, and were later passed out in the feces? Where animals and birds picked them up in beak, tooth, or foot, and then, seized by other Mothers in this oblique rape, transmitted the heredity-carrying agents to the conception-spots while attacking them, the nodules being scraped off and implanted in the skin and blood of the swelling even as others were harvested? Later, the mobiles were eaten, digested, and ejected in the obscure but ingenious and never-ending cycle? Thus ensuring the continual, if haphazard, recombining of genes, chances for variations in offspring, opportunities for mutations, and so on?

Mother pulsed that she was nonplussed.

Eddie gave up. He'd never know. After all, did it matter?

He decided not, and rose from his prone position to request water. She pursed up her iris and spouted a tepid quartful into his thermos. He dropped in a pill, swished it around till it dissolved, and drank a reasonable facsimile of Old Red Star. He preferred the harsh and powerful rye, though he could have afforded the smoothest. Quick results were what he wanted. Taste didn't matter, as he disliked all liquor tastes. Thus he drank what the Skid Row bums drank and shuddered even as they did, renaming it Old Rotten Tar and cursing the fate that had brought them so low they had to gag such stuff down.

The rye glowed in his belly and spread quickly through his limbs and up to his head, chilled only by the increasing scarcity of the capsules. When he ran out—then what? It was at times like this that he most missed his mother.

Thinking about her brought a few large tears. He snuffled and drank some more and when the biggest of the Sluggos nudged him for a back-scratching, he gave it instead a shot of Old Red Star. A slug for Sluggo. Idly, he wondered what effect a taste for rye would have on the future of the race when these virgins became Mothers.

At that moment he was shaken by what seemed a life-saving idea. These creatures could suck up the required elements from the earth and with them duplicate quite complex molecular structures. Provided, of course, they had a sample of the desired substance to brood over in some cryptic organ.

Well, what easier to do than give her one of the cherished capsules? One could become any number. Those, plus the abundance of water pumped up through hollow underground tendrils from the nearby creek, would give enough to make a master-distiller green!

He smacked his lips and was about to key her his request when what she was transmitting penetrated his mind.

Rather cattily, she remarked that her neighbor across the valley was putting on airs because she, too, held prisoner a communicating mobile.

6

The Mothers had a society as hierarchical as table-protocol in Washington or peck-order in a barnyard. Prestige was what counted, and prestige was determined by the broadcasting power, the height of the eminence on which the Mother sat, which governed the extent of her radar-territory, and the abundance and novelty and wittiness of her gossip. The creature that had snapped Eddie up was a queen. She had precedence over thirty-odd of her kind; they all had to let her broadcast first, and none dared start pulsing until she quit. Then, the next in order began, and so on down the line. Any of them could be interrupted at any time by Number One, and if any of the lower echelon had something interesting to transmit, she could break in on the one then speaking and get permission from the queen to tell her tale.

Eddie knew this, but he could not listen in directly to the hilltop-gabble. The thick pseudo-granite shell barred him from that and made him dependent upon her womb-stalk for relayed information.

Now and then Mother opened the door and allowed her young to crawl out. There they practiced beaming and broadcasting at the Sluggos of the Mother across the valley. Occasionally that Mother deigned herself to pulse the young, and Eddie's keeper reciprocated to her offspring.

Turnabout.

The first time children had inched through the exit-iris, Eddie had tried, Ulysses-like, to pass himself off as one of them and crawl out in the midst of the flock. Eyeless, but no Polyphemus, Mother had picked him out with her tentacles and hauled him back in.

It was following that incident that he had named her Polyphema.

He knew she had increased her own already powerful prestige tremendously by possession of that unique thing—a transmitting mobile. So much had her importance grown that the Mothers on the fringes of her area passed on the news to others. Before he had learned her language, the entire continent was hooked-up. Polyphema had become a veritable gossip columnist; tens of thousands of hillcrouchers listened in eagerly to her accounts of her dealings with the walking paradox: a semantic male.

That had been fine. Then, very recently, the Mother across the valley had captured a similar creature. And in one bound she had become Number Two in the area and would, at the slightest weakness on Polyphema's part, wrest the top position away.

Eddie became wildly excited at the news. He had often daydreamed about his mother and wondered what she was doing. Curiously enough, he ended many of his fantasies with lip-mutterings, reproaching her almost audibly for having left him and for making no try to rescue him. When he became aware of his attitude, he was ashamed. Nevertheless, the sense of desertion colored his thoughts.

Now that he knew she was alive and had been caught, probably while trying to get him out, he rose from the lethargy that had lately been making him doze the clock around. He asked Polyphema if she would open the entrance so he could talk directly with the other captive. She said yes. Eager to listen in on a conversation between two mobiles, she was very co-operative. There would be a mountain of gossip in what they would have to say. The only thing that dented her joy was that the other Mother would also have access.

Then, remembering she was still Number One and would

broadcast the details first, she trembled so with pride and ecstasy that Eddie felt the floor shaking.

Iris open, he walked through it and looked across the valley. The hillsides were still green, red, and yellow, as the plants on Baudelaire did not lose their leaves during winter. But a few white patches showed that winter had begun. Eddie shivered from the bite of cold air on his naked skin. Long ago he had taken off his clothes. The womb-warmth had made garments too uncomfortable; moreover, Eddie, being human, had had to get rid of waste products. And Polyphema, being a Mother, had had periodically to flush out the dirt with warm water from one of her stomachs. Every time the tracheae-vents exploded streams that swept the undesirable elements out through her door-iris, Eddie had become soaked. When he abandoned dress, his clothes had gone floating out. Only by sitting on his pack did he keep it from a like fate.

Afterward, he and the Sluggos had been dried off by warm air pumped through the same vents and originating from the mighty battery of lungs. Eddie was comfortable enough—he'd always liked showers—but the loss of his garments had been one more thing that kept him from escaping. He would soon freeze to death outside unless he found the yacht quickly. And he wasn't sure he remembered the path back.

So now, when he stepped outside, he retreated a pace or two and let the warm air from Polyphema flow like a cloak from his shoulders.

Then he peered across the half-mile that separated him from his mother, but he could not see her. The twilight state and the dark of the unlit interior of her captor hid her.

He tapped in Morse, "Switch to the talkie, same frequency." Paula Fetts did so. She began asking him frantically if he were all right.

He replied he was fine.

"Have you missed me terribly, son?"

"Oh, very much."

Even as he said this he wondered vaguely why his voice

sounded so hollow. Despair at never again being able to see her, probably.

"I've almost gone crazy, Eddie. When you were caught I ran away as fast as I could. I had no idea what horrible monster it was that was attacking us. And then, halfway down the hill, I fell and broke my leg. . . ."

"Oh, no, mother!"

"Yes. But I managed to crawl back to the ship. And there, after I'd set it myself, I gave myself B.K. shots. Only, my system didn't react like it's supposed to. There are people that way, you know, and the healing took twice as long.

"But when I was able to walk, I got a gun and a box of dynamite. I was going to blow up what I thought was a kind of rock-fortress, an outpost for some kind of extee. I'd no idea of the true nature of these beasts. First, though, I decided to reconnoiter. I was going to spy on the boulder from across the valley. But I was trapped by this thing.

"Listen, son. Before I'm cut off, let me tell you not to give up hope. I'll be out of here before long and over to rescue you."

"How?"

"If you remember, my lab kit holds a number of carcinogens for field work. Well, you know that sometimes a Mother's conception-spot when it is torn up during mating, instead of begetting young, goes into cancer—the opposite of pregnancy. I've injected a carcinogen into the spot and a beautiful carcinoma has developed. She'll be dead in a few days."

"Mom! You'll be buried in that rotting mass!"

"No. This creature has told me that when one of her species dies, a reflex opens the labia. That's to permit their young—if any—to escape. Listen, I'll—"

A tentacle coiled about him and pulled him back through the iris, which shut.

When he switched back to C.W., he heard, "Why didn't you communicate? What were you doing? Tell me! Tell me!"

Eddie told her. There was a silence that could only be interpreted as astonishment. After Mother had recovered her wits, she said, "From now on, you will talk to the other male through me."

Obviously, she envied and hated his ability to change wavebands, and, perhaps, had a struggle to accept the idea.

"Please," he persisted, not knowing how dangerous were the waters he was wading in, "please let me talk to my mother di—"

For the first time, he heard her stutter.

"Wha-wha-what? Your Mo-Mo-Mother?"

"Yes. Of course."

The floor heaved violently beneath his feet. He cried out and braced himself to keep from falling and then flashed on the light. The walls were pulsating like shaken jelly, and the vascular columns had turned from red and blue to gray. The entrance-iris sagged open, like a lax mouth, and the air cooled. He could feel the drop in temperature in her flesh with the soles of his feet.

It was some time before he caught on.

Polyphema was in a state of shock.

What might have happened had she stayed in it, he never knew. She might have died and thus forced him out into the winter before his mother could escape. If so, and he couldn't find the ship, he would die. Huddled in the warmest corner of the egg-shaped chamber, Eddie contemplated that idea and shivered to a degree for which the outside air couldn't account.

7

However, Polyphema had her own method of recovery. It consisted of spewing out the contents of her stew-stomach, which had doubtless become filled with the poisons draining out of her system from the blow. Her ejection of the stuff was the physical manifestation of the psychical catharsis. So furious was the flood that her foster son was almost swept out in the hot tide, but she, reacting instinctively, had coiled tentacles about him and the Sluggos. Then she followed the first upchucking by emptying her other three water-pouches, the second hot and the third lukewarm and the fourth, just filled, cold.

Eddie yelped as the icy water doused him.

Polyphema's irises closed again. The floor and walls gradually quit quaking; the temperature rose; and her veins and arteries regained their red and blue. She was well again. Or so she seemed.

But when, after waiting twenty-four hours, he cautiously approached the subject, he found she not only would not talk about it, she refused to acknowledge the existence of the other mobile.

Eddie, giving up hope of conversation, thought for quite a while. The only conclusion he could come to, and he was sure he'd grasped enough of her psychology to make it valid, was that the concept of a mobile female was utterly unacceptable.

Her world was split into two: mobile and her kind, the immobile. Mobile meant food and mating. Mobile meant—male. The Mothers were—female.

How the mobiles reproduced had probably never entered the hillcrouchers' minds. Their science and philosophy were on the instinctive body-level. Whether they had some notion of spontaneous generation or amoebalike fission being responsible for the continued population of mobiles, or they'd just taken for granted they "growed," like Topsy, Eddie never found out. To them, they were female and the rest of the protoplasmic cosmos was male.

That was that. Any other idea was more than foul and obscene and blasphemous. It was—unthinkable.

Polyphema had received a deep trauma from his words. And though she seemed to have recovered, somewhere in those tons of unimaginably complicated flesh a bruise was buried. Like a hidden flower, dark purple, it bloomed, and the shadow it cast was one that cut off a certain memory, a certain tract, from the light of consciousness. That bruise-stained shadow covered that time and event which the Mothers, for reasons unfathomable to the human being, found necessary to mark KEEP OFF.

Thus, though Eddie did not word it, he understood in the cells of his body, he felt and knew, as if his bones were prophesying and his brain did not hear, what came to pass.

Sixty-six hours later by the panrad clock, Polyphema's entrance-lips opened. Her tentacles darted out. They came back in, carrying his helpless and struggling mother.

Eddie, roused out of a doze, horrified, paralyzed, saw her toss her lab kit at him and heard an inarticulate cry from her. And saw her plunged, headforemost, into the stomach-iris.

Polyphema had taken the one sure way of burying the evidence.

Eddie lay face down, nose mashed against the warm and faintly throbbing flesh of the floor. Now and then his hands clutched spasmodically as if he were reaching for something that soneone kept putting just within his reach and then moving away.

How long he was there he didn't know, for he never again looked at the clock.

Finally, in the darkness, he sat up and giggled inanely, "Mother always did make good stew."

That set him off. He leaned back on his hands and threw his head back and howled like a wolf under a full moon.

Polyphema, of course, was dead-deaf, but she could radar his posture, and her keen nostrils deduced from his body-scent that he was in terrible fear and anguish.

A tentacle glided out and gently enfolded him.

"What is the matter?" zzted the panrad.

He stuck his finger in the keyhole.

"I have lost my mother!"

"?"

"She's gone away, and she'll never come back."

"I don't understand. *Here I am.*"

Eddie quit weeping and cocked his head as if he were listening to some inner voice. He snuffled a few times and wiped away the tears, slowly disengaged the tentacle, patted it, walked over to his pack in a corner, and took out the bottle of Old Red Star capsules. One he popped into the thermos; the other he gave to her with the request she duplicate it, if possible. Then he stretched out on his side, propped on one elbow like a Roman in his sensualities, sucked the rye through the nipple, and listened to a medley of Beethoven, Moussorgsky, Verdi, Strauss, Porter, Feinstein, and Waxworth.

So the time—if there were such a thing there—flowed around Eddie. When he was tired of music or plays or books, he listened in on the area hookup. Hungry, he rose and walked—or often just crawled—to the stew-iris. Cans of rations lay in his pack; he had planned to eat those until he was sure that—what was it he was forbidden to eat? Poison? Something had been devoured by Polyphema and the Sluggos. But sometime during the music-rye orgy, he had forgotten. He now ate quite hungrily and with thought for nothing but the satisfaction of his wants.

Sometimes the door-iris opened, and Billy Greengrocer hopped in. Billy looked like a cross between a cricket and a kangaroo. He was the size of a collie, and he bore in a marsupialian pouch vegetables and fruit and nuts. These he extracted with shiny green, chitinous claws and gave to Mother in return for meals of stew. Happy symbiote, he chirruped merrily while his many-faceted eyes, revolving independently of each other, looked one at the Sluggos and the other at Eddie.

Eddie, on impulse, abandoned the 1000 kc. band and roved the frequencies until he found that both Polyphema and Billy were emitting a 108 wave. That, apparently, was their natural signal. When Billy had his groceries to deliver, he broadcast. Polyphema, in turn, when she needed them, sent back to him. There was nothing intelligent on Billy's part; it was just his instinct to transmit. And the Mother was, aside from the "semantic" frequency, limited to that one band. But it worked out fine.

8

Everything was fine. What more could a man want? Free food, unlimited liquor, soft bed, air-conditioning, shower-baths, music, intellectual works (on the tape), interesting conversation (much of it was about him), privacy, and security.

If he had not already named her, he would have called her Mother Gratis.

Nor were creature comforts all. She had given him the answers to all his questions, all. . . .

Except one.

That was never expressed vocally by him. Indeed, he would have been incapable of doing so. He was probably unaware that he had such a question.

But Polyphema voiced it one day when she asked him to do her a favor.

Eddie reacted as if outraged.

"One does not—! One does not—!"

He choked, and then he thought, how ridiculous! She is not—And looked puzzled, and said, "But she is."

He rose and opened the lab kit. While he was looking for a scalpel, he came across the carcinogens. He threw them through the half-opened labia far out and down the hillside.

Then he turned and, scalpel in hand, leaped at the light gray swelling on the wall. And stopped, staring at it, while the instrument fell from his hand. And picked it up and stabbed feebly and did not even scratch the skin. And again let it drop.

"What is it? What is it?" crackled the panrad hanging from his wrist.

Suddenly, a heavy cloud of human odor—mansweat—was puffed in his face from a nearby vent.

"? ? ? ?"

And he stood, bent in a half-crouch, seemingly paralyzed. Until tentacles seized him in fury and dragged him toward the stomach-iris, yawning man-sized.

Eddie screamed and writhed and plunged his finger in the panrad and tapped, "All right! All right!"

And once back before the spot, he lunged with a sudden and wild joy; he slashed savagely; he yelled. "Take that! And that, P . . ." and the rest was lost in a mindless shout.

He did not stop cutting, and he might have gone on and on

until he had quite excised the spot had not Polyphema interfered by dragging him toward her stomach-iris again. For ten seconds he hung there, helpess and sobbing with a mixture of fear and glory.

Polyphema's reflexes had almost overcome her brain. Fortunately, a cold spark of reason lit up a corner of the vast, dark, and hot chapel of her frenzy.

The convolutions leading to the steaming, meat-laden pouch closed and the foldings of flesh rearranged themselves. Eddie was suddenly hosed with warm water from what he called the "sanitation" stomach. The iris closed. He was put down. The scalpel was put back in the bag.

For a long time Mother seemed to be shaken by the thought of what she might had done to Eddie. She did not trust herself to transmit until her nerves were settled. When they were, she did not refer to his narrow escape. Nor did he.

He was happy. He felt as if a spring, tight-coiled against his bowels since he and his wife had parted, was now, for some reason, released. The dull vague pain of loss and discontent, the slight fever and cramp in his entrails, and the apathy that sometimes afflicted him, were gone. He felt fine.

Meanwhile, something akin to deep affection had been lighted, like a tiny candle under the drafty and overtowering roof of a cathedral. Mother's shell housed more than Eddie; it now curved over an emotion new to her kind. This was evident by the next event that filled him with terror.

For the wounds in the spot healed and the swelling increased into a large bag. Then the bag burst and ten mouse-sized Sluggos struck the floor. The impact had the same effect as a doctor spanking a newborn baby's bottom; they drew in their first breath with shock and pain; their uncontrolled and feeble pulses filled the ether with shapeless SOS's.

When Eddie was not talking with Polyphema or listening in or drinking or sleeping or eating or bathing or running off the tape, he played with the Sluggos. He was, in a sense, their father. Indeed, as they grew to hog-size, it was hard for their female parent to distinguish him from her young. As he seldom walked anymore, and was often to be found on hands and knees in their midst, she could not scan him too well. Moreover, something in the heavywet air or in the diet had caused every hair on his body to drop off. He grew very fat. Generally speaking, he was one with the pale, soft, round, and bald offspring. A family likeness.

There was one difference. When the time came for the virgins to be expelled, Eddie crept to one end, whimpering, and stayed there until he was sure Mother was not going to thrust him out into the cold, hard, and hungry world.

That final crisis over, he came back to the center of the floor. The panic in his breast had died out, but his nerves were still quivering. He filled his thermos and then listened for a while to his own tenor singing the "Sea Things" aria from his favorite opera, Gianelli's *Ancient Mariner.* Suddenly, he burst out and accompanied himself, finding himself thrilled as never before by the concluding words.

> And from my neck so free
> The Albatross fell off, and sank
> Like lead into the sea.

Afterwards, voice silent but heart singing, he switched off the wire and cut in on Polyphema's broadcast.

Mother was having trouble. She could not precisely describe to the continent-wide hook-up this new and almost inexpressible emotion she felt about the mobile. It was a concept her language was not prepared for. Nor was she helped any by the gallons of Old Red Star in her bloodstream.

Eddie sucked at the plastic nipple and nodded sympathetically and drowsily at her search for words. Presently, the thermos rolled out of his hand.

He slept on his side, curled in a ball, knees on his chest and arms crossed, neck bent forward. Like the pilot room chronometer whose hands reversed after the crash, the clock of his body was ticking backwards, ticking backwards . . .

In the darkness, in the moistness, safe and warm, well fed, much loved.

The God Business
1954

IT WAS THE first time that the U.S. Marines had ever been routed with water pistols.

The screen flickered. Another scene replaced the first. But the afterimage had burned itself on my mind.

A distorted sun that had no business in a mid-Illinois sky made the scene bright for the long-range cameras. A regiment of Marines, helmeted, wearing full packs, toting rifles with bayonets and automatic weapons, were stumbling backward in full retreat before a horde of naked men and women. The nudists, laughing and capering, were aiming toy cowboy-sixshooters and Captain Orbit rayguns. These sprayed streams of liquid from tiny muzzles, streams that arched over desperately upraised guns and squirted off the faces under the helmets.

Then, the tough veterans were throwing their weapons down and running away. Or else standing foolishly, blinking, running their tongues over wet lips. And the victors were taking the victims by the hand and leading them away behind their own uneven lines.

Why didn't the Marines shoot? Simple. Their cartridges *refused* to explode.

Flamethrowers, burpguns, recoilless cannon? They might as well have been shillelaghs.

The screen went white. Lights flashed on. Major Alice Lewis, WHAM, put down her baton.

"Well, gentlemen, any questions? None? Mr. Temper, perhaps *you'd* like to tell us why you expect to succeed where so many others have failed. Mr. Temper, gentlemen, will give us the *bald* facts."

I rose. My face was flushed; my palms, sticky. I'd have been wiser to laugh at the major's nasty crack about my lack of hair, but a quarter century hadn't killed my self-consciousness over the eggishness of my head. When I was twenty, I came down with a near-fatal fever the doctors couldn't identify. When I rose from bed, I was a shorn lamb, and I'd stayed fleeced. Furthermore, I was allergic to toupées. So it was a trifle embarrassing to get up before an audience just after the beautiful Major Lewis had made a pun at the expense of my shining pate.

I walked to the table where she stood, pert and, dammit, pretty. Not until I got there did I see that the hand holding the stick was shaking. I decided to ignore her belligerent attitude. After all, the two of us were going to be together on our mission, and she couldn't help it any more than I. Moreoever, she had reason to be nervous. These were trying times for everybody, and especially for the military.

I faced a roomful of civilians and officers, all V.I.P. or loud brass. Through the window at the back, I could see a segment of snow-covered Galesburg, Illinois. The declining sun was perfectly normal. People were moving about as if it were customary for fifty thousand soldiers to be camped between them and the valley of the Illinois, where strange creatures roamed through the fantastically luxuriant vegetation.

I paused to fight down the wave of reluctance which invariably inundated me when I had to speak in public. For some reason, my upper plate always went into a tap dance at such crucial moments.

"Ladie-s-s and gentlemen, I s-s-saw S-s-susie on the s-s-seashore yes-s-sterday." You know what I mean. Even if you're describing the plight of the war orphans in Azerbaijan, you watch your listeners smile and cover their lower faces, and you feel like a fool.

I shouldn't have taken so long to summon my nerve, for the major spoke again. Her lip curled. It was a very pretty lip, but I didn't think even a nonpermanent wave improved its appearance at the moment.

"Mr. Temper believes he has the key to our problem. Perhaps he does. I must warn you, however, that his story combines such unrelated and unlikely events as the escape of a bull from the stockyards, the drunken caperings of a college professor who was noted for his dedicated sobriety, to say nothing of the disappearance of said professor of classical literature and two of his students on the same night."

I waited until the laughter died down. When I spoke, I said nothing about two other improbably connected facts. I did not mention the bottle I had purchased in an Irish tavern and shipped to the professor two years before. Nor did I say what I thought one of the camera shots taken by an Army balloon over the city of Onaback meant. This photograph had shown a huge red brick statue of a bull astride the football field of Traybell University.

"Gentlemen," I said, "before I say much about myself, I'll tell you why the Food and Drug Administration is sending a lone agent into an area where, so far, the combined might of the Army, Air Force, Coast Guard, and Marines have failed."

Red faces blossomed like flowers in springtime.

"The F.D.A. necessarily takes a part in the *affaire à l'Onaback*. As you know, the Illinois River, from Chillicothe to Havana, now runs with beer."

Nobody laughed. They'd long ago quit being amused by that. As for me, I loathed any alcoholic drink or drug. With good reason.

"I should modify that. The Illinois has an odor of hops, but those of our volunteers who have drunk from the river where the stuff begins to thin out don't react to it as they would to a regular alcoholic drink. They report a euphoria, plus an almost total lack of inhibition, which lasts even after all alcohol is oxidized from their bloodstream. And the stuff acts like a stimulant, not a depressant. There is no hangover. To add to our mystification, our scientists can't find any unknown substance in the water to analyze.

"However, you all know this, just as you know why the F.D.A. is involved. The main reason I'm being sent in, aside from the fact that I was born and raised in Onaback, is that my superiors, including the President of the United States, have been impressed with my theory about the identity of the man responsible for this whole fantastic mess.

"Besides," I added with a not entirely unmalicious glance at Major Lewis, "they believe that, since I first thought of psychologically conditioning an agent against the lure of the river-water, I should be the agent sent in.

"After this situation had come to the notice of the F.D.A. authorities, I was assigned to the case. Since so many Federal Agents had disappeared in Onabagian territory, I decided to do some checking from the outside. I went to the Congressional Library and began reading the Onaback *Morning Star* and *Evening Journal* backwards, from the day the Library quit receiving copies of them. Not until I came across the January 13 issues of two years ago, did I find anything significant."

I stopped. Now that I had to put my reasonings in spoken words before these hardheaded bigshots, I could weigh their reception. Zero. Nevertheless, I plunged ahead. I did have an ace-in-the-hole. Or, to be more exact, a monkey-in-a-cage.

"Gentlemen, the January 13 issues related, among other things, the disappearance on the previous night of Dr. Boswell Durham of Traybell University, along with two of his students in his survey course on classical literature. The reports were conflicting, but most of them agreed on the following. One, that during the day of the 13th, a male student, Andrew Polivinosel, made some slighting remark about classical literature. Dr. Durham, a man noted for his mildness and forbearance, called Polivinosel an ass. Polivinosel, a huge football player, rose and said he'd toss Durham out of the building by the seat of his pants. Yet, if we are to believe the witnesses, the timid, spindly, and middle-aged Durham took the husky Polivinosel by one hand and literally threw him out of the door and down the hall.

"Whereupon, Peggy Rourke, an extremely comely coed and

Polivinosel's 'steady,' persuaded him not to attack the professor. The athlete, however, didn't seem to need much persuasion. Dazed, he made no protest when Miss Rourke led him away.

"The other students in the class reported that there had been friction between the two and that the athlete bugged Dr. Durham in class. Durham now had an excellent opportunity for getting Polivinosel kicked out of school, even though Polivinosel was Little All-American. The professor didn't, however, report the matter to the Dean of Men. He was heard to mutter that Polivinosel was an ass and that this was a fact anyone could plainly see. One student said he thought he detected liquor on the professor's breath, but believed he must have been mistaken, since it was campus tradition that the good doctor never even touched Cokes. His wife, it seems, had a great deal to do with that. She was an ardent temperance worker, a latter-day disciple of Frances Willard.

"This may seem irrelevant, gentlemen, but I assure you it isn't. Consider two other students' testimony. Both swore they saw the neck of a bottle sticking from the professor's overcoat pocket as it hung in his office. It was uncapped. And, though it was freezing outside, the professor, a man famed for his aversion to cold, had both windows open. Perhaps to dispel the fumes from the bottle.

"After the fight, Peggy Rourke was asked by Dr. Durham to come into his office. An hour later, Miss Rourke burst out with her face red and her eyes full of tears. She told her roommate that the professor had acted like a madman. That he had told her he had loved her since the day she'd walked into his classroom. That he had known he was too old and ugly even to think of eloping with her. But, now that 'things' had changed, he wanted to run away with her. She told him she had always been fond of him, but she was by no stretch of the imagination in love with him. Whereupon, he had promised that by that same evening he would be a changed man, and that she would find him irresistible.

"Despite all this, everything seemed to be smooth that evening when Polivinosel brought Peggy Rourke to the Sophomore Frolic. Durham, a chaperon, greeted them as if nothing had happened. His wife did not seem to sense anything wrong. That in itself was strange, for Mrs. Durham was one of those faculty wives who has one end of the campus grapevine grown permanently into her ear. Moreover, a highly nervous woman, she was not one to conceal her emotions. Nor was she subdued by the doctor. He was the butt of many a joke behind his back because he was so obviously henpecked. Mrs. Durham often made a monkey of him and led him around like a bull with a ring in his nose. Yet that night . . ."

Major Lewis cleared her throat. "Mr. Temper, streamline the details, will you please? These gentlemen are very busy, and they'd like the bald facts. The *bald* facts, mind you."

I continued, "The bare facts are these. Late that night, shortly after the ball broke up, a hysterical Mrs. Durham called the police and said her husband was out of his mind. Never a word that he might be drinking. Such a thing to her was unthinkable. He wouldn't dare . . ."

Major Lewis cleared her throat again. I shot her a look of annoyance. Apparently, she failed to realize that some of the details were necessary.

"One of the policemen who answered her call reported later that the professor was staggering around in the snow, dressed only in his pants with a bottle sticking out of his hip pocket, shooting red paint at everybody with a spray gun. Another officer contradicted him. He said the doctor did all the damage with a bucket of paint and a brush.

"Whatever he used, he covered his own house and some of his neighbors' houses from roof to base. When the police appeared, he plastered their car with the paint and blinded them. While they were trying to clear their eyes, he walked off. A half-hour later, he streaked the girls' dorm with red paint and scared a number of the occupants into hysteria. He entered the building, pushed past the scandalized housemother, raced up and down the halls, threw paint over anybody who showed his head, seemingly from a bottomless can, and then, failing to find Peggy Rourke, disappeared.

"I might add that all this time he was laughing like a madman and announcing loudly to all and sundry that tonight he was painting the town red.

"Miss Rourke had gone with Polivinosel and some of his fraternity brothers and dates to a restaurant. Later, the couple dropped the others off at their homes and then proceeded, theoretically, to the girls' dormitory. Neither got there. Nor were they or the professor seen again during the two years that elapsed between that incident and the time the Onaback papers quit publishing. The popular theory was that the love-crazed professor had killed and buried them and then fled to parts unknown. But I choose, on good evidence, to believe otherwise."

Hurriedly, for I could see they were getting restless, I told them of the bull that had appeared from nowhere at the foot of Main Street. The stockyards later reported that none of their bulls was missing. Nevertheless, too many people saw the bull for the account to be denied. Not only that, they all testified that the last they saw of it, it was swimming across the Illinois River with a naked woman on its back. She was waving a bottle in her hand. It, and the woman, then plunged into the forest on the bluffs and disappeared.

At this there was an uproar. A Coast Guard Commander said "Are you trying to tell me that Zeus and Europa have come to life, Mr. Temper?"

There was no use in continuing. These men didn't believe unless they saw with their own eyes. I decided it was time to let them see.

I waved my hand. My assistants pushed in a large cage on wheels. Within it crouched a very large ape, wearing a little straw hat, a sour expression, and a pair of pink nylon panties. A hole cut in the bottom of the latter allowed her long tail to stick through. Strictly speaking, I suppose, she couldn't be classified as an ape. Apes have no tails.

An anthropologist would have seen at once that this wasn't a monkey, either. It was true that she did have a prognathous muzzle, long hair that covered her whole body, long arms, and a tail. But no monkey ever had such a smooth, high brow, or such a big hooked nose, or legs so long in proportion to her trunk.

When the cage had come to rest beside the platform, I said,

"Gentlemen, if everything I've said seemed irrevelant, I'm sure that the next few minutes will convince you I have not been barking up the wrong tree."

I turned to the cage, caught myself almost making a bow, and said, "Mrs. Durham, will you please tell these gentlemen what happened to you?"

Then I waited, in full expectation of the talk, torrential and disconnected but illuminating, that had overwhelmed me the previous evening after my buddies had captured her on the edge of the area. I was very proud, because I'd made a discovery that would shock and rock these gentlemen from their heads of bone to their heels of leather and show them that one little agent from the F.D.A. had done what the whole armed forces had not. Then they wouldn't snicker and refer to me as Out-of-Temper by Frothing-at-the-Mouth.

I waited . . .

And I waited . . .

And Mrs. Durham refused to say a word. Not one, though I all but got down on my knees and pleaded with her. I tried to explain to her what giant forces were in balance and that she held the fate of the world in the hollow of her pink hairless palm. She would not open her mouth. Somebody had injured her dignity, and she would do nothing but sulk and turn her back on all of us and wave her tail above her pink panties.

She was the most exasperating female I'd ever known. No wonder that her husband made a monkey of her.

Triumph had become fiasco. Nor did it convince the big shots when I played the recording of my last night's conversation with her. They still thought I had less brains than hair, and they showed it when they replied to my request for questions with silence. Major Alice Lewis smiled scornfully.

Well, it made no difference in my mission. I was under orders they hadn't power to countermand.

At 7:30 that evening, I was outside the area with a group of officers and my boss. Though the moon was just coming up, its light was bright enough to read by. About ten yards from us, the whiteness of snow and cold ended, and the green and warmth began.

General Lewis, Major Lewis' father, said, "We'll give you two days to contact Durham, Mr. Temper. Wednesday, 1400, we attack. Marines, equipped with bows and arrows and airguns, and wearing oxygen masks, will be loaded into gliders with pressurized cabins. These will be released from their tow-planes at high altitude. They will land upon U.S. Route 24 just south of the city limits, where there are now two large meadows. They will march up South Adams Street until they come to the downtown district. By then, I hope, you will have located and eliminated the source of this trouble."

For "eliminated," read "assassinated." By his expression, he thought I couldn't do it. General Lewis disliked me, not only because I was a civilian with authority, backed by the President himself, but because the conditions of my assignment with his daughter were unorthodox, to say the least. Alice Lewis was not only a major and a woman—she was a mightily attractive one and young for her rank.

She stood there, shivering, in her bra and panties, while I was stripped down to my own shorts. Once we were safely in the woods, we would take off the rest of our clothes. When in Rome . . .

Marines with bows and arrows and BB guns—no wonder the military was miserable. But, once inside the Area controlled by my former professor and his Brew, firearms simply refused to work. And the Brew *did* work, making addicts of all who tasted it.

All but me.

I was the only one who had thought to have myself conditioned against it.

Dr. Duerf asked me a few questions while someone strapped a three-gallon tank of distilled water to my back. The doctor was the Columbia psychiatrist who had conditioned me against the Brew.

Suddenly, in the midst of a casual remark, he grabbed the back of my head. A glass seemed to appear from nowhere in his fist. He tried to force its contents past my lips. I took just one sniff and knocked the glass from his grip and struck him with the other fist.

He danced back, holding the side of his face. "How do you feel now?" he asked.

"I'm all right," I said, "but I thought for a moment I'd choke. I wanted to kill you for trying to do that to me."

"I had to give you a final test. You passed it with a big A. You're thoroughly conditioned against the Brew."

The two Lewises said nothing. They were irked because I, a civilian, had thought of this method of combating the allure of the Brew. The thousand Marines, scheduled to follow me in two days, would have to wear oxygen masks to save them from temptation. As for my companion, she had been hastily put under hypnosis by Duerf, but he didn't know how successfully. Fortunately, her mission would not take as long as mine. She was supposed to go to the source of the Brew and bring back a sample. If, however, I needed help, I was to call on her. Also, though it was unstated, I was to keep her from succumbing to the Brew.

We shook hands all around, and we walked away. Warm air fell over us like a curtain. One moment, we were shivering; the next, sweating. That was bad. It meant we'd be drinking more water than we had provided ourselves with.

I looked around in the bright moonlight. Two years had changed the Illinois-scape. There were many more trees than there had been, trees of a type you didn't expect to see this far north. Whoever was responsible for the change had had many seeds and sprouts shipped in, in preparation for the warmer climate. I knew, for I had checked in Chicago on various shipments and had found that a man by the name of Smith—Smith!—had, two weeks after Durham's disappearance, begun ordering from tropical countries. The packages had gone to an Onaback house and had ended up in the soil hereabouts. Durham must have realized that this river-valley area couldn't support its customary 300,000 people, once the railroads and trucks quit shipping in cans of food and fresh milk and provisions. The countryside would have been stripped by the hungry hordes.

But when you looked around at the fruit trees, bananas, cherries, apples, pears, oranges, and others, most of them out of season and flourishing in soils thought unfavorable for their growth—when you noted the blackberry, blueberry, gooseberry, and raspberry bushes, the melons and potatoes and tomatoes on the ground—all large enough to have won county-fair first prizes in any pre-Brew age—then you realized there was no lack of food. All you had to do was pick it and eat.

"It looks to me," whispered Alice Lewis, "like the Garden of Eden."

"Stop talking treason, Alice!" I snapped.

She iced me with a look. "Don't be silly. And don't call me Alice. I'm a major in the Marines."

"Pardon," I said. "But we'd better drop the rank. The natives might wonder. What's more, we'd better shed these clothes before we run into somebody."

She wanted to object, but she had her orders. Even though we were to be together at least thirty-six hours, and would be mother-naked all that time, she insisted we go into the bushes to peel. I didn't argue.

I stepped behind a tree and took off my shorts. At the same time, I smelled cigar smoke. I slipped off the webbing holding the tank to my back and walked out onto the narrow trail. I got a hell of a shock.

A monster leaned against a tree, his short legs crossed, a big Havana sticking from the side of his carnivorous mouth, his thumbs tucked in an imaginary vest.

I shouldn't have been frightened. I should have been amused. This creature had stepped right out of a very famous comic strip. He stood seven feet high, had a bright green hide and yellow-brown plates running down his chest and belly. His legs were very short; his trunk, long. His face was half-man, half-alligator. He had two enormous bumps on top of his head and big dish-sized eyes. The same half-kindly, half-stupid, and arrogant look was upon his face. He was complete, even to having four fingers instead of five.

My shock came not only from the unexpectedness of his appearance. There is a big difference between something seen on paper and that seen in the flesh. This thing was cute and humorous and lovable in the strip. Transformed into living color and substance, it was monstrous.

"Don't get scared," said the apparition. "I grow on you after a while."

"Who are you?" I asked.

At that moment, Alice stepped out from behind a tree. She gasped, and she grabbed my arm.

He waved his cigar. "I'm the Allegory on the Banks of the Illinois. Welcome, strangers, to the domain of the Great Mahrud."

I didn't know what he meant by those last few words. And it took a minute to figure out that his title was a pun derived from the aforesaid cartoonist and from Sheridan's Mrs. Malaprop.

"Albert Allegory is the full name," he said. "That is, in this metamorph. Other forms, other names, you know. And you two, I suppose, are outsiders who wish to live along the Illinois, drink from the Brew, and worship the Bull."

He held out his hand with the two inside fingers clenched and the thumb and outside finger extended.

"This is the sign that every true believer makes when he meets another," he said. "Remember it, and you'll be saved much trouble."

"How do you know I'm from the outside?" I asked. I didn't try to lie. He didn't seem to be bent on hurting us.

He laughed, and his vast mouth megaphoned the sound. Alice, no longer the cocky WHAM officer, gripped my hand hard.

He said, "I'm sort of a demigod, you might say. When Mahrud, bull be his name, became a god, he wrote a letter to me—using the U.S. mails of course—and invited me to come here and demigod for him. I'd never cared too much for the world as it was so I slipped in past the Army cordon and took over the duties that Mahrud, bull be his name, gave me."

I, too, had received a letter from my former professor. It had arrived before the trouble developed, and I had not understood his invitation to come live with him and be his demigod. I'd thought he'd slipped a gear or two.

For lack of anything pertinent to say, I asked, "What are your duties?"

He waved his cigar again. "My job, which is anything but onerous, is to meet outsiders and caution them to keep their eyes open. They are to remember that not everything is what it seems, and they are to look beyond the surface of the deed for the symbol."

He puffed on his cigar and then said, "I have a question for you. I don't want you to answer it now, but I want you to think about it and give me an answer later." He blew smoke again. "My question is this—where do you want to go now?"

He didn't offer to expand his question. He said, "So long," and strolled off down a side-path, his short legs seeming to move almost independently of his elongated saurian torso. I stared for a moment, still shaking from the encounter. Then I returned to the tree behind which I'd left my water-tank and strapped it back on.

We walked away fast. Alice was so subdued that she did not seem conscious of our nudity. After a while, she said, "Something like that frightens me. *How* could a man assume a form like that?"

"We'll find out," I said with more optimism than I felt. "I think we'd better be prepared for just about anything."

"Perhaps the story Mrs. Durham told you back at Base was true."

I nodded. The Professor's wife had said that, shortly before the Area was sealed off, she had gone to the bluffs across the river, where she knew her husband was. Even though he had announced himself a god by then, she was not afraid of him.

Mrs. Durham had taken two lawyers along, just in case. She was highly incoherent about what happened across the river. But some strange force, apparently operated by Dr. Durham, had turned her into a large tailed ape, causing her to flee. The two lawyers, metamorphosed into skunks, had also beaten a retreat.

Considering these strange events, Alice said, "What I can't understand is how Durham could do these things. Where's his power? What sort of gadget does he have?"

Hot as it was, my skin developed gooseflesh. I could scarcely tell her that *I* was almost certainly responsible for this entire situation. I felt guilty enough without actually telling the truth. Moreover, if I *had* told her what I believed to be the truth, she'd have *known* I was crazy. Nevertheless, that was the way it was, and that was why I had volunteered for this assignment. I'd started it; I had to finish it.

"I'm thirsty," she said. "What about a drink, Pops? We may not get a chance at another for a long time."

"Damn it," I said as I slipped off the tank, "don't call me Pops! My name is Daniel Temper, and I'm not so old that I could be . . ."

I stopped. I *was* old enough to be her father. In the Kentucky mountains, at any rate.

Knowing what I was thinking, she smiled and held out the little cup she had taken from the clip on the tank's side. I growled, "A man's only as old as he feels, and I don't feel over thirty."

At that moment I caught the flicker of moonlight on a form coming down the path. "Duck!" I said to Alice.

She just had time to dive into the grass. As for me, the tank got in my way, so I decided to stay there and brazen things out.

When I saw what was coming down the path, I wished I had taken off the tank. Weren't there *any* human beings in this God-forsaken land? First it was the Allegory. Now it was the Ass.

He said, "Hello, brother," and before I could think of a good comeback, he threw his strange head back and loosed tremendous laughter that was half *ha-ha!* and half *hee-haw!*

I didn't think it was funny. I was far too tense to pretend amusement. Moreover, his breath stank of Brew. I was half-sick before I could back up to escape it.

He was tall and covered with short blond hair, unlike most asses, and he stood upon two manlike legs that ended in broad hoofs. He had two long hairy ears, but, otherwise, he was as human as anybody else you might meet in the woods—or on the street. And his name, as he wasn't backward in telling me, was Polivinosel.

He said, "Why are you carrying that tank?"

"I've been smuggling the Brew to the outside."

His grin revealed long yellow horselike teeth. "Bootlegging, eh? But what do they pay you with? Money's no good to a worshiper of the All-Bull."

He held up his right hand. The thumb and two middle fingers were bent. The index finger and little finger were held straight out. I didn't respond immediately, and he looked hard. I imitated his gesture, and he relaxed a little.

"I'm bootlegging for the love of it," I said. "And also to spread the gospel."

Where that last phrase came from, I had no notion. Perhaps from the reference to "worshiper" and the vaguely religious-looking sign that Polivinosel had made.

He reached out a big hairy hand and turned the spigot on my tank. Before I could move, he had poured out enough to fill his cupped palm. He raised his hand to his lips and slurped loudly. He blew the liquid out so it sprayed all over me. "Whee-oo! That's *water!*"

"Of course," I said. "After I get rid of my load of Brew, I fill the tank with ordinary water. If I'm caught by the border patrol, I tell them I'm smuggling pure water into our area."

Polivinosel went *hoo-hah-hah* and slapped his thigh so hard, it sounded like an axe biting into a tree.

"That's not all," I said. "I even have an agreement with some of the higher officers. They allow me to slip through if I bring them back some Brew."

He winked and brayed and slapped his thigh again. "Corruption, eh, brother? Even brass will rust. I tell you, it won't be long until the Brew of the Bull spreads everywhere."

Again he made that sign, and I did so almost at the same time.

He said, "I'll walk with you a mile or so. My worshipers—the local Cult of the Ass—are holding a fertility ceremony down the path a way. Care to join us?"

I shuddered. "No, thank you," I said fervently.

I had witnessed one of those orgies through a pair of fieldglasses one night. The huge bonfire had been about two hundred yards inside the forbidden boundary. Against its hellish flame, I could see the white and capering bodies of absolutely uninhibited men and women. It was a long time before I could get that scene out of my mind. I used to dream about it.

When I declined the invitation, Polivinosel brayed again and slapped me on the back, or where my back would have been if my tank hadn't been in the way. As it was, I fell on my hands and knees in a patch of tall grass. I was furious. I not only resented his too-high spirits, I was afraid he had bent the thin-walled tank and sprung a leak in its seams.

But that wasn't the main reason I didn't get up at once. I couldn't move because I was staring into Alice's big blue eyes.

Polivinosel gave a loud whoop and leaped through the air and landed beside me. He got down on his hands and knees and stuck his big ugly mule-eared face into Alice's and bellowed, "How now, white cow! How high browse thou?"

He grabbed Alice by the waist and lifted her up high, getting up himself at the same time. There he held her in the moonlight and turned her around and over and over, as if she were a strange-looking bug he had caught crawling in the weeds.

She squealed and gasped, "Damn you, you big jackass, take your filthy paws off me!"

"I'm Polivinosel, the local god of fertility!" he brayed. "It's my duty—and privilege—to inspect your qualifications. Tell me, daughter, have you prayed recently for a son or daughter? Are your crops coming along? How are your cabbages growing? What about your onions and your parsnips? Are your hens laying enough eggs?"

Instead of being frightened, Alice got angry. "All right, Your Asininity, would you please let me down? And quit looking at me with those big lecherous eyes. If you want what I think you do, hurry along to your own orgy. Your worshipers are waiting for you."

He opened his hands so she fell to the ground. Fortunately, she was quick and lithe and landed on her feet. She started to walk away, but he reached out and grabbed her by the wrist.

"You're going the wrong way, my pretty little daughter. The infidels are patrolling the border only a few hundred yards away.

You wouldn't want to get caught. Then you'd not be able to drink the divine Brew anymore. You wouldn't want that, would you?"

"I'll take care of myself, thank you," she said huskily. "Just leave me alone. It's getting so a girl can't take a snooze by herself in the grass without some minor deity or other wanting to wrestle!"

Alice was picking up the local lingo fast.

"Well, now, daughter, you can't blame us godlings for that. Not when you're built like a goddess yourself."

He gave that titanic bray that should have knocked us down, then grabbed both of us by the wrists and dragged us along the path.

"Come along, little ones. I'll introduce you around. And we'll all have a ball at the Feast of the Ass." Again, the loud offensive bray. I could see why Durham had metamorphosed this fellow into his present form.

That thought brought me up short. The question was, *how* had he done it? I didn't believe in supernatural powers, of course. If there were any, they weren't possessed by man. And anything that went on in this physical universe had to obey physical laws.

Take Polivinosel's ears and hoofs. I had a good chance to study them more closely as I walked with him. His ears may have been changed, like Bottom's, into a donkey's, but whoever had done it had not had an accurate picture in his mind. They were essentially human ears, elongated and covered over with tiny hairs.

As for the legs, they were human, not equine. It was true he had no feet. But his pale, shiny hoofs, though cast into a good likeness of a horse's, were evidently made of the same stuff as toenails. And there was still the faintest outline and curve of five toes.

It was evident that some biological sculptor had had to rechisel and then regrow the basic human form.

I looked at Alice to see what she thought of him. She was magnificent in her anger. As Polivinosel had been uncouth enough to mention, she had a superb figure. She was the sort of girl who is always president of her college sorority, queen of the Senior Prom, and engaged to a Senator's son. The type I had never had a chance with when I was working my way through Traybell University.

Polivinosel suddenly stopped and roared, "Look, you, what's your name?"

"Daniel Temper," I said.

"Daniel Temper? D.T.? Ah, *hah, hoo, hah, hah!* Listen, Old D.T., throw that tank away. It burdens you down, and you look like an ass, a veritable beast of burden, with it on your back. And I won't have anybody going around imitating me, see? *Hoohah-heehaw!* Get it?"

He punched me in the ribs with a big thumb as hard as horn. It was all I could do to keep from swinging at him. I never hated a man—or deity—so much. Durham had failed if he had thought to punish him. Polivinosel seemed to be proud of his transformation and had, if I understood him correctly, profited enough by his experience to start a cult. Of course, he wasn't the first to make a religion of his infirmity.

"How will I be able to bootleg the Brew out?" I asked.

"Who cares?" he said. "Your piddling little operations won't help the spread of the divine Drink much. Leave that up to the rivers of the world and to Mahrud, bull be his name."

He made that peculiar sign again.

I couldn't argue with him. He'd have torn the tank off my back. Slowly, I unstrapped it. He helped me by grabbing it and throwing it off into the darkness of the woods.

Immediately, I became so thirsty, I could hardly stand it.

"You don't want that filthy stuff!" Polivinosel brayed. "Come with me to the Place of the Ass! I have a nice little temple there— nothing fancy, understand, like the Flower Palace of Mahrud, may he be all bull—but it will do. And we do have a good time."

All this while, he was ogling Alice shamelessly and projecting more than his thoughts. Like all the degenerates in this area, he had absolutely no inhibitions. If I had had a gun, I think I would have shot him then and there. That is, if the cartridges could have exploded.

"Look here," I said, abandoning caution in my anger. "We're

going where we damn well please." I grabbed the girl's wrist. More wrist-grabbing going on lately. "Come on, Alice, let's leave this glorified donkey."

Polivinosel loomed in our way. The slightly Mongolian tilt of his eyes made him look more Missouri-mulish than ever. Big and mean and powerful, with the accent on mean.

"Don't think for a minute," he bellowed, "that you're going to get me mad enough to harm you so you can go tell your prayerman to report me to Mahrud! You can't tempt me into wrath! That would be a *mortal* sin, mortals!"

Shouting about my not being able to disturb his Olympian aloofness, he put his arm around my neck and with the other hand reached into my mouth and yanked out my upper plate.

"You and your mushmouthing annoy me!" he cried.

He released his choking grip around my neck and threw the plate into the shadows of the forest. I rushed toward the bush where I thought I'd seen the white teeth land. I got down on my hands and knees and groped frantically around, but I couldn't find them.

Alice's scream brought me upward. Too fast, for I bumped my head hard against a branch. Despite the pain, I turned back to see what was the trouble and charged through the brush. And I banged my shins hard against some object and fell flat on my face, knocking my breath out.

When I rose, I saw I'd tripped over my own watertank. I didn't stop to thank whatever gods might be for my good fortune. Instead, I picked the tank up and, running up to them, brought it crashing down against the back of his head. Soundlessly, he crumpled. I threw the container to one side and went to Alice.

"You all right?" I asked.

"Yes-s," she said, sobbing, and put her head on my shoulder.

I judged she was more frightened and mad than hurt. I patted her shoulder—she had beautifully smooth skin—and stroked her long black hair. But she wouldn't quit weeping.

"That filthy creep! First he ruins my sister, and now he tries to do the same to me."

"Huh?"

She raised her head to look at me. Look down at me, rather— she was an inch or two taller.

"Peggy was my half-sister, daughter by my father's first marriage. Her mother married a Colonel Rourke. But we were always close."

I wanted to hear more, but the immediate situation demanded my attention.

I turned Polivinosel over. His heart was still beating. Blood flowed from the gash in the back of his scalp, not the clear ichor you expect from a god's veins.

"Type O," said Alice. "Same as it was before. And don't worry about him. He deserves to die. He's a big stupid jerk of a Don Juan who got my sister in trouble and wouldn't . . ."

She stopped and gasped. I followed her stricken gaze and water had spilled into the dirt. And again I felt that sudden wrench of thirst. It was purely mental, of course, but that knowledge didn't make me less dry.

She put her hand to her throat and croaked, "All of a sudden, I'm thirsty."

"There's nothing we can do about it unless we find a source of uncontaminated water," I said. "And the longer we stand around talking about it, the thirstier we'll get."

The tank was empty. Stopping to check this sad fact, I saw light flash on something beneath a bush. I retrieved my upper plate. With my back toward Alice, I inserted the teeth and, feeling a little more assured, told her we'd better start walking on.

We did, but she still had the water problem on her mind. "Surely, there are wells and creeks that aren't infected. Only the river is filled with the Brew, isn't it?"

"If I were sure of that I'd not have taken the watertank," I was unkind enough to point out.

She opened her mouth to reply. But just then we heard voices down the path and saw the flare of approaching torches. Quickly, we stepped into the brush and hid.

The newcomers were singing. Their song owed its music to *The Battle Hymn of the Republic*, but the words were Latin. It was wretched Latin, for their accent paid allegiance to the beat of the original English meter. It didn't bother them at all. I doubt if many even knew what they were singing.

"Orientis partibus
Adventavit Asinus,
Pulcher et Fortissimus,
Sarcinis aptissimus.
Orientis partibus
Adventavit . . . Eeeeek!"

They had rounded the trail's bend and discovered their god, bleeding and unconscious.

Alice whispered, "Let's get out of here. If that mob catches us, they'll tear us apart."

I wanted to watch, to learn from their behavior how we should act when among the natives. I told her so, and she nodded. Despite our antagonism, I had to admit that she was intelligent and brave. If she was a little nervous, she had good reason to be.

These people didn't act at all as I'd thought they would. Instead of wailing and weeping, they stood away from him, huddled together, not quite sure what to do. I didn't see at first what caused their attitude. Then I realized from their expressions and whispers that they were afraid to interfere in the affairs of a demi-god—even one as demi as Polivinosel.

The thing that italicized their indecision was their youthfulness. There wasn't a man or woman in the group who looked over twenty-five, and all were of superb physique.

Something made a loud cracking noise down the path behind us. Alice and I jumped, as did the whole group. They took off like a bunch of scared rabbits. I felt like joining them, but I stayed. I did, however, pray that this wouldn't be another nerve-rocking monster.

It was merely a naked native, a tall lean one with a long thin nose, who looked as if he ought to be teaching in some college. The effect was intensified by the fact that he had his nose in a book. As I've said, the moonlight was strong enough for reading, but I hadn't really expected anyone to take advantage of it.

His scholarly appearance was somewhat marred by the dead squirrel, large as a collie, which hung around his neck and over his shoulders. He had been hunting, I suppose, though I'd never heard of hunting squirrels in the dark. Moreover, he carried no weapons.

All of this, except for the squirrel's size, was surprising. I'd seen camera shots of the great beasts taken along the Area's edge.

I watched him closely to see what he'd do when he saw Polivinosel. He disappointed me. When he came to the prostrate form, he did not hesitate or give any sign that he had seen the god except to lift his feet over the outstretched legs. His nose remained dipped in the book.

I took Alice's hand. "Come on. We're following him."

We walked behind the reader for perhaps a half-mile. When I thought it was safe to stop him, I called out to him. He halted and put his squirrel on the ground and waited for me.

I asked him if he had noticed Polivinosel lying on the path. Puzzled, he shook his head.

"I saw you step over him," I said.

"I stepped over nothing," he insisted. "The path was perfectly clear." He peered closely at me. "I can see you're a newcomer. Perhaps you've had your first taste of the Brew. Sometimes, at first, it gives strange sensations and visions. Takes a little time to get adjusted to it, you know."

I said nothing about that, but I did argue with him about Polivinosel. Not until I mentioned the name, however, did he look enlightened. He smiled in a superior manner and looked down his long nose.

"Ah, my good man, you mustn't believe everything you hear, you know. Just because the majority, who have always been ignorami and simpletons, choose to explain the new phenomena in terms of ancient superstition is no reason for an intelligent man such as yourself to put any credence in them. I suggest you discard anything you hear—with the exception of what I tell you, of course—and use the rational powers that you were lucky enough to be born with and to develop in some university, providing, that is, you didn't go to some institution which is merely a training ground for members of the Chamber of Commerce, Rotary, Odd Fellows, Knights of Columbus, Shriners, or the Lions, Moose, Elk, and other curious beasts. I scarcely—"

"But I *saw* Polivinosel!" I said, exasperated. "And if you hadn't lifted your feet, you'd have fallen over him!"

Again, he gave a superior smile. "Tut, tut! Self-hypnotism, mass delusion, something of that sort. Perhaps you are a victim of suggestion. Believe me, there are many unsettling things in this valley. You mustn't allow yourself to be bamboozled by the first charlatan who comes along and has an easy—if fantastic—explanation for all this."

"What's yours?" I challenged.

"Dr. Durham invented some sort of machine that generates the unknown chemical with which he is now infecting the Illinois River. And eventually, we hope, the waters of the world. One of its properties is a destruction of many of the sociologically and psychologically conditioned reflexes which some term inhibitions, mores, or neuroses. And a very good thing, too. It also happens to be a universal antibiotic and tonic—such a combination!—besides a number of other things, not all of which I approve.

"However, he has, I must admit, done away with such societal and politico-economic structurologies and agents as factories, shops, doctors, hospitals, schools—which have hitherto devoted most of their time and energy to turning out half-educated morons—bureaucracies, automobiles, churches, movies, advertising, distilleries, soap operas, armies, prostitutes, and innumerable other institutions until recently considered indispensable.

"Unfortunately, the rationalizing instinct in man is very hard to down, as is the power-drive. So you have charlatans posing as prophets and setting up all sorts of new churches and attracting the multitudes in all their moronic simplicity and pathetic eagerness to grasp at some explanation for the unknown."

I wanted to believe him, but I knew that the Professor had neither ability nor money enough to build such a machine.

"What is the peasants' explanation for the Brew?" I asked.

"They have none except that it comes from the Bottle," said

the Rational Man. "They swear that Durham derives his powers from this Bottle, which, by description, is nothing more than a common everyday beer bottle. Some declare, however, that it bears, *in stiacciato*, the image of a bull."

Guilt brought sweat out on my forehead. So, it *had* been my gift! And I'd thought I was playing a harmless little hoax on my likable but daffy old Classical-Lit prof!

"That story is probably derived from his name," I said hastily. "After all, his students used to call him 'Bull.' It wasn't only the fact that his name was Durham. His wife led him around with a ring in his nose, and—"

"In which case, he fooled his students," said the Rational Man. "For he was, beneath that mild and meek exterior, a prize bull, a veritable stallion, a lusty old goat. As you may or may not know, he has any number of nymphs stabled in his so-called Flower Palace, not to mention beautiful Peggy Rourke, now known as the—"

Alice gasped. "Then she *is* living! And with Durham!"

He raised his eyebrows. "Well that depends upon whether or not you listen to these charlatans. Some of them would have it that she has become transfigured in some mystical-muddled manner— *multiplied*, they call it—and is each and every one of those nymphs in Mahrud's seraglio, yet is in some way none of them and exists in essence only."

He shook his head and said, "Oh, the rationalizing species that must invent gods and dogmas!"

"Who's Mahrud?" I asked.

"Why, Durham spelled backward, of course. Don't you know that there is a tendency in every religion to avoid pronouncing the True Name? However, I believe that those fakers, the Scrambled Men, invented the name, mainly because they couldn't say it right. They insisted the predeity name be distinguished from the Real One. It caught on fast, probably because it sounded so Oriental and, therefore, in the minds of these peons, mystical."

I was getting so much data all at once that I was more mixed up than ever.

"Haven't you ever seen Mahrud?" I asked.

"No, and I never shall. Those so-called gods just don't exist, any more than the Allegory or the Ass. Nobody with a rational mind could believe in them. Unfortunately, the Brew, despite its many admirable qualities, does have a strong tendency to make one illogical, irrational, and susceptible to suggestion."

He tapped his high forehead and said, "But I accept all the good things and reject the others. I'm quite happy."

Shortly after this, we came out on a country road I recognized.

The Rational Man said, "We'll be coming soon to my house. Would you two care to stop? We'll have this squirrel to eat and lots of Brew from the well in the backyard. Some of my friends will be there, and we'll have a nice intellectual talk before the orgy starts. You'll find them congenial—they're all atheists or agnostics."

I shuddered at the idea of being asked to drink the hated Liquor. "Sorry," I said. "We must be going. But tell me, as a matter of curiosity, how you caught that squirrel. You're not carrying any weapon."

"Can't," he replied, waving his book.

"Can't? Why not?"

"No, not can't. K-a-n-t. Kant. You see, the Brew has had this extraordinary effect on stimulating certain animals' growth. More than that, it has, I'm sure, affected their cerebral systems. They seem much more intelligent than before. A combination of increase in size of brain and change in organization of neurons, probably. Whatever the effect, the change has been most remarkable in rodents. A good thing, too. Wonderful source of meat, you know.

"Anyway," he continued, as he saw my increasing impatience, "I've found that one doesn't need a gun, which no longer explodes in this area, anyway, nor a bow and arrow. All one has to do is locate an area abundant in squirrels and sit down and read aloud. While one is both enjoying and educating oneself, the squirrel, attracted by one's monotonous voice, descends slowly from his tree and draws nearer.

"One pays no attention to him—one reads on. The beast sits close to one, slowly waving its bushy tail, its big black eyes fixed on one. After a while, one rises, closes the book, and picks up the squirrel, which is by now completely stupefied and never comes out of its state, not even when one takes it home and cuts it throat.

"I've found by experiment that one gets the best results by reading *The Critique of Pure Reason*. Absolutely stuns them. However, rabbits, for some reason, are more easily seduced by my reading Henry Miller's *Tropic of Capricorn*. In the French translation, of course. Friend of mine says that the best book for the birds is Hubbard's *Dianetics*, but one ought to take pride in one's tools, you know. I've always caught my pheasants and geese with *Three Contributions to the Theory of Sex*."

We came to his estate and said good-by to him. Stepping up our pace, we walked for several miles past the many farmhouses along the gravel road. Some of these had burned down, but their occupants had simply moved into the barn. Or, if that had gone up in flames, had erected a lean-to.

"Photographs from Army balloons have shown that a good many houses in the city have burned down," I said. "Not only that, the grass is literally growing in the streets again. I've been wondering where the burned-out people were living, but this shows how they manage. They live like savages."

"Well, why not?" asked Alice. "They don't seem to have to work very hard to live in abundance. I've noticed we haven't been bitten by mosquitoes, so noxious insects must have been exterminated. Sanitation shouldn't bother them—the Brew kills all diseases, if we're to believe that squirrel-reader. They don't have much refuse in the way of tin cans, paper, and so on to get rid of. They all seem very happy and hospitable. We've had to turn down constant invitations to stop and eat and drink some Brew. And even," she added with a malicious smile, "to participate in orgies afterward. That seems to be quite a respectable word now. I noticed that beautiful blonde back at the last farm tried to drag you off the road. You'll have to admit that that couldn't have happened Outside."

"Maybe I *am* bald," I snarled, "but I'm not so damned repulsive that no good-looking girl could fall in love with me. I wish I had a photo of Bernadette to show you. Bernadette and I were just on the verge of getting engaged. She's only thirty and—"

"Has she got all her teeth?"

"Yes, she has," I retorted. "She didn't get hit in the mouth by a mortar fragment and then lose the rest of her upper teeth through an infection, with no antibiotics available because enemy fire kept her in a foxhole for five days."

I was so mad I was shaking.

Alice answered softly, "Dan, I'm sorry I said that. I didn't know."

"Not only that," I plunged on, ignoring her apology. "What have you got against me besides my teeth and hair and the fact that I thought of this conditioning idea and my superiors—including the President—thought enough of my abilities to send me into this area without ten thousand Marines paving the way for me? As far as that goes, why were you sent with me? Was it because your father happens to be a general and wanted to grab some glory for you and him by association with me? If that isn't militaristic parasitism, what is? And furthermore . . ."

I raved on, and every time she opened her mouth, I roared her down. I didn't realize how loud I was until I saw a man and a woman standing in the road ahead of us, watching intently. I shut up at once, but the damage was done.

As soon as we were opposite them, the man said, "Newcomer, you're awfully grumpy." He held out a bottle to me. "Here, drink. It's good for what ails you. We don't have any harsh words in Mahrudland."

I said, "No, thanks," and tried to go around them, but the woman, a brunette who resembled a cross between the two Russells, Jane and Lillian, grabbed me around my neck and said, "Aw, come on, skinhead, I think you're cute. Have a drink and come along with us. We're going to a fertility ceremony at Jonesy's farm. Polivinosel himself'll be there. He's deigning to mix with us mortals for tonight. And you can make love with me and ensure a good crop. I'm one of Poli's nymphs, you know."

"Sorry," I said. "I've got to go."

I felt something wet and warm flooding over my scalp. For a second, I couldn't guess what it was. But when I smelled the hop-like Brew, I knew! And I responded with all the violence and horror the stuff inspired in me. Before the man could continue pouring the liquid over my head, I tore the woman's grip loose and threw her straight into the face of her companion. Both went down.

Before they could rise, I grabbed Alice's hand and fled with her down the road.

After we had run about a quarter of a mile, I had to slow to a walk. My heart was trying to beat its way out of my chest, and my head was expanding to fill the dome of the sky. Even my setting-up exercises hadn't fitted me for this.

However, I didn't feel so bad when I saw that Alice, young and fit as she was, was panting just as hard.

"They're not chasing us," I said. "Do you know, we've penetrated this area so easily, I wonder how far a column of Marines could have gone if they'd come in tonight. Maybe it would have been better to try an attack this way."

"We've tried four already," said Alice. "Two by day, two by night. The first three marched in and never came back, and you saw what happened to the last."

We walked along in silence for a while. Then I said, "Look, Alice, I blew my top a while ago, and we almost got into trouble. So why don't we agree to let bygones be bygones and start out on a nice fresh foot?"

"Nothing doing! I will refrain from quarreling, but there'll be none of this buddy-buddy stuff. Maybe, if we drank this Brew, I might get to liking you. But I doubt if even that could do it."

I said nothing, determined to keep my mouth shut if it killed me.

Encouraged by my silence—or engaged—she said, "Perhaps we might end up by drinking the Brew. Our water is gone, and if you're as thirsty as I am, you're on fire. We'll be at least fourteen hours without water, maybe twenty. And we'll be walking all the time. What happens when we just *have* to have water and there's nothing but the river to drink from? It won't be as if the stuff was poison.

"As a matter of fact, we know we'll probably be very happy.

And that's the worst of it. That X substance, or Brew, or whatever you want to call it, is the most insidious drug ever invented. Its addicts not only seem to be permanently happy, they benefit in so many other ways from it."

I couldn't keep silent any longer. "'That's dangerous talk!"

"Not at all, *Mister* Temper. Merely the facts."

"I don't like it!"

"What are *you* so vehement about?"

"Why?" I asked, my voice a little harder. "There's no reason why I should be ashamed. My parents were hopheads. My father died in the state hospital. My mother was cured, but she burned to death when the restaurant she was cooking in caught fire. Both are buried in the old Meltonville cemetery just outside Onaback. When I was younger, I used to visit their graves at night and howl at the skies because an unjust God had allowed them to die in such a vile and beastly fashion. I . . ."

Her voice was small but firm and cool. "I'm sorry, *Dan*, that that happened to you. But you're getting a little melodramatic aren't you?"

I subsided at once. "You're right. It's just that you seem to needle me so I want to—"

"Bare your naked soul? No, thanks, Dan. It's bad enough to have to bare our bodies. I don't want to make you sore, but there's not much comparison between the old narcotics and this Brew."

"There's no degeneration of the body of the Brewdrinker? How do you *know* there isn't? Has this been going on long enough to tell? And if everybody's so healthy and harmless and happy, why did Polivinosel try to rape you?"

"I'm certainly not trying to defend that Jackass," she said. "But, Dan, can't you catch the difference in the psychic atmosphere around here? There seem to be no barriers between men and women doing what they want with each other. Nor are they jealous of each other. Didn't you deduce, from what that Russell-type woman said, that Polivinosel had his choice of women and nobody objected? He probably took it for granted that I'd want to roll in the grass with him."

"All right, all right," I said. "But it's disgusting, and I can't understand why Durham made him a god of fertility when he seems to have hated him so."

"What do you know about Durham?" she countered.

I told her that Durham had been a short, bald, and paunchy little man with a face like an Irish leprechaun, with a wife who henpecked him till the holes showed, with a poet's soul, with a penchant for quoting Greek and Latin classics, with a delight in making puns, and with an unsuppressed desire to get his book of essays, *The Golden Age*, published.

"Would you say he had a vindictive mind?" she asked.

"No, he was very meek and forbearing. Why?"

"Well, my half-sister Peggy wrote that her steady, Polivinosel, hated Durham because he had to take his course to get a credit in the Humanities. Not only that, it was evident that Durham was sweet on Peggy. So, Polivinosel upset the doctor every time he got a chance. In fact, she mentioned that in her last letter to me just before she disappeared. And when I read in the papers that Durham was suspected of having murdered them, I wondered if he hadn't been harboring his hate for a long time."

"Not the doc," I protested. "He might get mad, but not for long."

"There you are," she said triumphantly. "He changed Polivinosel into a jackass, and then he got soft-hearted and forgave him. Why not? He had Peggy."

"But why wasn't Polivinosel changed back to a man then?"

"All I know is that he was majoring in Agriculture, and, if I'm to believe Peggy's letters, he was a Casanova."

"No wonder you were a little sarcastic when I gave my lecture," I said. "You knew more about those two than I did. But that doesn't excuse your reference to my baldness and false teeth."

She turned away. "I don't know why I said that. All I do know is that I hated you because you were a civilian and were being given such authority and entrusted with such an important mission."

I wanted to ask her if she'd changed her mind. Also I was sure that wasn't all there was to it, but I didn't press the point. I went on to tell her all I knew about Durham. The only thing I kept back was the most important. I had to sound her out before I mentioned that.

"Then the way you see it," she said, "is that everything that's been happening here fits this Doctor Boswell Durham's description of the hypothetical Golden Age?"

"Yes," I said. "He often used to lecture to us on what an opportunity the ancient gods lost. He said that if they'd taken the trouble to look at their mortal subjects, they'd have seen how to do away with disease, poverty, unhappiness, and war. But he maintained the ancient gods were really men who had somehow or other gotten superhuman powers and didn't know how to use them because they weren't versed in philosophy, ethics, or science.

"He used to say he could do better, and he would then proceed to give us his lecture entitled *How to Be a God and Like It*. It used to make us laugh, because you couldn't imagine anyone less divine than Durham."

"I know that," she said. "Peggy wrote me about it. She said that was what irked Polivinosel so. He didn't understand that the doctor was just projecting his dream world into classroom terms. Probably he dreamed of such a place so he could escape from his wife's nagging. Poor little fellow."

"Poor little fellow, my foot!" I snorted. "He's done just what he said he wanted to do, hasn't he? How many others can say the same, especially on such a scale?"

"No one," she admitted. "But tell me, what was Durham's main thesis in *The Golden Age*?"

"He maintained that history showed that the so-called common man, Mr. Everyman, is a guy who wants to be left alone and is quite pleased if only his mundane life runs fairly smoothly. His ideal is an existence with no diseases, plenty of food and amusement and sex and affection, no worry about paying bills, just enough work to keep from getting bored with all play and someone to do his thinking for him. Most adults want a god of some sort to run things for them while they do just what they please."

"Why," exclaimed Alice, "he isn't any better than Hitler or Stalin!"

"Not at all," I said. "He *could* bring about Eden as we can see by looking around us. And he didn't believe in any particular ideology or in using force. He . . ."

I stopped, mouth open. I'd been defending the Professor!

Alice giggled. "Did you change your mind?"

"No," I said. "Not at all. Because the Professor, like my dictator, must have changed *his* mind. He *is* using force. Look at Polivinosel."

"He's no example. He always was an ass, and he still is. And how do we know he doesn't *like* being one?"

I had no chance to reply. The eastern horizon was lit up by a great flash of fire. A second or two later, the sound of the explosion reached us.

We were both shocked. We had come to accept the idea that such chemical reactions just didn't take place in this valley.

Alice clutched my hand and said sharply. "Do you think the attack has started ahead of schedule? Or is that one we weren't told about?"

"I don't think so. Why would an attack be launched around here? Let's go and see what's up."

"You know, I'd have thought that was lightning, except that— well, it was just the opposite of lightning."

"The negative, you mean?" I asked her.

She nodded. "The streak was—black."

"I've seen lightning streaks that branched out like trees," I said. "But this is the first tree that I ever . . ." I stopped and murmured. "No, that's crazy. I'll wait until I get there before I make any more comments."

We left the gravel road and turned right onto a paved highway. I recognized it as the state route that ran past the airfield and into Meltonville, about a mile and a half away. Another explosion lit up the eastern sky, but this time we saw it was much closer than we had first thought.

We hurried forward, tense, ready to take to the woods if danger threatened. We had traveled about half a mile when I stopped so suddenly that Alice bumped into me. She whispered, "What is it?"

"I don't remember that creekbed ever being there," I replied slowly. "In fact, I *know* it wasn't there. I took a lot of hikes along here when I was a Boy Scout."

And there it was. It came up from the east, from Onaback's general direction, and cut southwest, away from the river. It slashed through the state highway, leaving a thirty-foot gap in the road. Somebody had dragged two long tree trunks across the cut and laid planks between them to form a rough bridge.

We crossed it and walked on down the highway, but another explosion to our left told us we were off the trail. This one, very close, came from the edge of a large meadow that I remembered had once been a parking lot for a trucking company.

Alice sniffed and said, "Smell that burning vegetation?"

"Yes." I pointed to the far side of the creek where the moon shone on the bank. "Look at those."

Those were the partly burned and shattered stalks and branches of plants about the size of pine trees. They were scattered about forty feet apart. Some lay against the bank; some were stretched along the bottom of the creekbed.

What did it mean? The only way to find out was to investigate. So, as we came abruptly to the creek's end, which was surrounded by a ring of about a hundred people, we tried to elbow through to see what was so interesting.

We never made it, for at that moment a woman screamed, "He put in too much Brew!"

A man bellowed, "Run for your lives!"

The night around us was suddenly gleaming with bodies and clamorous with cries. Everybody was running and pushing everybody else to make room. Nevertheless, in spite of their reckless haste, they were laughing as if it was all a big joke. It was a strange mixture of panic and disdain for the panic.

I grabbed Alice's hand and started running with them. A man came abreast of us and I shouted. "What's the danger?"

He was a fantastic figure, the first person I had seen with any clothing on. He wore a red fez with a tassel and a wide green sash wound around his waist. A scimitar was stuck through it at such an angle it looked like a ducktail-shaped rudder. The illusion was furthered by the speed at which he was traveling.

When he heard my shout, he gave me a wild look that contributed to the weirdness of his garb and shouted something.

"Huh?"

Again he yelled at me and sped on.

"What'd he say?" I panted at Alice. "I'll swear he said 'Horatio Hornblower.'"

"Sounded more like 'Yorassiffencornblows,'" she replied.

That was when we found out why the crowd was running like mad. A lion the size of a mountain roared behind us—a blast knocked us flat on our faces—a wave of hot air succeeded the shock—a hail of rocks and clods of dirt pelted us. I yelped as I was hit in the back of one leg. For a moment, I could have sworn my leg was broken.

Alice screamed and grabbed me around the neck. "Save me!"

I'd have liked to, but who was going to save *me*?

Abruptly, the rocks quit falling, and the yells stopped. Silence, except for the drawing of thankful breaths. Then, giggles and yelps of pure delight and calls back and forth and white bodies were shining in the moonlight as they rose like ghosts from the grass. Fear among these uninhibited people could not last long. They were already joshing each other about the way they'd run and then were walking back to the cause of their flight.

I stopped a woman, a beautiful buxom wench of twenty-five— all the adult female Brew addicts, I later found, were pretty and well-shaped and looked youthful—and I said, "What happened?"

"Ah, the fool Scrambler put too much Brew in the hole," she replied, smiling. "Anybody could see what'd happen. But he wouldn't listen to us, and his own buddies are as scrambled as he is, thanks to Mahrud."

When she uttered *that* name, she made *that* sign. These people, no matter how lightly and irreverently they behaved in other matters, were always respectful toward their god Mahrud.

I was confused. "He? Who?" I said, inelegantly.

"He *haw?*" she brayed and my body turned cold as I thought

she was referring to Polivinosel. But she was merely mocking the form of my question. "The Scrambled Men, of course, Baldy." Looking keenly at me in a single sweep that began at my feet and ended at the top of my head, she added, "If it weren't for that, I'd think you hadn't tasted the Brew yet."

I didn't know what she meant by *that*. I looked upward, because she had pointed in that direction. But I couldn't see anything except the clear sky and the huge distorted moon.

I didn't want to continue my questioning and expose myself as such a newcomer. I left the woman and, with Alice, followed the crowd back. Their destination was the end of the creek, a newly blasted hole which showed me in a glance how the dry bed had so suddenly come into existence. Somebody has carved it out with a series of the tremendous blasts we'd heard.

A man brushed by me. His legs pumped energetically, his body was bent forward, and one arm was crooked behind his back. His right hand clutched the matted hair on his chest. Jammed sideways on his head was one of those plumed cocked hats you see the big brass of men's lodges wear during parades. A belt around his otherwise naked waist supported a sheathed sword. High-heeled cowboy boots completed his garb. He frowned deeply and carried, in the hand behind his back, a large map.

"Uh—Admiral," I called out.

He paid no attention but plowed ahead.

"General!"

Still he wouldn't turn his head.

"Boss. Chief. Hey, *you!*"

He looked up. "*Winkled tupponies?*" he queried.

"Huh?"

Alice said, "Close your mouth before your plate falls out, and come along."

We got to the excavation's edge before the crowd became too thick to penetrate. It was about thirty feet across and sloped steeply down to the center, which was about twenty feet deep. Exactly in the middle reared an enormous, blackened, and burning plant. Talk about Jack and your beanstalk. This *was* a cornstalk, ears, leaves, and all, and it was at least fifty feet high. It leaned perilously and would, if touched with a finger, fall flaming to the ground. Right on top of us, too, if it happened to be toppling our way. Its roots were as exposed as the plumbing of a half-demolished tenement.

The dirt had been flung away from the roots and piled up around the hole to complete the craterlike appearance of the excavation. It looked as if a meteor had plowed into the ground.

That's what I thought at first glance. Then I saw from the way the dirt scattered that the meteor must have come up from below.

There was no time to think through the full implication of what I saw, for the huge cornstalk began its long-delayed fall. I was busy, along with everybody else, in running away. After it had fallen with a great crash, and after a number of the oddly dressed men had hitched it up to a ten-horse team and dragged it away to one side, I returned with Alice. This time I went down into the crater. The soil was hard and dry under my feet. Something had sucked all the water out and had done it fast, too, for the dirt in the adjoining meadow was moist from a recent shower.

Despite the heat contained in the hole, the Scrambled Men swarmed in and began working with shovels and picks upon the western wall. Their leader, the man with the admiral's hat, stood in their middle and held the map before him with both hands, while he frowned blackly at it. Every once in a while he'd summon a subordinate with a lordly gesture, point out something on the map, and then designate a spot for him to use his shovel.

"*Olderen croakish richbags,*" he commanded.

"*Eniatipac nom, iuo, iuo,*" chanted the subordinate.

But the digging turned up nothing they were looking for. And the people standing on the lip of the crater—like the big city crowds that watch steam-shovel excavating—hooted and howled and shouted unheeded advice at the Scrambled Men. They passed bottles of Brew back and forth and had a good time, though I thought some of their helpful hints to the workers were definitely in bad taste.

Suddenly, the semi-Napoleon snorted with rage and threw his hands up so the map fluttered through the air.

"Shimsham the rodtammed shipshuts!" he howled.
"Rerheuf niem, lohwaj!" his men shouted.
"Frammistab the wormbattened frigatebarns!"

The result of all this was that everybody quit digging except for one man. He was dressed in a plug hat and two dozen slave bracelets. He dropped a seed of some sort within a six-foot-deep hole cut almost horizontally into the bank. He filled this with dirt, tamped it, then drove a thin wire down through the soil. Another man, wearing harlequin spectacles in which the glass had been knocked out, and a spiked Prussian officer's helmet from the First World War, withdrew the wire and poured a cascade of Brew from a huge vase. The thirsty soil gulped it eagerly.

There was silence as the Scrambled Men and the spectators intently watched the ceremony. Suddenly a woman on the excavation's edge shouted, "He's putting in too much again! Stop the fool!"

The Napoleon looked up fiercely and reprimanded, *"Fornicoot the onus squeered."*

Immediately, the ground rumbled, the earth shook, the crust quivered. Something was about to pop, and it was going to pop loud!

"Run for the hills! This time he's really done it!"

I didn't know what he'd done, but it didn't seem a time to be standing around asking questions.

We ran up the slope and out onto the meadow and across it. When we were halfway to the road, I overcame the contagious panic long enough to risk a glance over my shoulder. And I saw *it*.

You've heard of explosions flowering? Well, this was the first time I had ever seen the reverse—a colossal sunflower exploding, energized and accelerated fantastically in its growth by an overdose of that incredible stimulant, the Brew. It attained the size of a Sequoia within a split-second, its stalk and head blasting the earth in a hurry to get out. It was reaching high into the sky and burning, because of the tremendous energy poured out in its growth.

And then, its lower parts having been denied a grip because its foundations had been thrust aside, it was toppling, toppling, a flaming tower of destruction.

Alice and I got out of the way. But we barely made it and, for a second, I was sure that that titanic blazing hulk would smash us like beetles beneath a hard leather heel.

It went *whoosh!* And then *karoomp!* And we fell forward, stunned, unable to move. Or so we thought. The next instant we both leaped from our paralysis, bare rumps blistered.

Alice screamed. "Oh, God, Dan! It hurts!"

I knew that, for I had been burned too in that region. I think our expedition would have come to a bad end right then and there, for we needed immediate medical attention and would have had to go back to HQ to get it. These primitives had evidently forgotten all knowledge of up-to-date healing.

True enough—but they had forgotten because they no longer needed the knowledge. Attracted by our pitiful plight, two men, before I could object, had thrown the contents of two buckets over our backs.

I yelped with terror, but I had no place to run except back into the fire. Even the Brew was better than that. And I didn't get any in or even near my mouth.

Nevertheless, I was going to protest angrily at this horse-play while we were in such agony. But before I could say anything, I no longer felt pain.

I couldn't see what was happening to me, but I could see Alice's reaction. Her back was toward me, and she had quit whimpering.

Beneath the moist film of Brew, the blisters had fallen off, and a new healthy pink shone through.

Alice was so overcome, she even forgot her feud with me long enough to put her head on my chest and weep, "Oh, Dan, Dan, isn't it wonderful?"

I didn't want to give this evil drug too much credit. After all, like any narcotic, it had its beneficial effects if used correctly, but it could be horribly vicious if mishandled.

I said, "Come on, we have to go back," and I took her hand and led her to the new crater. I felt I *must* solve the puzzle of the Scrambled Men. And I thought of the credit I'd get for suggesting a new method of warfare—dropping bombcases filled with Brew and seeds from balloons. And what about cannon shooting shells whose propulsive power would also be seed and Brew? Only—how would you clean the cannon out afterward? You'd have to have a tree surgeon attached to every artillery team. Of course, you could use the rocket principle for your missiles. Only—wouldn't a Brobdingnagian pansy or cornstalk trailing out behind create an awful drag and a suddenly added weight? Wouldn't you have to train botanists to be aerodynamicists, or vice versa, and . . . ?

I rejected the whole idea. The brass at HQ would never believe me.

The Scrambled Men worked quickly and efficiently and with all the added vigor Brew-drinking gave. Inside of fifteen minutes, they had put out the fire and had then pulled the smoldering trunk out of the way. They at once began digging into the slopes and bottom of the excavation.

I watched them. They seemed to be obeying the orders of the man in the admiral's hat, and were continually conferring with him and their fellow workers. But not a single one could understand what the other was saying. All effective communication was done by facial expressions and gestures. Yet none would admit that to any of the others.

Well, I thought, this was scarcely a novelty, though I had never seen it carried out on such a thorough scale. And what—or who—was responsible?

Again, wearily this time, I asked a spectator what was going on. These people seemed to be incapable of making a serious statement, but there was always the chance that I'd find somebody who was an exception.

"I'll tell you, stranger. These men are living evidences of the fact that it doesn't pay to corrupt religion for your own purposes."

He drank from a flask he carried on a chain around his neck and then offered me a slug. He looked surprised at my refusal but took no offense.

"These were the leaders of the community just before Mahrud manifested himself as the Real Bull. You know—preachers, big and little businessmen, newspaper editors, gamblers, lawyers, bankers, union business agents, doctors, book reviewers, college professors. The men who are supposed to know how to cure your diseases social, economic, financial, administrative, psychological, spiritual, and so on, into the deep dark night. They knew the Right Word, comprehend? The Word that'd set Things straight, understand?

"The only trouble was that after the Brew began to flow freely, nobody who'd drunk from the Holy Bottle would pay any attention to these pillars of the community. They tried hard for a long time. Then, seeing which way the tide was inevitably foaming, they decided that maybe they'd better get in on a good thing. After all, if everybody was doing it, it must be the correct thing to do.

"So, after drinking enough Brew to give them courage, but not enough to change them into ordinary fun-loving but Mahrud-fearing citizens, they announced they were the prophets of a new religion. And from then on, according to their advertisements, none but them was fit to run the worship of the Big Bull. Of course, Sheed the Weather Prophet and Polivinosel and the Allegory ignored them, and so were denounced as false gods.

"Makes you laugh, doesn't it? But that's the way it goes. And that's the way it went until Mahrud—bibulous be his people forever—got mad. He announced, through Sheed, that these pillars of the community were just dummy-prophets, fakes. As punishment, he was going to give them a gift, as he had earlier done to the Dozen Diapered Darlings.

"So he said, in effect, 'You've been telling the people that you, and only you, have possession of the Real Bull, the Right Word. Well, you'll have it. Only it'll be the Word that nobody but you can understand, and to every other man it'll be a strange tongue. Now—scram!'

"But after he'd watched these poor characters stumbling around trying to talk to each other and the people and getting madder than the hops in the Brew or else sadder than the morning-after, Mahrud felt sorry. So he said, 'Look, I'll give you a chance. I've hidden the key to your troubles somewhere in this valley.

Search for it. If you find it, you'll be cured. And everybody will understand you, understand?'

"So he gave them a map—all of them, mind you—but this half-dressed Napoleon here grabbed the map, and he kept it by virtue of being the most un-understandable of the bunch. And, ever since, he's been directing the search for the key that'll unscramble them."

"That's why they're doing all this blasting and digging?" I asked, dazed.

"Yes, they're following the map," he said, laughing.

I thanked him and walked up behind the man with the admiral's hat and sword. I looked over his shoulder. The map was covered with long squiggly lines and many shorter branches. These, I supposed, were the lines he was following in his creekbed-making.

He looked around at me. "*Symfrantic gangleboys?*"

"You said it," I choked, and then I had to turn and walk away. "That map is a chart of the human nervous system," I gasped to Alice. "And he's following one of the branches of the vagus nerve."

"The *wandering* nerve," murmured Alice. "Or is it the *wondering* nerve? But what could all this mean?"

As we began our climb from the pit, I said, "I think we're seeing the birth-pangs of a new mythology. One of the demigods is based upon a famous comic strip character. Another is formed in the image of a pun on the translation of his name—though his new form does correspond to his lustful, asinine character. And we see that the chief deity bases his worship—and at least one of his epiphanies—on his mortal nickname. All this makes me wonder upon what foundations the old-time pantheons and myths were built. Were they also orginally based on such incongruous and unlikely features?"

"Daniel Temper!" Alice snapped. "You talk as if you believed the old pagan gods once existed and as if this Mahrud actually is a god!"

"Before I came here, I'd have laughed at any such theory," I said. "How do *you* explain what you've seen?"

We climbed up in silence. At the edge, I turned for one more glimpse of the Scrambled Men, the object lesson designed by Mahrud. They were digging just as busily as ever paying no attention to the ribald comments of the spectators. The funny thing about this, I thought, was that these unscrambled men had not yet caught on to the fact that the Scrambled Men were more than a wacky sect, that they were symbols of what the spectators must themselves do if they wished to travel beyond their own present carefree and happy but unprogressive state.

As plainly as the ears on the head of the Ass-God, the plight of these frantically digging sons of Bạbel said to everybody, "Look within yourselves to find the key."

That advice was probably uttered by the first philosopher among the cavemen.

I caught the glint of something metallic almost buried in the dirt of the slope. I went back and picked it up. It was a long-handled silver screwdriver.

If I hadn't known my old teacher so well, I don't think I ever would have understood its presence. But I'd been bombarded in his classes with his bizarre methods of putting things over. So I knew that I held in my hand another of his serious jokes—a utensil designed to take its place in the roster of myths springing up within this Valley Olympus.

You had the legend of Pandora's Box, of Philemon and Baucis' Pitcher, Medusa's Face, Odin's Pledged Eye. Why not the Silver Screwdriver?

I explained to Alice. "Remember the gag about the boy who was born with a golden screw in his navel? How all his life he wondered what it was for? How *ashamed* he was because he was different from anybody else and had to keep it hidden? Remember how he finally found a psychiatrist who told him to go home and dream of the fairy queen? And how Queen Titania slid down on a moonbeam and gave him a silver screwdriver? And how, when he'd unscrewed the golden screw from his navel, he felt so happy about being normal and being able to marry without making his bride laugh at him? Remember, he then forgot all his vain speculations upon the purpose of that golden screw? And how, very happy, he got up from his chair to reach for a cigarette? And his derrière, deprived of its former fastening, dropped off?"

"You don't mean it?" she breathed.

"But I do! How do we know the tale of the Golden Apples or the Golden Fleece didn't have their origin in jokes and that they later acquired a symbolic significance?"

She had no answer to that, any more than anybody did.

"Aren't you going to give it to the Scrambled Men?" she asked. "It'd save them all this blasting and digging. And they could settle down and quit talking gibberish."

"I imagine they've stumbled over it a hundred times before and kicked it to one side, refusing to recognize its meaning."

"Yes, but what does it mean?"

Exasperatedly, I said, "It's another clue to the fact that they ought to look within themselves, that they ought to consider the nature of their punishment and the lesson to be derived from it."

We walked away. The whole incident had left me plunged in gloom. I seemed to be getting deeper and deeper into a murk furnished by a being who, in the far dim background, mocked me. Was it mere coincidence that we'd been met by the Allegory, that he'd given us his vaguely ominous advice?

I didn't have much time to think, for we came to the side road which led to the State Hospital. I could look down it and see the white stones of the cemetery outside the high wire fence. I must have stood there longer than I thought, because Alice said, "What's the matter?"

"The State Hospital cemetery is just inside the fence. The Meltonville cemetery is on the other side. My father is buried in the state grounds; my mother lies in the village's cemetery. They are separated in death, as they were in life."

"Dan," she said softly, "we ought to get a few hours' sleep before we go on. We've walked a long way. Why don't we visit your parents' graves and then sleep there? Would you like that?"

"Very much. Thank you for the thought, Alice." The words came hard. "You're a pretty wonderful person."

"Not so much. It's merely the decent thing to do."

She would have to say that just when I was beginning to feel a little warmer toward her.

We went down the road. A big red-haired man walked toward us. He was all eyes for Alice, so much so that I expected the same sort of trouble we'd had with Polivinosel. But when he looked at me, he stopped, grinned, and burst into loud howls of laughter. As he passed me, I smelled his breath. It was loaded with the Brew.

"What's the matter with *him?*"

"I don't know," said Alice, looking at me. "Wait a minute! Of course! Polivinosel and the others must have known all the time that you were an Outsider!"

"Why?"

"Because you're bald! Have we seen any bald men? No! That's why this fellow laughed!"

"If that's so, I'm marked! All Polivinosel has to do is have his worshipers look for a skinhead."

"Oh, it's not that bad," she said. "You have to remember that Outsiders are constantly coming in, and that any number of ex-soldiers are in the process of changing. You could pass for one of those." She grabbed my hand. "Oh well, come along, let's get some sleep. Then we can think about it."

We came to the cemetery entrance. The shrubbery on either side of the stone arch had grown higher than my head. The iron gate in the arch was wide open and covered with rust. Inside, however, I did not see the expected desolate and wild expanse of tall weeds. They were kept trimmed by the goats and sheep that stood around like silvery statues in the moonlight.

I gave a cry and ran forward.

My mother's grave gaped like a big brown mouth. There was black water at the bottom, and her coffin was tilted on end. Evidently, it had been taken out and then slid carelessly back in. Its lid was open. It was empty.

Behind me, Alice said, "Easy, Dan. There's no cause for looking so alarmed."

"So *this* is your splendid people, Alice, the gods and nymphs of the New Golden Age. Grave-robbers! *Ghouls!*"

"I don't think so. They'd have no need or desire for money and jewels. Let's look around. There must be some other explanation."

We looked. We found Weepenwilly.

He was sitting with his back against a tombstone. He was so large and dark and quiet that he seemed to be cast out of bronze, a part of the monument itself. He looked like Rodin's *Thinker*—a *Thinker* wearing a derby hat and white loincloth. But there was something alive about him and, when he raised his head, we saw tears glistening in the moonlight.

"Could you tell me," I asked excitedly, "why all these graves are dug up?"

"Bless you, my bhoy," he said in a slight brogue. "Sure, now, and have you a loved one buried here?"

"My mother," I said.

His tears flowed faster. "Faith, bhoy, and is it so? Then you'll be happy when I tell you the glorious news. Me own dear wife was buried here, you know."

I didn't see anything about that to make me happy, but I kept quiet and waited.

"Yes, me bhoy—you'll pardon my calling you that, won't you? After all, I was a veteran o' the Spanish-American War, and I outrank you by quite a few years. In fact, if it hadn't been for the blessed ascent o' Mahrud—may he stub his divine toe and fall on his glorious face, bless him—I would now be dead of old age and me bones resting in the boat along with me wife's, and so—"

"What boat?" I interrupted.

"What *boat?* Where have you been? Ah, yes, you're new." He pointed his finger at his head, to indicate my baldness, I suppose.

"Faith, bhoy, you must hurry to Onaback in the morning and see the boatload o'bones leave. 'Twill be big doings then, you can count on that, with lots o' Brew and barbecued beef and pork and enough love-making to last you for a week."

After repeated questioning, I learned that Mahrud had had the remains of the dead in all the graveyards of the Area dug up and transported to Onaback. The next day, a boat carrying the bones would cross the Illinois and deposit the load upon the eastern shore. What would happen after that, not even the minor gods knew—or else would not tell—but everybody was sure that Mahrud intended to bring the dead back to life. And everybody was thronging into the city to witness such an event.

That news made me feel better. If there were to be many people on the roads and in the city itself, then it would be easy to stay lost in the crowds.

The man with the derby said, "As sure as they call me Weepenwilly, children, the All-Bull is going too far. He'll try to raise the dead, and he won't be able to do it. And then where will the people's faith in him be? Where will *I* be?"

He sobbed, "I'll be out o'work again, me position lost—me that served the Old God faithfully until I saw He was losing ground and that Mahrud was the up-and-coming deity nowadays. A God such as they had in the ancient days in Erin when gods was gods and men was giants. But now Mahrud—bull be his name, curse him—will lose face, and he'll never get it back. Then I'll be that most miserable o' all things, a prophet without honor. What's worse, I was just about to be promoted to a hemi-semi-demigod—I've been coming up fast all on account o' me faithful and hard work and keeping me mouth shut—when this big promotional stunt has to enter the All-Bull's head. Why can't he leave well enough alone?"

At last, I got out of him that he wasn't so much afraid Mahrud would fail as he was that he might succeed.

"If Mahrud does clothe the old bones with new flesh, me ever-loving wife will be out looking for me, and me life won't be worth a pre-Brew nickel. She'll never forget nor forgive that 'twas me who pushed her down those steps ten years ago and broke her stringy neck. 'Twill make no difference to her that she'll come back better than ever, with a lovely new figure and a pretty face instead o' that hatchet. Not her, the black-hearted, stone-livered wrath o' God!

"Sure, and I've had an unhappy life ever since the day I opened me innocent blue eyes—untainted except for the old original sin, but Mahrud says that's no dogma o' his—and first saw the light o' day. Unhappy I've been, and unhappy I'll live. I can't even taste the sweet sting o' death—because, as sure as the sun rises in the east, as sure as Durham became a bull and swam the Illinois with the lovely Peggy on his back and made her his bride upon the high bluffs—I can't even die because me everloving wife would search out me bones and ship them to Mahrud and be standing there facing me when I arose."

I was getting weary of listening to this flow of hyperbole, interminable as the Illinois itself. I said, "Thank you, Mr. Weepenwilly, and good night. We've got a long trip ahead of us."

"Sure, me bhoy, and that's not me given name. 'Tis a nickname given me by the bhoys down at the town hall because . . ."

I heard no more. I went back to my mother's grave and lay down by it. I couldn't get to sleep, because Alice and Weepenwilly were talking. Then, just as I'd managed almost to drop off, Alice sat down by me. She insisted on retelling me the story Weepenwilly had just told her.

I'd seen his white loincloth, hadn't I? Well, if Weepenwilly had stood up, I'd have perceived the three-cornered fold of it. And I'd have seen its remarkable resemblance to early infant apparel. That resemblance was not coincidental, for Weepenwilly was one of the Dozen Diapered Darlings.

Moreover, if he had stood up, I'd have noticed the yellow glow that emanated from his posterior, the nimbus so much like a firefly's in color and position.

It seemed that, shortly after the Brew began taking full effect, when the people of Onaback had turned their backs to the outside world, numerous self-styled prophets had tried to take advantage of the new religion. Each had presented his own variation of an as-yet-misunderstood creed. Among them had been twelve politicians who had long been bleeding the city's treasury dry. Because it was some time before the Bottle's contents began affecting the nature of things noticeably, they had not been aware at first of what was happening.

The wheels of industry slowed by degrees. Grass and trees

subtly encroached upon pavement. People gradually lost interest in the cares of life. Inhibitions were imperceptibly dissolved. Enmities and bitternesses and diseases faded. The terrors, burdens, and boredoms of life burned away as magically as the morning mist under the rising sun.

A time came when people quit flying to Chicago for business or pleasure. When nobody went to the library to take out books. When the typographers and reporters of the daily newspapers failed to show up for work. When the Earthgripper Diesel Company and Myron Malker's Distillery—biggest on earth of their kind, both of them—blew the final whistle. When people everywhere seemed to realize that all had been wrong with the world, but that it was going to be fine and dandy in the future.

About then, the mail-carriers quit. Frantic telegrams and letters were sent to Washington and the state capital—though from other towns, because the local operators had quit. This was when the Food and Drug Administration, and the Internal Revenue Bureau, and the F.B.I. sent agents into Onaback to investigate. These agents did not come back and others were sent in, only to succumb to the Brew.

The Brew had not yet reached its full potency, when Durham had just revealed himself, through the prophet Sheed, as Mahrud. There was still some opposition, and the most vigorous came from the twelve politicians. They organized a meeting in the courthouse square and urged the people to follow them in an attack on Mahrud. First they would march on Traybell University, where Sheed lived in the Meteorological Building.

"Then," said one of the twelve, shaking his fist at the long thin line of Brew geysering from the Bottle up on the hills, "we'll lynch this mad scientist who calls himself Mahrud, this lunatic we know is a crazy university professor and a reader of poetry and philosophy. Friends, citizens, Americans, if this Mahrud is indeed a god, as Sheed, another mad scientist claims, let him strike me with lightning! My friends and I dare him to!"

The dozen were standing on a platform in the courthouse yard. They could look down Main Street and across the river to the

hills. They faced the east defiantly. No bellowings came, no light-
nings. But in the next instant, the dozen were forced to flee
ignominiously, never again to defy the All-Bull.

Alice giggled. "They were struck by an affliction which was
not as devastating as lightning nor as spectacular. But it was far
more demoralizing. Mahrud wished on them a disability which
required them to wear diapers for much the same reason babies
have to. Of course, this convinced the Dozen Diapered Darlings.
But that brassy-nerved bunch of ex-ward-heelers switched right
around and said they'd known all along that Mahrud was the Real
Bull. They'd called the meeting so they could make a dramatic
announcement of their change of heart. Now he'd given them a
monopoly on divine relevation. If anybody wanted to get in touch
with him, let them step up and pay on the line. They still hadn't
realized that money was no good anymore.

"They even had the shortsightedness and the crust to pray to
Mahrud for a special sign to prove their prophethood. And the All-
Bull did send them signs of their sanctity. He gave them permanent
halos, blazing yellow lights."

Sitting up and hugging her knees, Alice rocked back and forth
with laughter. "Of course, the Dozen should have been ecstatically
happy. But they weren't. For Mahrud had slyly misplaced their
halos, locating them in a place where, if the Darlings wished to
demonstrate their marks of sainthood, they would be forced to
stand up.

"And, would you believe it, this thick-headed Dozen refuses to
admit that Mahrud has afflicted them. Instead, they brag continually about their halos' location, and they attempt to get everybody else to wear diapers. They say a towel around the middle is as
much a sign of a true believer in Mahrud as a turban or fez is that
of a believer in Allah.

"Naturally, their real reason is that they don't want to be
conspicuous. Not that they mind being outstanding. It's just that
they don't want people to be reminded of their disability or their
original sin."

Tears ran from her eyes. She choked with laughter.

I failed to see anything funny about it, and I told her so.

"You don't get it, Temper," she said. "This condition is curable. All the Darlings have to do is pray to Mahrud to be relieved of it, and they will be. But their pride won't let them. They insist it's a benefit and a sign of the Bull's favor. They suffer, yes, but they like to suffer. Just as Weepenwilly likes to sit on his wife's tombstone— as if that'd keep her under the ground—and wail about his misfortune. He and his kind wouldn't give up their punishment for the world—literally!"

She began laughing loudly again. I sat up and grabbed her shoulders and pulled her close to smell her breath. There was no hint of the Brew, so she hadn't been drinking from Weepenwilly's bottle. She was suffering from hysteria, plain and simple.

The normal procedure for bringing a woman back to normality is to slap her resoundingly upon the cheek. But in this case Alice turned the tables by slapping me first—resoundingly. The effect was the same. She quit laughing and glared at me.

I held my stinging cheek. "What was that for?"

"For trying to take advantage of me," she said.

I was so angry and taken aback that I could only stutter, "Why, I—why, I—"

"Just keep your hands to yourself," she snapped. "Don't mistake my sympathy for love. Or think, because these Brew-bums have no inhibitions or discrimination, that I've also succumbed."

I turned my back on her and closed my eyes. But the longer I lay there, and the more I thought of her misinterpretation, the madder I became. Finally, boiling within, I sat up and said tightly, "Alice!"

She must not have been sleeping either. She raised up at once and stared at me, her eyes big. "What—what is it?"

"I forgot to give you this." I let her have it across the side of her face. Then, without waiting to see the effect of my blow, I lay down and turned my back again. For a minute, I'll admit, my spine was cold and tense, waiting for the nails to rake down my naked skin.

But nothing like that happened. First, there was the sort of silence that breathes. Then, instead of the attack, came a racking breath, followed by sobs, which sloped off into snifflings and the wiping of tears.

I stood it as long as I could. Then I sat up again and said, "All right, so maybe I shouldn't have hit you. But you had no business taking it for granted that I was trying to make love to you. Look, I know I'm repulsive to you, but that's all the more reason why I wouldn't be making a pass at you. I have some pride. And you don't exactly drive me out of my mind with passion, you know. What makes you think you're any Helen of Troy or Cleopatra?"

There I went. I was always trying to smooth things over, and every time I ended by roughing them up. Now she was mad and she showed it by getting up and walking off. I caught her as she reached the cemetery gate.

"Where do you think you're going?" I asked.

"Down to the foot of Main Street, Onaback, Illinois, and I'm bottling a sample of the Brew there. Then I'm reporting to my father as soon as possible."

"You little fool, you can't do that. You're supposed to stick with me."

She tossed her long black hair. "My orders don't say I have to. If, in my opinion, your presence becomes a danger to my mission, I may leave you. And I think you're a definite danger—if not to my mission, at least to me!"

I grabbed her wrist and whirled her around. "You're acting like a little girl, not like a major in the U.S. Marines. What's the matter with you?"

She tried to jerk her wrist loose. That made me madder, but when her fist struck me, I saw red. I wasn't so blinded that I couldn't find her cheek again with the flat of my hand. Then she was on me with a hold that would have broken my arm if I hadn't applied the counterhold. Then I had her down on her side with both her arms caught behind her back. This was where a good little man was better than a good big girl.

"All right," I gritted, "what is it?"

She wouldn't reply. She twisted frantically, though she knew she couldn't get loose and groaned with frustration.

"Is it the same thing that's wrong with me?"

She quit struggling and said, very softly. "Yes, that's it."

I released her arms. She rolled over on her back, but she didn't try to get up. "You mean," I said, still not able to believe it, "that you're in love with me, just as I am with you?"

She nodded again. I kissed her with all the pent-up desire that I'd been taking out on her in physical combat a moment ago.

I said, "I still can't believe it. It was only natural for me to fall in love with you, even if you did act as if you hated my guts. But why did you fall in love with me? Or, if you can't answer that, why did you ride me?"

"You won't like this," she said. "I could tell you what a psychologist would say. We're both college graduates, professional people, interested in the arts and so on. That wouldn't take in the differences, or course. But what does that matter? It happened.

"I didn't want it to. I fought against it. And I used the reverse of the old Jamesian principle that, if you pretend to be something or to like something, you will be that something. I tried to act as if I loathed you."

"Why?" I demanded. She turned her head away, but I took her chin and forced her face to me. "Let's have it."

"You know I was nasty about your being bald. Well, I didn't really dislike that. Just the opposite—I loved it. And that was the whole trouble. I analyzed my own case and decided I loved you because I had an Electra complex. I—"

"You mean," I said, my voice rising, "that because I was bald like your father and somewhat older than you, you fell for me?"

"Well, no, not really. I mean that's what I told myself so I'd get over it. That helped me to pretend to hate you so that I might end up doing so."

Flabbergasted was no word for the way I felt. If I hadn't been lying on the ground, I'd have been floored. Alice Lewis was one of those products of modern times, so psychology-conscious that she tended to regard an uninhibited affection of parent and child as a sign that both ought to rush to the nearest psychoanalyst.

"I'm in a terrible fix," said Alice. "I don't know if you fulfill my father-image or if I'm genuinely in love with you. I think I am, yet . . ."

She put her hand up to stroke my naked scalp. Knowing what I did, I resented the caress. I started to jerk my head away, but she clamped her hand on it and exclaimed, "Dan, your scalp's *fuzzy!*"

I said, "Huh?" and ran my own palm over my head. She was right. A very light down covered my baldness.

"So," I said, delighted and shocked at the same time, "that's what the nymph meant when she pointed at my head and said that if it weren't for *that*, she'd think I hadn't tasted the Brew yet! The Brew that fellow poured on my head—*that's* what did it!"

I jumped up and shouted, "Hooray!"

And scarcely had the echoes died down than there was an answering call, one that made my blood chill. This was a loud braying laugh from far off, a bellowing hee-haw!

"Polivinosel!" I said. I grabbed Alice's hand, and we fled down the road. Nor did we stop until we had descended the hill that runs down into U.S. Route 24. There, puffing and panting from the half-mile run and thirstier than ever, we walked toward the city of Onaback, another half-mile away.

I looked back from time to time, but I saw no sign of the Ass. There was no guarantee he wasn't on our trail, however. He could have been lost in the great mass of people we'd encountered. These carried baskets and bottles and torches and were, as I found out from conversation with a man, latecomers going to view the departure of the bone-boat from the foot of Main Street.

"Rumor says that Mahrud—may his name be bull—will raise the dead at the foot of the hill the Fountain of the Bottle spurts from. Whether that's so or not, we'll all have fun. Barbecue, Brew, and bundling make the world go round."

I couldn't argue with that statement. They certainly were the principal amusements of the natives.

During our progress down Adams Street, I learned much about the valley's setup. My informant was very talkative, as were all his fellow Brew-drinkers. He told me that the theocracy began on the lowest plane with his kind, Joe Doe. Then there were the prayer-men. These received the petitions of the populace, sorted them out, and passed on those that needed attention to prophets like the Forecaster Sheed, who screened them. Then these in turn were relayed to demigods like Polivinosel, Albert Allegory, and a dozen others I had not heard of before then. They reported directly to Mahrud or Peggy.

Mahrud handled godhood like big business. He had delegated various departments to his vice-presidents such as the Ass, who handled fertility, and Sheed, who was probably the happiest forecaster who'd ever lived. Once a professor of physics at Traybell and the city's meteorologist, Sheed was now the only weatherman whose prophecies were one hundred percent correct. There was a good reason for that. He made the weather.

All this was very interesting, but my mind wasn't as intent on the information as it should have been. For one thing, I kept looking back to see if Polivinosel was following us. For another, I worried about Alice's attitude toward me. Now that I had hair, would she stop loving me? Was it a—now I was doing it—fixation that attracted her to me, or was it a genuine affection?

If my situation hadn't been so tense, I'd have laughed at myself. Who would have thought that some day I might not leap with joy at the possibility of once again having a full head of hair and a beautiful girl in love with me?

The next moment, I did leap. It was not from joy, however. Somebody behind me had given a loud braying laugh. There was no mistaking the Ass's hee-haw. I whirled and saw, blazing golden in both the light of the moon and the torches, the figure of Polivinosel galloping toward us. There were people in the way, but they ran to get out of his path, yelling as they did so. His hoofs rang on the pavement even above their cries. Then he was on us and bellowing, "What now, little man? What now?"

Just as he reached us, I fell flat on my face. He was going so fast, he couldn't stop. His hoofs didn't help him keep his balance either, nor did Alice when she shoved him. Over he went, carrying with him bottles and baskets of fruit and corn and little cages of chickens. Women shrieked, baskets flew, glass broke, chickens squawked and shot out of sprung doors—Polivinosel was buried in the whole mess.

Alice and I burst through the crowd, turned a corner and raced down to Washington Street, which ran parallel to Adams. There was a much smaller parade of pilgrims here, but it was better than nothing. We ducked among these while, a block away, the giant throat of the Ass called again and again, "Little man, what now? What now, little man?"

I could have sworn he was galloping toward us. Then his voice, mighty as it was, became smaller, and the fast cloppety-clop died away.

Panting, Alice and I walked down Washington. We saw that the three bridges across the Illinois had been destroyed. A native told us that Mahrud had wrecked them with lightning one stormy night.

"Not that he needed to worry about crossing to the other side," he said, swiftly making the sign of the bull. "All of what used to be East Onaback is now sacred to the owner of the Bottle."

His attitude verified what I had noticed already. These people, though uninhibited by the Brew in other respects, retained enough awe to give the higher gods plenty of privacy. Whatever the priests relayed to them was enough to keep them happy.

When we came to the foot of Main Street, which ran right into the Illinois, we looked for a place to rest. Both of us were bone-weary. It was almost dawn. We had to have some sleep, if we wanted to be at all efficient for our coming work.

First, though, we had to watch the Fountain. This was a thin arc of the Brew which rose from the Bottle, set on the top of the bluffs across the river from Onaback, and ended in the middle of the waters. The descending moon played a rainbow of wavering and bright colors along it. How that trick was done, I didn't know, but it was one of the most beautiful sights I've ever seen.

I studied it and concluded that some force was being exerted linearly to keep the winds from scattering it into fine spray. And I saw how easy it would be to locate the Bottle. Follow the fountain to its source, a mile and a half away. Then destroy it, so the power

of the Bull would be gone. After that, sit back and watch the
Marines glide in and begin the conquest of Onaback.

It was as simple as that.

We looked around some more and found a place on the riverside park to lie down. Alice, snuggled in my arms, said, "Dan, I'm
awfully thirsty. Are you?"

I admitted that I was, but that we'd have to stand it. Then I
said, "Alice, after you get your sample, are you going to hike right
back to H.Q.?"

"No," she said, kissing my chest, "I'm not. I'm sticking with
you. After all, I want to see if your hair turns out curly or straight.
And don't tell me!"

"I won't. But you're going to get awfully thirsty before this
assignment is over."

Secretly, I was pleased. If she wanted to be with me, then my
returning hair wasn't putting a roadblock in the course of true love.
Maybe it was the real thing, not just something laid by a trauma
and hatched by a complex. Maybe . . .

*There I was in the tavern in the little town of Croncruachshin.
I'd just fulfilled my mother's deathbed wish that I visit her mother,
who was living when I stepped aboard the plane for Ireland and died
the day I set foot on the green sod.*

*After the funeral, I'd stopped in Bill O'basean's for a bite, and
Bill, who was wearing horns like a Texas steer's, picked the bottle off
the shelf where he kept his other curios, and bellowed, "Danny
Temper, look at the bull on the side o' that piece of glass! Know what
that means? 'Tis the bottle that Goibniu, the smith o' the gods,
fashioned. 'Twill run forever with magical brew for him that knows
the words, for him that has a god hidden within himself."*

*"What happened to the owner?" I said, and he answered,
"Sure and bejasus, all the Old Ones—Erse and Greek and Dutch
and Rooshian and Chinee and Indian—found they was crowdin'
each other, so they had a trooce and left Airth and went elsewhere.
Only Pan stayed here for a few centuries, and he flew away on the*

wings o'light when the New Ones came. He didn't die as the big mouths claim.

"*And then, in the eighteenth century, the New Ones, who'd become Old Ones now, thought that, begorry, they'd better be leavin,' too, now that they was crowdin' each other and makin' a mess o'things. But the Bottle o' Goibniu has been lyin' around here collectin' dust and stories and here ye are, my bhoy, for ten American dollars, and what do ye intend doin' with it?*"

So I said, "I'll wrap it up and send it on to my old professor as a joke. It'll tickle him when I tell him it's for sure the genuine everflowing bottle o' Goibniu."

And Bill O'basean winked and said, "And him a teetotaller. What'll his wife, the old hag and wicked witch, say to that?"

And I said, "Wouldn't it be funny if the old prof thought this really was Goibniu's bottle?"

And Bill, who had now become the Rational Man, looked severely at me and said to the squirrel crouched on his shoulder, "O Nuciferous One, what this simpleton don't know nohow! Hasn't he intellect enough, begorry, to see that the bottle was destined from its making for Boswell Durham? 'Bos,' which is Latin for the bovine species, and 'well,' a combination of the Anglo-Saxon 'wiella,' meaning fountain or well-spring 'wiellan' or 'wellen,' meaning to pour forth, and the Anglo-Saxon adverb 'wel,' meaning worthily or abundantly, and the adjective, meaning healthy. Boswell—the fountaining, abundantly healthy bovine. And of course, Durham. Everybody knows that that is sign and symbol for a bull."

"And he was born under Taurus too," I said.

And then the bartender, who was bald Alice by now—bald alas!—handed me the Bottle. "Here, have a drink on the house." And then I was on the steeply sloping rooftop and sliding fast toward the edge. "Drink, drink, drink!" screamed Alice. "Or you're lost, lost, lost!"

But I wouldn't do it, and I awoke moaning, with the sun in my eyes and Alice shaking me and saying, "Dan, Dan, what's the matter?"

I told her about my dream and how it was mixed up with things that had actually happened. I told her how I had bought this bottle from O'basean and sent it to the Professor as a hoax. But she didn't pay much attention because, like me, she had one thing uppermost in the cells of both body and mind. Thirst. Thirst was a living lizard that, with a hot rough skin, forced its swelling body down our throats and pulsed there, sucking moisture from us with every breath.

She licked her dry, cracked lips and then, glancing wistfully toward the river, where bathers shouted and plunged with joy, asked, "I don't suppose it'd hurt me if I sat in it, do you?"

"Be careful," I said, my words rattling like pebbles in a dried gourd. I ached to join her, but I couldn't even get near the water. I was having trouble enough combatting the panic that came with the odor of the Brew blowing from the river on the morning breeze.

While she waded out until the water was hip-deep and cupped it in her hands and poured it over her breasts, I examined my surroundings in the daylight. To my left was a warehouse and a wharf. Tied alongside the latter was an old coal barge that had been painted bright green. A number of men and women, ignoring the festivities, were busy carrying bags and long mummy-shaped bundles from the warehouse to the boat. These were the bones that had been dug up recently. If my information was correct, they'd be ferried across to the other side after the ceremonies.

That was fine. I intended to go over with them. As soon as Alice came back out of the water, I'd unfold my plans to her and if she thought she could go through with it, we'd . . .

A big grinning head emerged from the water just behind Alice. It belonged to one of those jokers on every beach who grabs you from behind and pulls you under. I opened my mouth to yell a warning, but it was too late. I don't suppose I'd have been heard above the crowd's noise, anyway.

After sputtering and blowing the water out, she stood there with the most ecstatic expression, then bent over and began drinking great mouthfuls. That was enough for me. I was dying within, because she was now on the enemy's side, and I'd wanted so badly to do something for her that I hurt. But I had to get going before she saw me and yelled, "Come on in, Dan, the beer's fine!"

I trotted through the crowd, moaning to myself at losing her, until I came to the far end of the warehouse, where she couldn't possibly see me enter. There, under the cool cavernous roof, I paused until I saw a lunch-basket sitting by a pile of rags. I scooped it up, untied one of the bags, put the basket inside, and hoisted the bag over my shoulder. I stepped, unchallenged, into the line of workers going out to the barge. As if I belonged there, I briskly carried my burden over the gangplank.

But instcad of depositing it where everybody else was, I walked around the mountain of bags. Out of view on the riverside, I took the basket out and dumped the bones inside the bag over the railing into the river. I took one peek around my hiding place. Alice was nowhere to be seen.

Satisfied she would not be able to find me, and glad that I'd not disclosed my plans to her last night, I took the basket and crawled backward into the bag.

Once there, I succumbed to the three things that had been fighting within me—grief, hunger, and thirst. Tears ran as I thought of Alice. At the same time, I greedily devoured, in rapid succession, an orange, a leg and breast of chicken, a half-loaf of fresh bread, and two great plums.

The fruit helped my thirst somewhat, but there was only one thing that could fully ease that terrible ache in my throat—water. Moreover, the bag was close and very hot. The sun beat down on it and, though I kept my face as close to the open end as I dared, I suffered. But as long as I kept sweating and could draw some fresh air now and then, I knew I'd be all right. I wasn't going to give up when I'd gotten this far.

I crouched within the thick leather bag like—I couldn't help thinking—an embryo within its sac. I was sweating so much that I felt as if I were floating in amniotic fluid. The outside noises came through dimly; every once in a while I'd hear a big shout.

When the workers quit the barge, I stuck my head out long enough to grab some air and look at the sun. It seemed to be about eleven o'clock, although the sun, like the moon, was so distorted that I couldn't be sure. Our scientists had said the peculiar warmth of the valley and the elongation of the sun and moon were due to some "wave-focusing force field" hanging just below the stratosphere. This had no more meaning than calling it a sorcerer's spell, but it had satisfied the general public and the military.

About noon, the ceremonies began. I ate the last two plums in the basket, but I didn't dare open the bottle at its bottom. Though it felt like a wine-container, I didn't want to chance the possibility that the Brew might be mixed in it.

From time to time, I heard, intermingled with band music, snatches of chants. Then, suddenly, the band quit playing and there was a mighty shout of, "Mahrud is Bull—Bull is all—and Sheed is the prophet!"

The band began playing the Semiramis overture. When it was almost through, the barge trembled with an unmistakable motion. I had not heard any tug, nor did I think there was one. After all I'd seen, the idea of a boat moving by itself was just another miracle.

The overture ended in a crash of chords. Somebody yelled, "Three cheers for Albert Allegory!" and the crowd responded.

The noises died. I could hear, faintly, the slapping of the waves against the side of the barge. For a few minutes, that was all. Then heavy footsteps sounded close by. I ducked back within the bag and lay still. The steps came very near and stopped.

The rumbling unhuman voice of The Allegory said, "Looks as if somebody forgot to tie up this bag."

Another voice said, "Oh, Al, leave it. What's the difference?"

I would have blessed the unknown voice except for one thing—it sounded so much like Alice's.

I'd thought that was a shock, but a big green four-fingered hand appeared in the opening of the bag's mouth and seized the cords, intending to draw them close and tie them up. At the same time, the tag, which was strung on the cord, became fixed in my vision long enough for me to read the name.

Mrs. Daniel Temper.

I had thrown my mother's bones into the river!

For some reason, this affected me more than the fact that I was now tied into a close and suffocating sack, with no knife to cut my way out.

The voice of The Allegory, strange in its saurian mouth-structure, boomed out. "Well, Peggy, was your sister quite happy when you left her?"

"Alice'll be perfectly happy as soon as she finds this Dan Temper," said the voice, which I now realized was Peggy Rourke's. "After we'd kissed, as sisters should who haven't seen each other for three years, I explained everything that had happened to me. She started to tell me of her adventures, but I told her I knew most of them. She just couldn't believe that we'd been keeping tabs on her and her lover ever since they crossed the border."

"Too bad we lost track of him after Polivinosel chased them down Adams Street," said Allegory. "And if we'd been one minute earlier, we'd have caught him, too. Oh, well, we know he'll try to destroy the Bottle—or steal it. He'll be caught there."

"If he does get to the Bottle," said Peggy, "he'll be the first man to do so. That F.B.I. agent only got as far as the foot of the hill, remember."

"If anybody can do it," chuckled Allegory, "Dan H. Temper can. Or so says Mahrud, who should know him well enough."

"Won't Temper be surprised when he finds out that his every move since he entered Mahrudland has been not only a reality, but a symbol of reality? And that we've been leading him by the nose through the allegorical maze?"

Allegory laughed with all the force of a bull-alligator's roar.

"I wonder if Mahrud isn't asking too much of him by demanding that he read into his adventures a meaning outside of themselves? For instance, could he see that he entered this valley as a baby enters the world, bald and toothless? Or that he met and conquered the ass that is in all of us? But that, in order to do so, he had to lose his outer strength and visible burden—the water-tank? And then operate upon his own strength with no source of external strength to fall back on? Or that, in the Scrambled Men, he met the living punishment of human self-importance in religion?"

Peggy said, "He'll die when he finds out that the real Polivinosel was down South and that you were masquerading as him."

"Well," rumbled Allegory, "I hope Temper can see that Mahrud kept Polivinosel in his asinine form as an object lesson to everybody that, if Polivinosel could become a god, then anybody could. If he can't, he's not very smart."

I was thinking that I had, strangely enough, thought that very thing about the Ass. And then the cork in the bottle in the basket decided to pop, and the contents—Brew—gushed out over my side.

I froze, afraid that the two would hear it. But they went on talking as if they hadn't noticed. It was no wonder—the Allegory's voice thundered on.

"He met Love, Youth, and Beauty—which are nowhere to be found in abundance except in this valley—in the form of Alice Lewis. And she, like all three of those qualities, was not won easily, nor without a change in the wooer. She rejected him, lured him, teased him, almost drove him crazy. She wanted him, yet she didn't. And he had to conquer some of his faults—such as shame of his baldness and toothlessness—before he could win her, only to find out his imagined faults were, in her eyes, virtues."

"Do you think he'll know the answer to the question you, in your metamorphosis, asked him?" Peggy said.

"I don't know. I wish I'd first taken the form of the Sphinx and asked him her questions, so he'd have had a clue to what was expected of him. He'd have known, of course, that the answer to the Sphinx is that man himself is the answer to all the old questions. Then he might have seen what I was driving at when I asked him where Man—Modern Man—was going."

"And when he finds the answer to that, then he too will be a god."

"If!" said Allegory. "If! Mahrud says that Dan Temper is quite a few cuts above the average man of this valley. He is the reformer, the idealist who won't be happy unless he's tilting his lance against some windmill. In his case, he'll not only have to defeat the windmills within himself—his neuroses and traumas—he'll have to reach deep within himself and pull up the drowned god in the abyss of himself by the hair. If he doesn't, he'll die."

"Oh, no, not that!" gasped Peggy. "I didn't know Mahrud *meant* that!"

"Yes," thundered the Allegory, "he does! He says that Temper will have to find himself or die. Temper himself would want it that way. He'd not be satisfied with being one of the happy-go-lucky, let-the-gods-do-it Brew-bums who loaf beneath this uninhibited sun. He'll either be first in this new Rome, or else he'll die."

The conversation was interesting, to say the least, but I lost track of the next few sentences because the bottle had not quit gushing. It was spurting a gentle but steady stream against my side. And, I suddenly realized that the bag would fill and the bottle's contents would run out the mouth of the bag and reveal my presence.

Frantically, I stuck my finger in the bottle's neck and succeeded in checking the flow.

"So," said Allegory, "he fled to the cemetery, where he met Weepenwilly. Weepenwilly who mourns eternally yet would resent the dead being brought back. Who refuses to take his cold and numbed posterior from the gravestone of his so-called beloved. That man was the living symbol of himself, Daniel Temper, who grieved himself into baldness at an early age, though he blamed his mysterious sickness and fever for it. Yet who, deep down, didn't want his mother back, because she'd been nothing but trouble to him."

The pressure in the bottle suddenly increased and expelled my finger. The Brew in it burst over me despite my efforts to plug it up again, gushing out at such a rate that the bag would fill faster than its narrow mouth could let it out. I was facing two dangers—being discovered and being drowned.

As if my troubles weren't enough, somebody's heavy foot descended on me and went away. A voice succeeded it. I recognized it, even after all these years. It was that of Doctor Boswell Durham, the god now known as Mahrud. But it had a basso quality and richness it had not possessed in his predeity days.

"All right, Dan Temper, the masquerade is over!"

Frozen with terror, I kept silent and motionless.

"I've sloughed off the form of the Allegory and taken my own,"

Durham went on. "That was really I talking all the time. I was the Allegory you refused to recognize. Myself—your old teacher. But then you always did refuse to see any of the allegories I pointed out to you.

"How's this one, Danny? Listen! You crawled aboard Charon's ferry—this coal barge—and into the sack which contained your mother's bones. Not only that, but as a further unconscious symbol of your rejection of the promise of life for your mother, you threw her bones overboard. Didn't you notice her name on the tag? Why not? Subconsciously on purpose?

"Well, Dan my boy, you're right back where you started—in your mother's womb where, I suspect you've always wanted to be. How do I know so much? Brace yourself for a real shock. I was Doctor Duerf, the psychologist who conditioned you. Run that name backward and remember how I love a pun or an anagram."

I found all this hard to believe. The Professor had always been kindly, gentle, and humorous. I would have thought he was pulling my leg if it hadn't been for one thing! that was the Brew, which was about to drown me. I really thought he was carrying his joke too far.

I told him so, as best I could in my muffled voice.

He yelled back, "'Life is real—life is earnest!' You've always said so, Dan. Let's see now if you meant it. All right, you're a baby due to be born. Are you going to stay in this sac, and die, or are you going to burst out from the primal waters into life?

"Let's put it another way, Dan. I'm the midwife, but my hands are tied. I can't assist in the accouchment directly. I have to coach you via long distance, symbolically, so to speak. I can tell you what to do to some extent, but you, being an unborn infant, may have to guess at the meaning of some of my words."

I wanted to cry out a demand that he quit clowning around and let me out. But I didn't. I had my pride.

Huskily, weakly, I said, "What do you want me to do?"

"Answer the questions I, as Allegory and Ass, asked you. Then you'll be able to free yourself. And rest assured, Dan, that I'm not opening the bag for you."

What was it he had said? My mind groped frantically; the rising tide of the Brew made thinking difficult. I wanted to scream and tear at the leather with my naked hands. But if I did that, I'd go under and never come up again.

I clenched my fists, forced my mind to slow down, to go back over what Allegory and Polivinosel had said.

What was it? What was it?

The Allegory had said, "Where do you want to go now?"

And Polivinosel, while chasing me down Adams Street—*Adam's* Street?—had called out, "Little man, what now?"

The answer to the *Sphinx's* question was:

Man.

Allegory and Ass had proposed *their* questions in the true scientific manner so that they contained their own answer.

That answer was that man was *more* than man.

In the next second, with that realization acting like a powerful motor within me, I snapped the conditioned reflex as if it were a wishbone. I drank deeply of the Brew, both to quench my thirst and to strip myself of the rest of my predeity inhibitions. I commanded the bottle to stop fountaining. And with an explosion that sent Brew and leather fragments flying over the barge, I rose from the bag.

Mahrud was standing there, smiling. I recognized him as my old prof, even though he was now six and a half feet tall, had a thatch of long black hair, and had pushed his features a little here and there to make himself handsome. Peggy stood beside him. She looked like her sister, Alice, except that she was red-haired. She was beautiful, but I've always preferred brunettes—specifically, Alice.

"Understand everything now?" he asked.

"Yes," I said, "including the fact that much of this symbolism was thought up on the spur of the moment to make it sound impressive. Also, that it wouldn't have mattered if I *had* drowned, for you'd have brought me back to life."

"Yes, but you'd never have become a god. Nor would you have succeeded me."

"What do you mean?" I asked blankly.

"Peggy and I deliberately led you and Alice toward this dénouement so we could have somebody to carry on our work here. We're a little bored with what we've done, but we realize that we can't just leave. So I've picked you as a good successor. You're conscientious, you're an idealist, and you've discovered your potentialities. You'll probably do better than I have at this suspension of 'natural' laws. You'll make a better world than I could. After all, Danny, my godling, I'm the Old Bull, you know, the one for having fun.

"Peggy and I want to go on a sort of Grand Tour to visit the former gods of Earth, who are scattered all over the Galaxy. They're all young gods, you know, by comparison with the age of the Universe. You might say they've just got out of school—this Earth—and are visiting the centers of genuine culture to acquire polish."

"What about me?"

"You're a god now, Danny. You make your own decisions. Meanwhile, Peggy and I have places to go."

He smiled one of those long slow smiles he used to give us students when he was about to quote a favorite line of his.

"'. . . listen: there's a hell
of a good universe next door.
Let's go.'"

Peggy and he did go. Like thistles, swept away on the howling winds of space, they were gone.

And after they had vanished, I was left staring at the river and the hills and the sky and the city, where the assembled faithful watched, awestruck. It was mine, all mine.

Including one black-haired figure—and what a figure—that stood on the wharf and waved at me.

Do you think I stood poised in deep reverie and pondered on my duty to mankind or the shape of teleology now that I was personally turning it out on my metaphysical potter's wheel?

Not I. I leaped into the air and completed sixteen entrechats of pure joy before I landed. Then I walked across the water—*on* the water—to Alice.

The next day, I sat upon the top of a hill overlooking the valley. As the giant troop-carrying gliders soared in, I seized them with psychokinesis, or what-have you, and dunked them one by one in the river. And as the Marines threw away their arms and swam toward shore, I plucked away their oxygen masks and thereafter forgot about them, unless they seemed to be having trouble swimming. Then I was kind enough to pick them up and deposit them on shore.

I do think it was rather nice of me. After all, I wasn't in too good a mood. That whole night and morning, my legs and my upper gums had been very sore. They were making me somewhat irritable, despite liberal potions of Brew.

But there was a good reason.

I had growing pains, and I was teething.

The Alley Man
1959

"THE MAN FROM the puzzle factory was here this morning," said Gummy. "While you was out fishin."

She dropped the piece of wiremesh she was trying to tie with string over a hole in the rusty window screen. Cursing, grunting like a hog in a wallow, she leaned over and picked it up. Straightening, she slapped viciously at her bare shoulder.

"Figurin skeeters! Must be a million outside, all tryin to get away from the burnin garbage."

"Puzzle factory?" said Deena. She turned away from the battered kerosene-burning stove over which she was frying sliced potatoes and perch and bullheads caught in the Illinois River, half a mile away.

"Yeah!" snarled Gummy. "You heard Old Man say it. Nuthouse. Booby hatch. So . . . this cat from the puzzle factory was named John Elkins. He gave Old Man all those tests when they had him locked up last year. He's the skinny little guy with a moustache 'n never lookin you in the eye 'n grinnin like a skunk eatin a shirt. The cat who took Old Man's hat away from him 'n woun't give it back to him until Old Man promised to be good. Remember now?"

Deena, tall, skinny, clad only in a white terrycloth bathrobe, looked like a surprised and severed head stuck on a pike. The great

110

purple birthmark on her cheek and neck stood out hideously against her paling skin.

"Are they going to send him back to the State hospital?" she asked.

Gummy, looking at herself in the cracked full-length mirror nailed to the wall, laughed and showed her two teeth. Her frizzy hair was a yellow brown, chopped short. Her little blue eyes were set far back in tunnels beneath two protruding ridges of bone; her nose was very long, enormously wide, and tipped with a broken-veined bulb. Her chin was not there, and her head bent forward in a permanent crook. She was dressed only in a dirty once-white slip that came to her swollen knees. When she laughed, her huge breasts, resting on her distended belly, quivered like bowls of fermented cream. From her expression, it was evident that she was not displeased with what she saw in the broken glass.

Again she laughed. "Naw, they din't come to haul him away. Elkins just wanted to interduce this chick he had with him. A cute little brunette with big brown eyes behint real thick glasses. She looked just like a collidge girl, 'n she was. This chick has got a B.M. or somethin in sexology. . . ."

"Psychology?"

"Maybe it was societyology. . . ."

"Sociology?"

"Umm. Maybe. Anyway, this foureyed chick is doin a study for a foundation. She wants to ride aroun with Old Man, see how he collects his junk, what alleys he goes up 'n down, what his, uh, habit patterns is, 'n learn what kinda bringin up he had. . . ."

"Old Man'd never do it!" burst out Deena. "You know he can't stand the idea of being watched by a False Folker!"

"Umm. Maybe. Anyway, I tell em Old Man's not goin to like their slummin on him, 'n they say quick they're not slummin, it's for science. 'N they'll pay him for his trouble. They got a grant from the foundation. So I say maybe that'd make Old Man take another look at the color of the beer, 'n they left the house. . . ."

"You *allowed* them in the house? Did you hide the birdcage?"

"Why hide it? His hat wasn't in it."

Deena turned back to frying her fish, but over her shoulder she said, "I don't think Old Man'll agree to the idea, do you? It's rather degrading."

"You *kiddin?* Who's lower'n Old Man? A snake's belly, maybe. Sure, he'll agree. He'll have an eye for the foureyed chick, sure."

"Don't be absurd," said Deena. "He's a dirty stinking one-armed middle-aged man, the ugliest man in the world."

"Yeah, it's the uglies he's got, for sure. 'N he smells like a goat that fell in a outhouse. But it's the smell that gets em. It got me, it got you, it got a whole stewpotful a others, includin that high society dame he used to collect junk off of. . . ."

"Shut up!" spat Deena. "This girl must be a highly refined and intelligent girl. She'd regard Old Man as some sort of ape."

"You know them apes," said Gummy, and she went to the ancient refrigerator and took out a cold quart of beer.

Six quarts of beer later, Old Man had still not come home. The fish had grown cold and greasy, and the big July moon had risen. Deena, like a long lean dirty-white nervous alley cat on top of a backyard fence, patrolled back and forth across the shanty. Gummy sat on the bench made of crates and hunched over her bottle. Finally, she lurched to her feet and turned on the battered set. But, hearing a rattling and pounding of a loose motor in the distance, she turned it off.

The banging and popping became a roar just outside the door. Abruptly, there was a mighty wheeze, like an old rusty robot coughing with double pneumonia in its iron lungs. Then, silence.

But not for long. As the two women stood paralyzed, listening apprehensively, they heard a voice like the rumble of distant thunder.

"Take it easy, kid."

Another voice, soft, drowsy, mumbling.

"Where . . . we?"

The voice like thunder, "Home, sweet home, where we rest our dome."

Violent coughing.

"It's this smoke from the burnin garbage, kid. Enough to make a maggot puke, ain't it? Lookit! The smoke's risin t'ward the full moon like the ghosts a men so rotten even their spirits're carryin the contamination with em. Hey, li'l chick, you din't know Old Man knew them big words like contamination, didja? That's what livin on the city dump does for you. I hear that word all a time from the big shots that come down inspectin the stink here so they kin get away from the stink a City Hall. I ain't no illitcrate. I got a TV set. Hor, hor, hor!"

There was a pause, and the two women knew he was bending his knees and tilting his torso backward so he could look up at the sky.

"Ah, you lovely lovely moon, bride a The Old Guy In The Sky! Some day to come, rum-a-dum-a-dum, one day I swear it, Old Woman a The Old Guy In The Sky, if you help me find the longlost headpiece a King Paley that I and my fathers been lookin for for fifty thousand years, so help me, Old Man Paley'll spread the freshly spilled blood a a virgin a the False Folkers out acrosst the ground for you, so you kin lay down in it like a red carpet or a new red dress and wrap it aroun you. And then you won't have to crinkle up your lovely shinin nose at me and spit your silver spit on me. Old Man promises that, just as sure as his good arm is holdin a daughter a one a the Falsers, a virgin, I think, and bringin her to his home, however humble it be, so we shall see. . . ."

"Stoned out a his head," whispered Gummy.

"My God, he's bringing a girl in here!" said Deena. "*The* girl!"

"Not the *collidge* kid?"

"Does the idiot want to get lynched?"

The man outside bellowed, "Hey, you wimmen, get off your fat asses and open the door 'fore I kick it in! Old Man's home with a fistful a dollars, a armful a sleepin lamb, and a gutful a beer! Home like a conquerin hero and wants service like one, too!"

Suddenly unfreezing, Deena opened the door.

Out of the darkness and into the light shuffled something so squat and blocky it seemed more a tree trunk come to life than a man. It stopped, and the eyes under the huge black homburg hat blinked glazedly. Even the big hat could not hide the peculiar lengthened-out bread-loaf shape of the skull. The forehead was abnormally low; over the eyes were bulging arches of bone. These were tufted with eyebrows like Spanish moss that made even more cavelike the hollows in which the little blue eyes lurked. Its nose was very long and very wide and flaring-nostriled. The lips were thin but pushed out by the shoving jaws beneath them. Its chin was absent, and head and shoulders joined almost without intervention from a neck, or so it seemed. A corkscrew forest of rusty-red hairs sprouted from its open shirt front.

Over his shoulder, held by a hand wide and knobbly as a coral branch, hung the slight figure of a young woman.

He shuffled into the room in an odd bent-kneed gait, walking on the sides of his thick-soled engineer's boots. Suddenly, he stopped again, sniffed deeply, and smiled, exposing teeth thick and yellow, dedicated to biting.

"Jeez, that smells good. It takes the old garbage stink right off. Gummy! You been sprinklin yourself with that perfume I found in a ash heap up on the bluffs?"

Gummy, giggling, looked coy.

Deena said, sharply, "Don't be a fool, Gummy. He's trying to butter you up so you'll forget he's bringing this girl home."

Old Man Paley laughed hoarsely and lowered the snoring girl upon an Army cot. There she sprawled out with her skirt around her hips. Gummy cackled, but Deena hurried to pull the skirt down and also to remove the girl's thick shell-rimmed glasses.

"Lord," she said, "how did this happen? What'd you do to her?"

"Nothin," he growled, suddenly sullen.

He took a quart of beer from the refrigerator, bit down on the cap with teeth thick and chipped as ancient gravestones, and tore it off. Up went the bottle, forward went his knees, back went his torso and he leaned away from the bottle, and down went the amber liquid, gurgle, gurgle, glub. He belched, then roared. "There I was, Old Man Paley, mindin my own figurin business, packin a bunch a papers and magazines I found, and here comes a blue fifty-one

Ford sedan with Elkins, the doctor jerk from the puzzle factory. And this little foureyed chick here, Dorothy Singer. And . . ."

"Yes," said Deena. "We know who they are, but we didn't know they went after you."

"Who asked you? Who's tellin this story? Anyway, they tole me what they wanted. And I was gonna say no, but this little collidge broad says if I'll sign a paper that'll agree to let her travel aroun with me and even stay in our house a couple a cvenins, with us actin natural, she'll pay me fifty dollars. I says yes! Old Guy In The Sky! That's a hundred and fifty quarts a beer! I got principles, but they're washed away in a roarin foamin flood of beer.

"I says yes, and the cute little runt give me the paper to sign, then advances me ten bucks and says I'll get the rest seven days from now. Ten dollars in my pocket! So she climbs up into the seat a my truck. And then this figurin Elkins parks his Ford and says he thinks he ought a go with us to check on if everythin's gonna be OK."

"He's not foolin Old Man. He's after Little Miss Foureyes. Everytime he looks at her, the lovejuice runs out a his eyes. So, I collect junk for a couple a hours, talkin all the time. And she is scared a me at first because I'm so figurin ugly and strange. But after a while she busts out laughin. Then I pulls the truck up in the alley back a Jack's Tavern on Ames Street. She asks me what I'm doin. I says I'm stoppin for a beer, just as I do every day. And she says she could stand one, too. So . . ."

"You actually went inside with her?" asked Deena.

"Naw. I was gonna try, but I started gettin the shakes. And I hadda tell her I coun't do it. She asks me why. I say I don't know. Ever since I quit bein a kid, I kin't. So she says I got a . . . somethin like a fresh flower, what is it?"

"Neurosis?" said Deena.

"Yeah. Only I call it a taboo. So Elkins and the little broad go into Jack's and get a cold six-pack, and brin it out, and we're off. . . ."

"So?"

"So we go from place to place, though always stayin in alleys, and she thinks it's funnier'n hell gettin loaded in the backs a taverns. Then I get to seein double and don't care no more and I'm over my fraidies, so we go into the Circle Bar. And get in a fight there with one a the hillbillies in his sideburns and leather jacket that hangs out there and tries to take the foureyed chick home with him."

Both the women gasped, "Did the cops come?"

"If they did, they was late to the party. I grab this hillbilly by his leather jacket with my one arm—the strongest arm in this world—and throw him clean acrosst the room. And when his buddies come after me, I pound my chest like a figurin gorilla and make a figurin face at em, and they all of a sudden get their shirts up their necks and go back to listenin to their hillbilly music. And I pick up the chick—she's laughin so hard she's chokin—and Elkins, white as a sheet out a the laundromat, after me, and away we go, and here we are."

"Yes, you fool, here you are!" shouted Deena. "Bringing that girl here in that condition! She'll start screaming her head off when she wakes up and sees you!"

"Go figure yourself!" snorted Paley. "She was scared a me a first, and she tried to stay upwind a me. But she got to *likin* me. I could tell. And she got so she liked my smell, too. I knew she would. Don't all the broads? These False wimmen kin't say no once they get a whiff of us. Us Paleys got the gift in the blood."

Deena laughed and said, "You mean you have it in the head. Honest to God, when are you going to quit trying to forcefeed me with that bull? You're insane!"

Paley growled. "I tole you not never to call me nuts, not never!" and he slapped her across the cheek.

She reeled back and slumped against the wall, holding her face and crying, "You ugly stupid stinking ape, you hit me, the daughter of people whose boots you aren't fit to lick. *You* struck *me!*"

"Yeah, and ain't you glad I did," said Paley in tones like a complacent earthquake. He shuffled over to the cot and put his hand on the sleeping girl.

"Uh, feel that. No sag there, you two flabs."

"You beast!" screamed Deena. "Taking advantage of a helpless little girl!"

Like an alley cat, she leaped at him with claws out.

Laughing hoarsely, he grabbed one of her wrists and twisted it so she was forced to her knees and had to clench her teeth to keep from screaming with pain. Gummy cackled and handed Old Man a quart of beer. To take it, he had to free Deena. She rose, and all three, as if nothing had happened, sat down at the table and began drinking.

About dawn a deep animal snarl awoke the girl. She opened her eyes but could make out the trio only dimly and distortedly. Her hands, groping around for her glasses, failed to find them.

Old Man, whose snarl had shaken her from the high tree of sleep, growled again. "I'm tellin you, Deena, I'm tellin you, don't laugh at Old Man, don't laugh at Old Man, and I'm tellin you again, three times, don't laugh at Old Man!"

His incredible bass rose to a high-pitched scream of rage.

"Whassa matter with your figurin brain? I show you proof after proof, and you sit there in all your stupidity like a silly hen that sits down too hard on its eggs and breaks em but won't get up and admit she's squattin on a mess. I—I—Paley—Old Man Paley—kin prove I'm what I say I am, a Real Folker."

Suddenly, he propelled his hand across the table toward Deena.

"Feel them bones in my lower arm! Them two bones ain't straight and dainty like the arm bones a you False Folkers. They're thick as flagpoles, and they're curved out from each other like the backs a two tomcats outbluffin each other over a fishhead on a garbage can. They're built that way so's they kin be real strong anchors for my muscles, which is bigger'n False Folkers'. Go ahead, feel em.

"And look at them brow ridges. Like the tops a those shell-rimmed spectacles all them intelleckchooalls wear. Like the spectacles this collidge chick wears.

"And feel the shape a my skull. It ain't a ball like yours but a loaf a bread."

"Fossilized bread!" sneered Deena. "Hard as a rock, through and through."

Old Man roared on, "Feel my neck bones if you got the strength to feel through my muscles! They're bent forward, not—"

"Oh, I know you're an ape. You can't look overhead to see if that was a bird or just a drop of rain without breaking your back."

"Ape, hell! I'm a Real Man! Feel my heel bone! Is it like yours? No, it ain't! It's built diff'runt, and so's my whole foot!"

Is that why you and Gummy and all those brats of yours have to walk like chimpanzees?"

"Laugh, laugh, laugh!"

"I am laughing, laughing, laughing. Just because you're a freak of nature, a monstrosity whose bones all went wrong in the womb, you've dreamed up this fantastic myth about being descended from the Neanderthals. . . ."

"Neanderthals!" whispered Dorothy Singer. The walls whirled about her, looking twisted and ghostly in the halflight, like a room in Limbo.

". . . all this stuff about the lost hat of Old King," continued Deena, "and how if you ever find it you can break the spell that keeps you so-called Neanderthals on the dumpheaps and in the alleys, is garbage, and not very appetizing. . . ."

"And you," shouted Paley, "are headin for a beatin!"

"Thass what she wants," mumbled Gummy. "Go ahead. Beat her. She'll get her jollies off, 'n quit needlin you. 'N we kin all get some shuteye. Besides, you're gonna wake up the chick."

"That chick is gonna get a wakin up like she never had before when Old Man gets his paws on her," rumbled Paley. "Guy In The Sky, ain't it somethin she should a met me and be in this house? Sure as an old shirt stinks, she ain't gonna be able to tear herself away from me.

"Hey, Gummy, maybe she'll have a kid for me, huh? We ain't had a brat aroun here for ten years. I kinda miss my kids. You gave me six that was Real Folkers, though I never was sure about that

Jimmy, he looked too much like O'Brien. Now you're all dried up, dry as Deena always was, but you kin still raise em. How'd you like to raise the collidge chick's kid?"

Gummy grunted and swallowed beer from a chipped coffee mug. After belching loudly, she mumbled, "Don't know. You're crazier'n even I think you are if you think this cute little Miss Foureyes'd have anythin to do with you. 'N even if she was out of her head enough to do it, what kind a life is this for a brat? Get raised in a dump? Have a ugly old maw 'n paw? Grow up so ugly nobody'd have nothin to do with him 'n smellin so strange all the dogs'd bite him?"

Suddenly, she began blubbering.

"It ain't only Neanderthals has to live on dumpheaps. It's the crippled 'n sick 'n the stupid 'n the queer in the head that has to live here. 'N they become Neanderthals just as much as us Real Folk. No diff'runce, no diff'runce. We're all ugly 'n hopeless 'n rotten. We're all Neander . . ."

Old Man's fist slammed the table.

"Name me no names like that! That's a G'yaga name for us Paleys—Real Folkers. Don't let me never hear that other name again! It don't mean a man; it means somethin like a high-class gorilla."

"Quit looking in the mirror!" shrieked Deena.

There was more squabbling and jeering and roaring and confusing and terrifying talk, but Dorothy Singer had closed her eyes and fallen asleep again.

Some time later, she awoke. She sat up, found her glasses on a little table beside her, put them on, and stared about her.

She was in a large shack built of odds and ends of wood. It had two rooms, each about ten feet square. In the corner of one room was a large kerosene-burning stove. Bacon was cooking in a huge skillet; the heat from the stove made sweat run from her forehead and over her glasses.

After drying them off with her handkerchief, she examined the furnishings of the shack. Most of it was what she had expected, but three things surprised her. The bookcase, the photograph on the wall, and the birdcage.

The bookcase was tall and narrow and of some dark wood, badly scratched. It was crammed with comic books, Blue Books, and Argosies, some of which she supposed must be at least twenty years old. There were a few books whose ripped backs and water-stained covers indicated they'd been picked out of ash heaps. Haggard's *Allan and the Ice Gods*, Wells's *Outline of History*, Vol. I, and his *The Croquet Player*. Also *Gog and Magog, A Prophecy of Armageddon* by the Reverend Caleb G. Harris. Burroughs' *Tarzan the Terrible* and *In the Earth's Core*. Jack London's *Beyond Adam*.

The framed photo on the wall was that of a woman who looked much like Deena and must have been taken around 1890. It was very large, tinted in brown, and showed an aristocratic handsome woman of about thirty-five in a high-busted velvet dress with a high neckline. Her hair was drawn severely back to a knot on top of her head. A diadem of jewels was on her breast.

The strangest thing was the large parrot cage. It stood upon a tall support which had nails driven through its base to hold it to the floor. The cage itself was empty, but the door was locked with a long narrow bicycle lock.

Her speculation about it was interrupted by the two women calling to her from their place by the stove.

Deena said, "Good morning, Miss Singer. How do you feel?"

"Some Indian buried his hatchet in my head," Dorothy said. "And my tongue is molting. Could I have a drink of water, please?"

Deena took a pitcher of cold water out of the refrigerator, and from it filled up a tin cup.

"We don't have any running water. We have to get our water from the gas station down the road and bring it here in a bucket."

Dorothy looked dubious, but she closed her eyes and drank.

"I think I'm going to get sick," she said. "I'm sorry."

"I'll take you to the outhouse," said Deena, putting her arm around the girl's shoulder and heaving her up with surprising strength.

"Once I'm outside," said Dorothy faintly, "I'll be all right."

"Oh, I know," said Deena. "It's the odor. The fish, Gummy's cheap perfume, Old Man's sweat, the beer. I forgot how it first affected me. But it's no better outside."

Dorothy didn't reply, but when she stepped through the door, she murmured, "Ohh!"

"Yes, I know," said Deena. "It's awful, but it won't kill you. . . ."

Ten minutes later, Deena and a pale and weak Dorothy came out of the ramshackle outhouse.

They returned to the shanty, and for the first time Dorothy noticed that Elkins was sprawled face-up on the seat of the truck. His head hung over the end of the seat, and the flies buzzed around his open mouth.

"This is horrible," said Deena. "He'll be very angry when he wakes up and finds out where he is. He's such a respectable man."

"Let the heel sleep it off," said Dorothy. She walked into the shanty, and a moment later Paley clomped into the room, a smell of stale beer and very peculiar sweat advancing before him in a wave.

"How you feel?" he growled in a timbre so low the hairs on the back of her neck rose.

"Sick. I think I'll go home."

"Sure. Only try some a the hair."

He handed her a half-empty pint of whiskey. Dorothy reluctantly downed a large shot chased with cold water. After a brief revulsion, she began feeling better and took another shot. She then washed her face in a bowl of water and drank a third whiskey.

"I think I can go with you now," she said. "But I don't care for breakfast."

"I ate already," he said. "Let's go. It's ten-thirty accordin to the clock on the gas station. My alley's prob'ly been cleaned out by now. Them other ragpickers are always moochin in on my territory when they think I'm stayin home. But you kin bet they're scared out a their pants every time they see a shadow cause they're afraid it's Old Man and he'll catch em and squeeze their guts out and crack their ribs with this one good arm."

Laughing a laugh so hoarse and unhuman it seemed to come

from some troll deep in the caverns of his bowels, he opened the refrigerator and took another beer.

"I need another to get me started, not to mention what I'll have to give that damn balky bitch, Fordiana."

As they stepped outside, they saw Elkins stumble toward the outhouse and then fall headlong through the open doorway. He lay motionless on the floor, his feet sticking out of the entrance. Alarmed, Dorothy wanted to go after him, but Paley shook his head.

"He's a big boy; he kin take care a hisself. We got to get Fordiana up and goin."

Fordiana was the battered and rusty pickup truck. It was parked outside Paley's bedroom window so he could look out at any time of the night and make sure no one was stealing parts or even the whole truck.

"Not that I ought a worry about her," grumbled Old Man. He drank three-fourths of the quart in four mighty gulps, then uncapped the truck's radiator and poured the rest of the beer down it.

"She knows nobody else'll give her beer, so I think that if any a these robbin figurers that live on the dump or at the shacks aroun the bend was to try to steal anythin off'n her, she'd honk and backfire and throw rods and oil all over the place so's her Old Man could wake up and punch the figurin shirt off a the thievin figurer. But maybe not. She's a female. And you kin't trust a figurin female."

He poured the last drop down the radiator and roared, "There! Now don't you dare *not* turn over. You're robbin me a the good beer I could be havin! If you so much as backfire, Old Man'll beat hell out a you with a sledgehammer!"

Wide-eyed but silent, Dorothy climbed onto the ripped open front seat beside Paley. The starter whirred, and the motor sputtered.

"No more beer if you don't work!" shouted Paley.

There was a bang, a fizz, a sput, a *whop, whop, whop,* a clash of gears, a monstrous and triumphant showing of teeth by Old Man, and they were bumpbumping over the rough ruts.

"Old Man knows how to handle all them bitches, flesh or tin, two-legged, four-legged, wheeled. I sweat beer and passion and promise em a kick in the tailpipe if they don't behave, and that gets em all. I'm so figurin ugly I turn their stomachs. But once they get a whiff a the out-a-this-world stink a me, they're done for, they fall prostrooted at my big hairy feet. That's the way it's always been with us Paley men and the G'yaga wimmen. That's why their menfolks fear us, and why we got into so much trouble."

Dorothy did not say anything, and Paley fell silent as soon as the truck swung off the dump and onto U.S. Route 24. He seemed to fold up into himself, to be trying to make himself as inconspicuous as possible. During the three minutes it took the truck to get from the shanty to the city limits, he kept wiping his sweating palm against his blue workman's shirt.

But he did not try to release the tension with oaths. Instead, he muttered a string of what seemed to Dorothy nonsense rhymes.

"Eenie, meenie, minie, moe. Be a good Guy, help me go. Hoola boola, teenie weenie, ram em, damn em, figure em, duck em, watch me go, don't be a shmoe. Stop em, block em, sing a go go go."

Not until they had gone a mile into the city of Onaback and turned from 24 into an alley did he relax.

"Whew! That's torture, and I been doin it ever since I was sixteen, some years ago. Today seems worse'n ever, maybe cause you're along. G'yaga men don't like it if they see me with one a their wimmen, specially a cute chick like you."

Suddenly, he smiled and broke into a song about being covered all over "with sweet violets, sweeter than all the roses." He sang other songs, some of which made Dorothy turn red in the face though at the same time she giggled. When they crossed a street to get from one alley to another, he cut off his singing, even in the middle of a phrase, and resumed it on the other side.

Reaching the west bluff, he slowed the truck to a crawl while his little blue eyes searched the ash heaps and garbage cans at the rears of the houses. Presently, he stopped the truck and climbed down to inspect his find.

"Guy In The Sky, we're off to a flyin start! Look!—some old grates from a coal furnace. And a pile a coke and beer bottles, all redeemable. Get down, Dor'thy—if you want to know how us ragpickers make a livin, you gotta get in and sweat and cuss with us. And if you come acrosst any hats, be sure to tell me."

Dorothy smiled. But when she stepped down from the truck, she winced.

"What's the matter?"

"Headache."

"The sun'll boil it out. Here's how we do this collectin, see? The back end a the truck is boarded up into five sections. This section here is for the iron and the wood. This, for the paper. This, for the cardboard. You get a higher price for the cardboard. This, for rags. This, for bottles we kin get a refund on. If you find any int'restin books or magazines, put em on the seat. I'll decide if I want to keep em or throw em in with the old paper."

They worked swiftly, and then drove on. About a block later, they were interrupted at another heap by a leaf of a woman, withered and blown by the winds of time. She hobbled out from the back porch of a large three-storied house with diamond-shaped panes in the windows and doors and cupolas at the corners. In a quavering voice she explained that she was the widow of a wealthy lawyer who had died fifteen years ago. Not until today had she made up her mind to get rid of his collection of law books and legal papers. These were all neatly cased in cardboard boxes not too large to be handled.

Not even, she added, her pale watery eyes flickering from Paley to Dorothy, not even by a poor one-armed man and a young girl.

Old Man took off his homburg and bowed.

"Sure, ma'am, my daughter and myself'd be glad to help you out in your housecleanin."

"Your daughter?" croaked the old woman.

"She don't look like me a tall," he replied. "No wonder. She's my foster daughter, poor girl, she was orphaned when she was still fillin her diapers. My best friend was her father. He died savin my life, and as he laid gaspin his life away in my arms, he begged me to take care a her as if she was my own. And I kept my promise to my dyin friend, may his soul rest in peace. And even if I'm only a poor ragpicker, ma'am, I been doin my best to raise her to be a decent Godfearin obedient girl."

Dorothy had to run around to the other side of the trunk where she could cover her mouth and writhe in an agony of attempting to smother her laughter. When she regained control, the old lady was telling Paley she'd show him where the books were. Then she started hobbling to the porch.

But Old Man, instead of following her across the yard, stopped by the fence that separated the alley from the backyard. He turned around and gave Dorothy a look of extreme despair.

"What's the matter?" she said. "Why're you sweating so? And shaking? And you're so pale."

"You'd laugh if I tole you, and I don't like to be laughed at."

"Tell me. I won't laugh."

He closed his eyes and began muttering. "Never mind, it's in the mind. Never mind, you're just fine." Opening his eyes, he shook himself like a dog just come from the water.

"I kin do it. I got the guts. All them books're a lotta beer money I'll lose if I don't go down into the bowels a hell and get em. Guy In The Sky, give me the guts a a goat and the nerve a a pork dealer in Palestine. You know Old Man ain't got a yellow streak. It's the wicked spell a the False Folkers workin on me. Come on, let's go, go, go."

And sucking in a deep breath, he stepped through the gateway. Head down, eyes on the grass at his feet, he shuffled toward the cellar door where the old lady stood peering at him.

Four steps away from the cellar entrance, he halted again. A small black spaniel had darted from around the corner of the house and begun yapyapping at him.

Old Man suddenly cocked his head to one side, crossed his eyes, and deliberately sneezed.

Yelping, the spaniel fled back around the corner, and Paley walked down the steps that led to the cool dark basement. As he did so, he muttered, "That puts the evil spell on em figurin dogs."

When they had piled all the books in the back of the truck, he took off his homburg and bowed again.

"Ma'am, my daughter and myself both thank you from the rockbottom a our poor but humble hearts for this treasure trove you give us. And if ever you've anythin else you don't want, and a strong back and a weak mind to carry it out . . . well, please remember we'll be down this alley every Blue Monday and Fish Friday about time the sun is three-quarters acrosst the sky. Providin it ain't rainin cause The Old Guy In The Sky is cryin in his beer over us poor mortals, what fools we be."

Then he put his hat on, and the two got into the truck and chugged off. They stopped by several other promising heaps before he announced that the truck was loaded enough. He felt like celebrating; perhaps they should stop off behind Mike's Tavern and down a few quarts. She replied that perhaps she might manage a drink if she could have a whiskey. Beer wouldn't set well.

"I got some money," rumbled Old Man, unbuttoning with slow clumsy fingers his shirt pocket and pulling out a roll of worn tattered bills while the truck's wheels rolled straight in the alley ruts.

"You brought me luck, so Old Man's gonna pay today through the hose, I mean, nose, har, har, har!"

He stopped Fordiana behind a little neighborhood tavern. Dorothy, without being asked, took the two dollars he handed her and went into the building. She returned with a can opener, two quarts of beer, and a half pint of V.O.

"I added some of my money. I can't stand cheap whiskey."

They sat on the running board of the truck, drinking, Old Man doing most of the talking. It wasn't long before he was telling her of the times when the Real Folk, the Paleys, had lived in Europe and Asia by the side of the woolly mammoths and the cave lion.

"We worshiped The Old Guy In The Sky who says what the thunder says and lives in the east on the tallest mountain in the world. We faced the skulls a our dead to the east so they could see

The Old Guy when he came to take them to live with him in the mountain.

"And we was doin fine for a long long time. Then, out a the east come them motherworshipin False Folk with their long straight legs and long straight necks and flat faces and thundermug round heads and their bows and arrows. They claimed they was sons a the goddess Mother Earth, who was a virgin. But we claimed the truth was that a crow with stomach trouble sat on a stump and when it left the hot sun hatched em out.

"Well, for a while we beat em hands-down because we was stronger. Even one a our wimmen could tear their strongest man to bits. Still, they had that bow and arrow, they kept pickin us off, and movin in and movin in, and we kept movin back slowly, till pretty soon we was shoved with our backs against the ocean.

"Then one day a big chief among us got a bright idea. 'Why don't we make bows and arrows, too?' he said. And so we did, but we was clumsy at makin and shootin em cause our hands was so big, though we could draw a heavier bow'n em. So we kept gettin run out a the good huntin grounds.

"There was one thin might a been in our favor. That was, we bowled the wimmen a the Falsers over with our smell. Not that we smell good. We stink like a pig that's been makin love to a billy goat on a manure pile. But, somehow, the wimmen folk a the Falsers was all mixed up in their chemistry, I guess you'd call it, cause they got all excited and developed roundheels when they caught a whiff a us. If we'd been left alone with em, we could a Don Juan'd them Falsers right off a the face a the earth. We would a mixed our blood with theirs so much that after a while you coun't tell the diff'runce. Specially since the kids lean to their pa's side in looks, Paley blood is so much stronger.

"But that made sure there would always be war tween us. Specially after our king, Old King Paley, made love to the daughter a the Falser king, King Raw Boy, and stole her away.

"Gawd, you should a seen the fuss then! Raw Boy's daughter flipped over Old King Paley. And it was her give him the bright idea a callin in every able-bodied Paley that was left and organizin em into one big army. Kind a puttin all our eggs in one basket, but it seemed a good idea. Every man big enough to carry a club went out in one big mob on Operation False Folk Massacre. And we ganged up on every little town a them motherworshipers we found. And kicked hell out a em. And roasted the men's hearts and ate em. And every now and then took a snack off the wimmen and kids, too.

"Then, all of a sudden, we come to a big plain. And there's a army a them False Folk, collected by Old King Raw Boy. They outnumber us, but we feel we kin lick the world. Specially since the magic strength a the G'yaga lies in their wimmen folk, cause they worship a woman god, The Old Woman In The Earth. And we've got their chief priestess, Raw Boy's daughter.

"All our own personal power is collected in Old King Paley's hat—his magical headpiece. All a us Paleys believed that a man's strength and his soul was in his headpiece.

"We bed down the night before the big battle. At dawn there's a cry that'd wake up the dead. It still sends shivers down the necks a us Paley's fifty thousand years later. It's King Paley roarin and cryin. We ask him why. He says that that dirty little sneakin little hoor, Raw Boy's daughter, has stole his headpiece and run off with it to her father's camp.

"Our knees turn weak as nearbeer. Our manhood is in the hands a our enemies. But out we go to battle, our witch doctors out in front rattlin their gourds and whirlin their bullroarers and prayin. And here comes the G'yaga medicine men doin the same. Only thing, their hearts is in their work cause they got Old King's headpiece stuck on the end a a spear.

"And for the first time they use dogs in war, too. Dogs never did like us any more'n we like em.

"And then we charge into each other. Bang! Wallop! Crash! Smash! Whack! Owwwrrroooo! And they kick hell out a us, do it to us. And we're never again the same, done forever. They had Old King's headpiece and with it our magic, cause we'd all put the soul a us Paleys in that hat.

"The spirit and power a us Paleys was prisoners cause that headpiece was. And life became too much for us Paleys. Them as wasn't slaughtered and eaten was glad to settle down on the garbage heaps a the conquerin Falsers and pick for a livin with the chickens, sometimes comin out second best.

"But we knew Old King's headpiece was hidden somewhere, and we organized a secret society and swore to keep alive his name and to search for the headpiece if it took us forever. Which it almost has, it's been so long.

"But even though we was doomed to live in shantytowns and stay off the streets and prowl the junkpiles in the alleys, we never gave up hope. And as time went on some a the nocounts a the *G'yaga* came down to live with us. And we and they had kids. Soon, most a us had disappeared into the bloodstream a the low-class *G'yaga*. But there's always been a Paley family that tried to keep their blood pure. No man kin do no more, kin he?"

He glared at Dorothy. "What d'ya think a that?"

Weakly, she said, "Well, I've never heard anything like it."

"Gawdamighty!" snorted Old Man. "I give you a history longer'n a hoor's dream, more'n fifty thousand years a history, the secret story a a longlost race. And all you kin say is that you never heard nothin like it before."

He leaned toward her and clamped his huge hand over her thigh.

"Don't flinch from me!" he said fiercely. "Or turn your head away. Sure, I stink, and I offend your dainty figurin nostrils and upset your figurin delicate little guts. But what's a minute's whiff a me on your part compared to a lifetime on my part a havin all the stinkin garbage in the universe shoved up my nose, and my mouth filled with what you woun't say if your mouth was full a it? What do you say to that, huh?"

Coolly, she said, "Please take your hand off me."

"Sure, I din't mean nothin by it. I got carried away and forgot my place in society."

"Now, look here," she said earnestly. "That has nothing at all to do with your so-called social position. It's just that I don't allow anybody to take liberties with my body. Maybe I'm being ridiculously Victorian, but I want more than just sensuality. I want love, and—"

"OK, I get the idea."

Dorothy stood up and said, "I'm only a block from my apartment. I think I'll walk on home. The liquor's given me a headache."

"Yeah," he growled. "You sure it's the liquor and not me?"

She looked steadily at him. "I'm going, but I'll see you tomorrow morning. Does that answer your question?"

"OK," he grunted. "See you. Maybe."

She walked away very fast.

Next morning, shortly after dawn, a sleepy-eyed Dorothy stopped her car before the Paley shanty. Deena was the only one home. Gummy had gone to the river to fish, and Old Man was in the outhouse. Dorothy took the opportunity to talk to Deena, and found her, as she had suspected, a woman of considerable education. However, although she was polite, she was reticent about her background. Dorothy, in an effort to keep the conversation going, mentioned that she had phoned her former anthropology professor and asked him about the chances of Old Man being a genuine Neanderthal. It was then that Deena broke her reserve and eagerly asked what the professor had thought.

"Well," said Dorothy, "he just laughed. He told me it was an absolute impossibility that a small group, even an inbred group isolated in the mountains, could have kept their cultural and genetic identity for fifty thousand years.

"I argued with him. I told him Old Man insisted he and his kind had existed in the village of Paley in the mountains of the Pyrenees until Napoleon's men found them and tried to draft them. Then they fled to America, after a stay in England. And his group was split up during the Civil War, driven out of the Great Smokies. He, as far as he knows, is the last purebreed, Gummy being a half or quarter-breed.

"The professor assured me that Gummy and Old Man were cases of glandular malfunctioning, of acromegaly. That they may have a superficial resemblance to the Neanderthal man, but a physical anthropologist could tell the difference at a glance. When I got a little angry and asked him if he wasn't taking an unscientific and prejudiced attitude, he became rather irritated. Our talk ended somewhat frostily.

"But I went down to the university library that night and read everything on what makes *Homo Neanderthalensis* different from *Homo sapiens.*"

"You almost sound as if you believe Old Man's private little myth is the truth," said Deena.

"The professor taught me to be convinced only by the facts and not to say anything is impossible," replied Dorothy. "If he's forgotten his own teachings, I haven't."

"Well, Old Man is a persuasive talker," said Deena. "He could sell the devil a harp and halo."

Old Man, wearing only a pair of blue jeans, entered the shanty. For the first time Dorothy saw his naked chest, huge, covered with long redgold hairs so numerous they formed a matting almost as thick as an orangutan's. However, it was not his chest but his bare feet at which she looked most intently. Yes, the big toes were widely separated from the others, and he certainly tended to walk on the outside of his feet.

His arm, too, seemed abnormally short in proportion to his body.

Old Man grunted a good morning and didn't say much for a while. But after he had sweated and cursed and chanted his way through the streets of Onaback and had arrived safely at the alleys of the west bluff, he relaxed. Perhaps he was helped by finding a large pile of papers and rags.

"Well, here we go to work, so don't you dare to shirk. Jump, Dor'thy! By the sweat a your brow, you'll earn your brew!"

When that load was on the truck, they drove off. Paley said, "How you like this life without no strife? Good, huh? You like alleys, huh?"

Dorothy nodded. "As a child, I liked alleys better than streets. And they still preserve something of their first charm for me. They were more fun to play in, so nice and cozy. The trees and bushes and fences leaned in at you and sometimes touched you as if they had hands and liked to feel your face to find out if you'd been there before, and they remembered you. You felt as if you were sharing a secret with the alleys and the things of the alleys. But streets, well, streets were always the same, and you had to watch out the cars didn't run you over, and the windows in the houses were full of faces and eyes, poking their noses in your business, if you can say that eyes had noses."

Old Man whopped and slapped his thigh so hard it would have broke if it had been Dorothy's.

"You must be a Paley! We feel that way, too! We ain't allowed to hang aroun streets, so we make our alleys into little kingdoms. Tell me, do you sweat just crossin a street from one alley to the next?"

He put his hand on her knee. She looked down at it but said nothing, and he left it there while the truck putputted along, its wheels following the ruts of the alley.

"No, I don't feel that way at all."

"Yeah? Well, when you was a kid, you wasn't so ugly you hadda stay off the streets. But I still wasn't too happy in the alleys because a them figurin dogs. Forever and forever they was barkin and bitin at me. So I took to beatin the bejesus out a them with a big stick I always carried. But after a while I found out I only had to look at em in a certain way. Yi, yi, yi, they'd run away yapping, like that old black spaniel did yesterday. Why? Cause they knew I was sneezin evil spirits at em. It was then I began to know I wasn't human. A course, my old man had been tellin me that ever since I could talk.

"As I grew up I felt every day that the spell a the G'yaga was gettin stronger. I was gettin dirtier and dirtier looks from em on the streets. And when I went down the alleys, I felt like I really *belonged* there. Finally, the day came when I coun't cross a street without gettin sweaty hands and cold feet and a dry mouth and breathin hard. That was cause I was becomin a full-grown Paley, and the curse a the G'yaga gets more powerful as you get more hair on your chest."

"Curse?" said Dorothy. "Some people call it a neurosis."

"It's a curse."

Dorothy didn't answer. Again, she looked down at her knee,

and this time he removed his hand. He would have had to do it, anyway, for they had come to a paved street.

On the way down to the junk dealer's, he continued the same theme. And when they got to the shanty, he elaborated upon it.

During the thousands of years the Paley lived on the garbage piles of the G'yaga, they were closely watched. So, in the old days, it had been the custom for the priests and warriors of the False Folk to descend on the dumpheap dwellers whenever a strong and obstreperous Paley came to manhood. And they had gouged out an eye or cut off his hand or leg or some other member to ensure that he remembered what he was and where his place was.

"That's why I lost this arm," Old Man growled, waving the stump. "Fear a the G'yaga for the Paley did this to me."

Deena howled with laughter and said, "Dorothy, the truth is that he got drunk one night and passed out on the railroad tracks, and a freight train ran over his arm."

"Sure, sure, that's the way it was. But it coun't a happened if the Falsers din't work through their evil black magic. Nowadays, stead a cripplin us openly, they use spells. They ain't got the guts anymore to do it themselves."

Deena laughed scornfully and said, "He got all those psychopathic ideas from reading those comics and weird tale magazines and those crackpot books and from watching that TV program, *Alley Oop and the Dinosaur.* I can point out every story from which he's stolen an idea."

"You're a liar!" thundered Old Man.

He struck Deena on the shoulder. She reeled away from the blow, then leaned back toward him as if into a strong wind. He struck her again, this time across her purple birthmark. Her eyes glowed, and she cursed him. And he hit her once more, hard enough to hurt but not to injure.

Dorothy opened her mouth as if to protest, but Gummy lay a fat sweaty hand on her shoulder and lifted her finger to her own lips.

Deena fell to the floor from a particularly violent blow. She did not stand up again. Instead, she got to her hands and knees and crawled toward the refuge behind the big iron stove. His naked foot shoved her rear so that she was sent sprawling on her face, moaning, her long stringy black hair falling over her face and birthmark.

Dorothy stepped forward and raised her hand to grab Old Man. Gummy stopped her, mumbling, "'S all right. Leave em alone."

"Look at that figurin female bein happy!" snorted Old Man. "You know why I *have* to beat the hell out a her, when all I want is peace and quiet? Cause I look like a figurin caveman, and they're supposed to beat their hoors silly. That's why she took up with me."

"You're an insane liar," said Deena softly from behind the stove, slowly and dreamily nursing her pain like the memory of a lover's caresses. "I came to live with you because I'd sunk so low you were the only man that'd have me."

"She's a retired high society mainliner, Dor'thy," said Paley. "You never seen her without a longsleeved dress on. That's cause her arms're full a holes. It was me that kicked the monkey off a her back. I cured her with the wisdom and magic a the Real Folk, where you coax the evil spirit out by talkin it out. And she's been livin with me ever since. Kin't get rid a her.

"Now, you take that toothless bag there. I ain't never hit her. That shows I ain't no woman-beatin bastard, right? I hit Deena cause she likes it, wants it, but I don't ever hit Gummy. . . . Hey, Gummy, that kind a medicine ain't what you want, is it?"

And he laughed his incredibly hoarse, *hor, hor, hor.*

"You're a figurin liar," said Gummy, speaking over her shoulder because she was squatting down, fiddling with the TV controls. "You're the one knocked most a my teeth out."

"I knocked out a few rotten stumps you was gonna lose anyway. You had it comin cause you was runnin aroun with that O'Brien in his green shirt."

Gummy giggled and said, "Don't think for a minute I quit goin with that O'Brien in his green shirt just cause you slapped me aroun a little bit. I quit cause you was a better man 'n him."

Gummy giggled again. She rose and waddled across the room toward a shelf which held a bottle of her cheap perfume. Her enormous brass earrings swung, and her great hips swung back and forth.

"Look at that," said Old Man. "Like two bags a mush in a windstorm."

But his eyes followed them with kindling appreciation, and, on seeing her pour that reeking liquid over her pillow-sized bosom, he hugged her and buried his huge nose in the valley of her breasts and sniffed rapturously.

"I feel like a dog that's found an old bone he buried and forgot till just now," he growled, "Arf, arf, arf!"

Deena snorted and said she had to get some fresh air or she'd lose her supper. She grabbed Dorothy's hand and insisted she take a walk with her. Dorothy, looking sick, went with her.

The following evening, as the four were drinking beer around the kitchen table, Old Man suddenly reached over and touched Dorothy affectionately. Gummy laughed, but Deena glared. However, she did not say anything to the girl but instead began accusing Paley of going too long without a bath. He called her a flatchested hophead and said that she was lying, because he had been taking a bath every day. Deena replied that, yes he had, ever since Dorothy had appeared on the scene. An argument raged. Finally, he rose from the table and turned the photograph of Deena's mother so it faced the wall.

Wailing, Deena tried to face it outward again. He pushed her away from it, refusing to hit her despite her insults—even when she howled at him that he wasn't fit to lick her mother's shoes, let alone blaspheme her portrait by touching it.

Tired of the argument, he abandoned his post by the photograph and shuffled to the refrigerator.

"If you dare turn her aroun till I give the word, I'll throw her in the creek. And you'll never see her again."

Deena shrieked and crawled onto her blanket behind the stove and there lay sobbing and cursing him softly.

Gummy chewed tobacco and laughed while a brown stream ran down her toothless jaws. "Deena pushed him too far that time."

"Ah, her and her figurin mother," snorted Paley. "Hey, Dor'thy, you know how she laughs at me cause I think Fordiana's got a soul.

And I put the evil eye on em hounds? And cause I think the salvation a us Paleys'll be when we find out where Old King's hat's been hidden?

"Well, get a load a this. This here intellekchooall purple-faced dragon, this retired mainliner, this old broken-down nag for a monkey-jockey, she's the sooperstishus one. She thinks her mother's a god. And she prays to her and asks forgiveness and asks what's gonna happen in the future. And when she thinks nobody's aroun, she talks to her. Here she is, worshipin her mother like The Old Woman In The Earth, who's The Old Guy's enemy. And she knows that makes The Old Guy sore. Maybe that's the reason he ain't allowed me to find the longlost headpiece a Old King, though he knows I been lookin in every ash heap from here to God-knowswhere, hopin some fool *G'yaga* would throw it away never realizin what it was.

"Well, by all that's holy, that pitcher stays with its ugly face on the wall. Aw, shut up, Deena, I wanna watch *Alley Oop*."

Shortly afterward, Dorothy drove home. There she again phoned her sociology professor. Impatiently, he went into more detail. He said that one reason Old Man's story of the war between the Neanderthals and the invading *Homo sapiens* was very unlikely was that there was evidence to indicate that *Homo sapiens* might have been in Europe before the Neanderthals—it was very possible the *Homo Neanderthalensis* was the invader.

"Not invader in the modern sense," said the professor. "The influx of a new species or race or tribe into Europe during the Paleolithic would have been a sporadic migration of little groups, an immigration which might have taken a thousand to ten thousand years to complete.

"And it is more than likely that *Neanderthalensis* and *sapiens* lived side by side for millennia with very little fighting between them because both were too busy struggling for a living. For one reason or another, probably because he was outnumbered, the Neanderthal was absorbed by the surrounding peoples. Some anthropologists have speculated that the Neanderthals were blonds and that they had passed their light hair directly to North Europeans.

"Whatever the guesses and surmises," concluded the professor, "it would be impossible for such a distinctly different minority to keep its special physical and cultural characteristics over a period of half a hundred millennia. Paley has concocted this personal myth to compensate for his extreme ugliness, his inferiority, his feelings of rejection. The elements of the myth came from the comic books and TV.

"However," concluded the professor, "in view of your youthful enthusiasm and naïveté, I will consider my judgment if you bring me some physical evidence of his Neanderthaloid origin. Say you could show me that he had a taurodont tooth. I'd be flabbergasted, to say the least."

"But, Professor," she pleaded, "why can't you give him a personal examination? One look at Old Man's foot would convince you, I'm sure."

"My dear, I am not addicted to wild-goose chases. My time is valuable."

That was that. The next day, she asked Old Man if he had ever lost a molar tooth or had an X-ray made of one.

"No," he said. "I got more sound teeth than brains. And I ain't gonnna lose em. Long as I keep my headpiece, I'll keep my teeth and my digestion and my manhood. What's more, I'll keep my good sense, too. The loose-screw tighteners at the State Hospital really gave me a good goin-over, fore and aft, up and down, in and out, all night long, don't never take a hotel room right by the elevator. And they proved I wasn't hatched in a cuckoo clock. Even though they tore their hair and said somethin must be wrong. Specially after we had that row about my hat. I woun't let them take my blood for a test, you know, because I figured they was going to mix it with water—G'yaga magic—and turn my blood to water. Somehow, that Elkins got wise that I hadda wear my hat—cause I woun't take it off when I undressed for the physical, I guess—and he snatched my hat. And I was done for. Stealin it was stealin my soul; all Paleys wears their souls in their hats. I hadda get it back. So I ate humble pie; I let em poke and pry all over and take my blood."

There was a pause while Paley breathed in deeply to get power to launch another verbal rocket. Dorothy, who had been struck by an idea, said, "Speaking of hats, Old Man, what does this hat that the daughter of Raw Boy stole from King Paley look like? Would you recognize it if you saw it?"

Old Man stared at her with wide blue eyes for a moment before he exploded.

"Would I recognize it? Would the dog that sat by the railroad tracks recognize his tail after the locomotive cut it off? Would you recognize your own blood if somebody stuck you in the guts with a knife and it pumped out with every heartbeat? Certainly, I would recognize the hat a Old Kind Paley! Every Paley at his mother's knees get a detailed description a it. You want to hear about the hat? Well, hang on, chick, and I'll describe every hair and bone a it."

Dorothy told herself more than once that she should not be doing this. If she was trusted by Old Man, she was, in one sense, a false friend. But, she reassured herself, in another sense she was helping him. Should he find the hat, he might blossom forth, actually tear himself loose from the taboos that bound him to the dumpheap, to the alleys, to fear of dogs, to the conviction he was an inferior and oppressed citizen. Moreover, Dorothy told herself, it would aid her scientific studies to record his reactions.

The taxidermist she hired to locate the necessary materials and fashion them into the desired shape was curious, but she told him it was for an anthropological exhibit in Chicago and that it was meant to represent the headpiece of the medicine man of an Indian secret society dedicated to phallic mysteries. The taxidermist sniggered and said he'd give his eyeteeth to see those ceremonies.

Dorothy's intentions were helped by the run of good luck Old Man had in his alleypicking while she rode with him. Exultant, he swore he was headed for some extraordinary find; he could feel his good fortune building up.

"It's gonna hit," he said, grinning with his huge widely spaced gravestone teeth. "Like lightnin."

Two days later, Dorothy rose even earlier than usual and drove to a place behind the house of a well-known doctor. She had read in the society column that he and his family were vacationing in Alaska, so she knew they wouldn't be wondering at finding a garbage can already filled with garbage and a big cardboard box full of cast-off clothes. Dorothy had brought the refuse from her own apartment to make it seem as if the house were occupied. The old garments, with one exception, she had purchased at a Salvation Army store.

About nine that morning, she and Old Man drove down the alley on their scheduled route.

Old Man was first off the truck; Dorothy hung back to let him make the discovery.

Old Man picked the garments out of the box one by one.

"Here's a velvet dress Deena kin wear. She's been complainin she hasn't had a new dress in a long time. And here's a blouse and skirt big enough to wrap aroun an elephant. Gummy kin wear it. And here . . ."

He lifted up a tall conical hat with a wide brim and two balls of felted horsemane attached to the band. It was a strange headpiece, fashioned of roan horsehide over a ribwork of split bones. It must have been the only one of its kind in the world, and it certainly looked out of place in the alley of a mid-Illinois city.

Old Man's eyes bugged out. Then they rolled up, and he fell to the ground, as if shot. The hat, however, was still clutched in his hand.

Dorothy was terrified. She had expected any reaction but this. If he had suffered a heart attack, it would, she thought, be her fault.

Fortunately, Old Man had only fainted. However, when he regained consciousness, he did not go into ecstasies as she had expected. Instead, he looked at her, his face gray and said, "It kin't be! It must be a trick The Old Woman In The Earth's playing on me so she kin have the last laugh on me. How could it be the hat a Old King Paley's? Woun't the G'yaga that been keepin it in their famley all these years know what it is?"

"Probably not," said Dorothy. "After all, the G'yaga, as you call them, don't believe in magic anymore. Or it might be that the present owner doesn't even know what it is."

"Maybe. More likely it was thrown out by accident durin housecleanin. You know how stupid them wimmen are. Anyway, let's take it and get goin. The Old Guy In The Sky might a had a hand in fixin up this deal for me, and if he did, it's better not to ask questions. Let's go."

Old Man seldom wore the hat. When he was home, he put it in the parrot cage and locked the cage door with the bicycle lock. At nights, the cage hung from the stand; days, it sat on the seat of the truck. Old Man wanted it always where he could see it.

Finding it had given him a tremendous optimism, a belief he could do anything. He sang and laughed even more than he had before, and he was even able to venture out onto the streets for several hours at a time before the sweat and shakings began.

Gummy, seeing the hat, merely grunted and made a lewd remark about its appearance. Deena smiled grimly and said, "Why haven't the horsehide and bones rotted away long ago?"

"That's just the kind a question a G'yaga dummy like you'd ask," said Old Man, snorting. "How kin the hat rot when there's a million Paley souls crowded into it, standin room only? There ain't even elbow room for germs. Besides, the horsehide and the bones're jampacked with the power and the glory a all the Paleys that died before our battle with Raw Boy, and all the souls that died since. It's seethin with soul-energy, the lid held on it by the magic a the G'yaga."

"Better watch out it don't blow up 'n wipe us all out," said Gummy, sniggering.

"Now you have the hat, what are you going to do with it?" asked Deena.

"I don't know. I'll have to sit down with a beer and study the situation."

Suddenly, Deena began laughing shrilly.

"My God, you've been thinking for fifty thousand years about this hat, and now you've got it, you don't know what to do about it! Well, I'll tell you what you'll do about it! You'll get to thinking big, all right! You'll conquer the world, rid it of all False Folk, all right! You fool! Even if your story isn't the raving of a lunatic, it would still be too late for you! You're alone! The last! One against two billion! Don't worry, World, this ragpicking Rameses, this alley Alexander, this junkyard Julius Caesar, he isn't going to conquer you! No, he's going to put on his hat, and he's going forth! To do what?

"To become a wrestler on TV, that's what! That's the height of his halfwit ambition—to be billed as the One-Armed Neanderthal, the Awful Apeman. That is the culmination of fifty thousand years ha, ha, ha!"

The others looked apprehensively at Old Man, expecting him to strike Deena. Instead, he removed the hat from the cage, put it on, and sat down at the table with a quart of beer in his hand.

"Quit your cacklin, you old hen," he said. "I got my thinkin cap on!"

The next day Paley, despite a hangover, was in a very good mood. He chattered all the way to the west bluff and once stopped the truck so he could walk back and forth on the street and show Dorothy he wasn't afraid.

Then, boasting he could lick the world, he drove the truck up an alley and halted it by the backyard of a huge but somewhat run-down mansion. Dorothy looked at him curiously. He pointed to the jungle-thick shrubbery that filled a corner of the yard.

"Looks like a rabbit coun't get in there, huh? But Old Man knows thins the rabbits don't. Folly me."

Carrying the caged hat, he went to the shrubbery, dropped to all threes, and began inching his way through a very narrow passage. Dorothy stood looking dubiously into the tangle until a hoarse growl came from its depths.

"You scared? Or is your fanny too broad to get through here?"

"I'll try anything once," she announced cheerfully. In a short time she was crawling on her belly, then had come suddenly into a little clearing. Old Man was standing up. The cage was at his feet, and he was looking at a red rose in his hand.

She sucked in her breath. "Roses! Peonies! Violets!"

"Sure, Dor'thy," he said, swelling out his chest. "Paley's Garden a Eden, his secret hothouse. I found this place a couple a years ago, when I was lookin for a place to hide if the cops was lookin for me or I just wanted a place to be alone from everybody, including myself.

"I planted these rosebushes in here and these other flowers. I come here every now and then to check on em, spray em, prune em. I never take any home, even though I'd like to give Deena some. But Deena ain't no dummy, she'd know I was gettin em out a a garbage pail. And I just din't want to tell her about this place. Or anybody."

He looked directly at her as if to catch every twitch of a muscle in her face, every repressed emotion.

"You're the only person besides myself knows about this place." He held out the rose to her. "Here. It's yours."

"Thank you. I am proud, really proud, that you've shown this place to me."

"Really are? That makes me feel good. In fact, great."

"It's amazing. This, this spot of beauty. And . . . and . . ."

"I'll finish it for you. You never thought the ugliest man in the world, a dumpheaper, a man that ain't even a man or a human bein, a—I hate the word—a Neanderthal, could appreciate the beauty of a rose. Right? Well, I growed these because I love em.

"Look, Dor'thy. Look at this rose. It's round, not like a ball but a flattened roundness. . . ."

"Oval."

"Sure. And look at the petals. How they fold in on one another, how they're arranged. Like one ring a red towers protectin the next ring a red towers. Protectin the gold cup on the inside, the precious source a life, the treasure. Or maybe that's the golden hair a the princess a the castle. Maybe. And look at the bright green leaves under the rose. Beautiful, huh? The Old Guy knew what he was doin when he made these. He was an artist then.

"But he must a been sufferin from a hangover when he shaped me, huh? His hands was shaky that day. And he gave up after a while and never bothered to finish me but went on down to the corner for some a the hair a the dog that bit him."

Suddenly, tears filled Dorothy's eyes.

"You shouldn't feel that way. You've got beauty, sensitivity, a genuine feeling, under . . ."

"Under this?" he said, pointing his finger at his face. "Sure. Forget it. Anyway, look at these green buds on these baby roses. Pretty, huh? Fresh with promise a the beauty to come. They're shaped like the breasts a young virgins."

He took a step toward her and put his arm around her shoulders.

"Dor'thy."

She put her hands on his chest and gently tried to shove herself away.

"Please," she whispered, "please, don't. Not after you've shown me how fine you really can be."

"What do you mean?" he said, not releasing her. "Ain't what I want to do with you just as fine and beautiful a thin as this rose here? And if you really feel for me, you'd want to let your flesh say what your mind thinks. Like the flowers when they open up for the sun."

She shook her head. "No. It can't be. Please. I feel terrible because I can't say yes. But I can't. I—you—there's too much diff—"

"Sure, we're diff'runt. Goin in diff'runt directions and then, comin roun the corner—bam!—we run into each other, and we wrap ours arms aroun each other to keep from fallin."

He pulled her to him so her face was pressed against his chest.

"See!" he rumbled. "Like this. Now, breathe deep. Don't turn your head. Sniff away. Lock yourself to me, like we was glued and nothin could pull us apart. Breathe deep. I got my arm aroun you, like these trees roun these flowers. I'm not hurtin you: I'm givin you life and protectin you. Right? Breathe deep."

"Please," she whimpered. "Don't hurt me. Gently . . ."

"Gently it is. I won't hurt you. Not too much. That's right, don't hold yourself stiff against me, like you're stone. That's right, melt like butter. I'm not forcin you, Dor'thy, remember that. You want this, don't you?"

"Don't hurt me," she whispered. "You're so strong, oh my God, so strong."

For two days, Dorothy did not appear at the Paleys'. The third morning, in an effort to fire her courage, she downed two double shots of V.O. before breakfast. When she drove to the dumpheap, she told the two women that she had not been feeling well. But she had returned because she wanted to finish her study, as it was almost at an end and her superiors were anxious to get her report.

Paley, though he did not smile when he saw her, said nothing. However, he kept looking at her out of the corners of his eyes when he thought she was watching him. And though he took the hat in its cage with him, he sweated and shook as before while crossing streets. Dorothy sat staring straight ahead, unresponsive to the few remarks he did make. Finally, cursing under his breath, he abandoned his effort to work as usual and drove to the hidden garden.

"Here we are," he said. "Adam and Eve returnin to Eden."

He peered from beneath the bony ridges of his brows at the sky. "We better hurry in. Looks as if The Old Guy got up on the wrong side a the bed. There's gonna be a storm."

"I'm not going in there with you," said Dorothy. "Not now or ever."

"Even after what we did, even if you said you loved me, I still make you sick?" he said. "You sure din't act then like Old Ugly made you sick."

"I haven't been able to sleep for two nights," she said tonelessly. "I've asked myself a thousand times why I did it. And each time I could only tell myself I didn't know. Something seemed to leap from you to me and take me over. I was powerless."

"You certainly wasn't paralyzed," said Old Man, placing his hand on her knee. "And if you was powerless, it was because you wanted to be."

"It's no use talking," she said. "You'll never get a chance again. And take your hand off me. It makes my flesh crawl."

He dropped his hand.

"All right. Back to business. Back to pickin people's piles a junk. Let's get out a here. Forget what I said. Forget this garden, too. Forget the secret I told you. Don't tell nobody. The dump-heapers'd laugh at me. Imagine Old Man Paley, the one-armed candidate for the puzzle factory, the fugitive from the Old Stone Age, growin peonies and roses! Big laugh, huh?"

Dorothy did not reply. He started the truck and, as they emerged onto the alley, they saw the sun disappear behind the clouds. The rest of the day, it did not come out, and Old Man and Dorothy did not speak to each other.

As they were going down Route 24 after unloading at the junkdealer's, they were stopped by a patrolman. He ticketed Paley for not having a chauffeur's license and made Paley follow him downtown to court. There Old Man had to pay a fine of twenty-five dollars. This, to everybody's amazement, he produced from his pocket.

As if that weren't enough, he had to endure the jibes of the police and the courtroom loafers. Evidently he had appeared in the police station before and was known as *King Kong, Alley Oop,* or just plain Chimp. Old Man trembled, whether with suppressed rage or nervousness Dorothy could not tell. But later, as Dorothy drove him home, he almost frothed at the mouth in a tremendous outburst of rage. By the time they were within sight of his shanty, he was shouting that his life savings had been wiped out and that it was all a plot by the *G'yaga* to beat him down to starvation.

It was then that the truck's motor died. Cursing, Old Man jerked the hood open so savagely that one rusty hinge broke. Further enraged by this, he tore the hood completely off and threw it away into the ditch by the roadside. Unable to find the cause of the breakdown, he took a hammer from the toolchest and began to beat the sides of the truck.

"I'll make her go, go, go!" he shouted. "Or she'll wish she had! Run, you bitch, purr, eat gasoline, rumble your damn belly and eat gasoline but run, run, run! Or your ex-lover, Old Man, sells you for junk, I swear it!"

Undaunted, Fordiana did not move.

Eventually, Paley and Dorothy had to leave the truck by the ditch and walk home. And as they crossed the heavily traveled highway to get to the dumpheap, Old Man was forced to jump to keep from getting hit by a car.

He shook his fist at the speeding auto.

"I know you're out to get me!" he howled. "But you won't! You been tryin for fifty thousand years, and you ain't made it yet! We're still fightin!"

At that moment, the black sagging bellies of the clouds overhead ruptured. The two were soaked before they could take four steps. Thunder bellowed, and lightning slammed into the earth on the other end of the dumpheap.

Old Man growled with fright, but seeing he was untouched, he raised his fist to the sky.

"OK, OK, so you got it in for me, too. I get it. OK, OK!"

Dripping, the two entered the shanty, where he opened a quart of beer and began drinking. Deena took Dorothy behind a curtain and gave her a towel to dry herself with and one of her white terrycloth robes to put on. By the time Dorothy came out from behind the curtain, she found Old Man opening his third quart. He was accusing Deena of not frying the fish correctly, and when she answered him sharply, he began accusing her of every fault, big or small, real or imaginary, of which he could think. In fifteen minutes, he was nailing the portrait of her mother to the wall with its face inward. And she was whimpering behind the stove and tenderly stroking the spots where he had struck her. Gummy protested, and he chased her out into the rain.

Dorothy at once put her wet clothes on and announced she was leaving. She'd walk the mile into town and catch the bus.

Old Man snarled, "Go! You're too snotty for us, anyway. We ain't your kind, and that's that."

"Don't go," pleaded Deena. "If you're not here to restrain him, he'll be terrible to us."

"I'm sorry," said Dorothy. "I should have gone home this morning."

"You sure should," he growled. And then began weeping, his pushed-out lips fluttering like a bird's wings, his face twisted like a gargoyle's.

"Get out before I forget myself and throw you out," he sobbed.

Dorothy, with pity on her face, shut the door gently behind her.

The following day was Sunday. That morning, her mother phoned her she was coming down from Waukegan to visit her. Could she take Monday off?

Dorothy said yes, and then, sighing, she called her supervisor. She told him she had all the data she needed for the Paley report and that she would begin typing it out.

Monday night, after seeing her mother off on the train, she decided to pay the Paleys a farewell visit. She could not endure another sleepless night filled with fighting the desire to get out of bed again and again, to scrub herself clean, and the pain of having to face Old Man and the two women in the morning. She felt that if she said goodbye to the Paleys, she could say farewell to those feelings, too, or, at least, time would wash them away more quickly.

The sky had been clear, star-filled, when she left the railroad station. By the time she had reached the dumpheap clouds had swept out from the west, and a blinding rainstorm was deluging the city. Going over the bridge, she saw by the lights of her headlamps that the Kickapoo Creek had become a small river in the two days of heavy rains. Its muddy frothing current roared past the dump and on down to the Illinois River, a half mile away.

So high had it risen that the waters lapped at the doorsteps of the shanties. The trucks and jalopies parked outside them were piled high with household goods, and their owners were ready to move at a minute's notice.

Dorothy parked her car a little off the road, because she did not want to get it stuck in the mire. By the time she had walked to the Paley shanty, she was in stinking mud up to her calves, and night had fallen.

In the light streaming from a window stood Fordiana, which Old Man had apparently succeeded in getting started. Unlike the other vehicles, it was not loaded.

Dorothy knocked on the door and was admitted by Deena. Paley was sitting in the ragged easy chair. He was clad only in a pair of faded and patched blue jeans. One eye was surrounded by a big black, blue, and green bruise. The horsehide hat of Old King was firmly jammed onto his head, and one hand clutched the neck of a quart of beer as if he were choking it to death.

Dorothy looked curiously at the black eye but did not comment on it. Instead, she asked him why he hadn't packed for a possible flood.

Old Man waved the naked stump of his arm at her.

"It's the doins a The Old Guy In The Sky. I prayed to the old idiot to stop the rain, but it rained harder'n ever. So I figure it's really The Old Woman In The Earth who's kickin up this rain. The Old Guy's too feeble to stop her. He needs strength. So . . . I thought about pouring out the blood a a virgin to him, so he kin lap it up and get his muscles back with that. But I give that up, cause there ain't no such thin anymore, not within a hundred miles a here, anyway.

"So . . . I been thinkin about goin outside and doin the next best thing, that is pouring a quart or two a beer out on the ground for him. What the Greeks call pourin a liberation to the Gods. . . ."

"Don't let him drink none a that cheap beer," warned Gummy. "This rain fallin on us is bad enough. I don't want no god pukin all over the place."

He hurled the quart at her. It was empty, because he wasn't so far gone he'd waste a full or even half-full bottle. But it was smashed against the wall, and since it was worth a nickel's refund, he accused Gummy of malicious waste.

"If you'd a held still, it woun't a broke."

Deena paid no attention to the scene. "I'm pleased to see you, child," she said. "But it might have been better if you had stayed home tonight."

She gestured at the picture of her mother, still nailed face inward. "He's not come out of his evil mood yet."

"You kin say that again," mumbled Gummy. "He got a pistol-whippin from that young Limpy Doolan who lives in that packin-box house with the Jantzen bathin suit ad pasted on the side, when Limpy tried to grab Old King's hat off a Old Man's head just for fun."

"Yeah, he tried to grab it," said Paley. "But I slapped his hand hard. Then he pulls a gun out a his coat pocket with the other hand and hit me in this eye with its butt. That don't stop me. He sees me comin at him like I'm late for work, and he says he'll shoot me if I touch him again. My old man din't raise no silly sons, so I don't charge him. But I'll get him sooner or later. And he'll be limpin in both legs, if he walks at all.

"But I don't know why I never had nothing but bad luck ever since I got this hat. It ain't supposed to be that way. It's supposed to be bringin me all the good luck the Paleys ever had."

He glared at Dorothy and said, "Do you know what? I had good luck until I showed you that place, you know, the flowers. And then, after you know what, everythin went sour as old milk. What did you do, take the power out a me by doin what you did? Did The Old Woman In The Earth send you to me so you'd draw the muscle and luck and life out a me if I found the hat when Old Guy placed it in my path?"

He lurched up from the easy chair, clutched two quarts of beer from the refrigerator to his chest, and staggered toward the door.

"Kin't stand the smell in here. Talk about *my* smell. I'm sweet violets, compared to the fish a some a you. I'm goin out where the air's fresh. I'm goin out and talk to The Old Guy In The Sky, hear what the thunder has to say to me. He understands me; he don't give a damn if I'm a ugly old man that's ha'f-ape."

Swiftly, Deena ran in front of him and held out her claws at him like a gaunt, enraged alley cat.

"So that's it! You've had the indecency to insult this young girl! You evil beast!"

Old Man halted, swayed, carefully deposited the two quarts on the floor. Then he shuffled to the picture of Deena's mother and ripped it from the wall. The nails screeched; so did Deena.

"What are you going to do?"

"Somethin I been wantin to do for a long long time. Only I felt sorry for you. Now I don't. I'm gonna throw this idol a yours into the creek. Know why? Cause I think she's a delegate a The Old Woman In The Earth, Old Guy's enemy. She's been sent here to watch on me and report to Old Woman on what I was doin. And you're the one brought her in this house."

"Over my dead body you'll throw that in the creek!" screamed Deena.

"Have it your way," he growled, lurching forward and driving her to one side with his shoulder.

Deena grabbed at the frame of the picture he held in his hand, but he hit her over the knuckles with it. Then he lowered it to the floor, keeping it from falling over with his leg while he bent over and picked up the two quarts in his huge hand. Clutching them, he squatted until his stump was level with the top part of the frame. The stump clamped down over the upper part of the frame, he straightened, holding it tightly, lurched toward the door, and was gone into the driving rain and crashing lightning.

Deena stared into the darkness for a moment, then ran after him.

Stunned, Dorothy watched them go. Not until she heard Gummy mumbling, "They'll kill each other," was Dorothy able to move.

She ran to the door, looked out, turned back to Gummy.

"What's got into him?" she cried. "He's so cruel, yet I know he has a soft heart. Why must he be this way?"

"It's you," said Gummy. "He thought it din't matter how he looked, what he did, he was still a Paley. He thought his sweat would get you like it did all em chicks he was braggin about, no matter how uppity the sweet young thin was. 'N you hurt him when you din't dig him. Specially cause he thought more a you 'n anybody before.

"Why'd you think life's been so miserable for us since he found you? What the hell, a man's a man, he's always got the eye for the chicks, right? Deena din't see that. Deena hates Old Man. But Deena kin't do without him, either. . . ."

"I have to stop them," said Dorothy, and she plunged out into the black and white world.

Just outside the door, she halted, bewildered. Behind her, light streamed from the shanty, and to the north was a dim glow from the city of Onaback. But elsewhere was darkness. Darkness, except when the lightning burned away the night for a dazzling frightening second.

She ran around the shanty toward the Kickapoo, some fifty yards away—she was sure that they'd be somewhere by the back of the creek. Halfway to the stream, another flash showed her a white figure by the bank.

It was Deena in her terrycloth robe, Deena now sitting up in the mud, bending forward, shaking with sobs.

"I got down on my knees," she moaned. "To him, to him. And I begged him to spare my mother. But he said I'd thank him later for freeing me from worshiping a false goddess. He said I'd kiss his hand."

Deena's voice rose to a scream. "And then he did it! He tore my blessed mother to bits! Threw her in the creek! I'll kill him! I'll kill him!"

Dorothy patted Deena's shoulder. "There, there. You'd better get back to the house and get dry. It's a bad thing he's done, but he's not in his right mind. Where'd he go?"

"Toward that clump of cottonwoods where the creek runs into the river."

"You go back," said Dorothy. "I'll handle him. I can do it."
Deena seized her hand.

"Stay away from him. He's hiding in the woods now. He's dangerous, dangerous as a wounded boar. Or as one of his ancestors when they were hurt and hunted by ours."

"Ours?" said Dorothy. "You mean you believe his story?"

"Not all of it. Just part. That tale of his about the mass

invasion of Europe and King Paley's hat is nonsense. Or, at least it's been distorted through God only knows how many thousands of years. But it's true he's at least part Neanderthal. Listen! I've fallen low, I'm only a junkman's whore. Not even that, now—Old Man never touches me anymore, except to hit me. And that's not his fault, really. I ask for it; I want it.

"But I'm not a moron. I got books from the library, read what they say about the Neanderthal. I studied Old Man carefully. And I *know* he must be what he says he is. Gummy, too—she's at least a quarter-breed."

Dorothy pulled her hand out of Deena's grip.

"I have to go. I have to talk to Old Man, tell him I'm not seeing him anymore."

"Stay away from him," pleaded Deena, again seizing Dorothy's hand. "You'll go to talk, and you'll stay to do what I did. What a score of others did. We let him make love to us becuase he isn't human. Yet, we found Old Man as human as any man, and some of us stayed after the lust was gone because love had come in."

Dorothy gently unwrapped Deena's fingers from her hand and began walking away.

Soon she came to the group of cottonwood trees by the bank where the creek and the river met and there she stopped.

"Old Man!" she called in a break between the rolls of thunder. "Old Man! It's Dorothy!"

A growl as of a bear disturbed in his cave answered her, and a figure like a tree trunk come to life stepped out of the inkiness between the cottonwoods.

"What you come for?" he said, approaching so close to her that his enormous nose almost touched hers. "You want me just as I am, Old Man Paley, descendant a the Real Folk—Paley, who loves you? Or you come to give the batty old junkman a tranquillizer so you kin take him by the hand like a lamb and lead him back to the slaughterhouse, the puzzle factory, where they'll stick a ice pick back a his eyeball and rip out what makes him a man and not an ox."

"I came . . ."

"Yeah?"

"For this!" she shouted, and she snatched off his hat and raced away from him, toward the river.

Behind her rose a bellow of agony so loud she could hear it even above the thunder. Feet splashed as he gave pursuit.

Suddenly, she slipped and sprawled facedown in the mud. At the same time, her glasses fell off. Now it was her turn to feel despair, for in this halfworld she could see nothing without her glasses except the lightning flashes. She must find them. But if she delayed to hunt for them, she'd lose her headstart.

She cried out with joy, for her groping fingers found what they sought. But the breath was knocked out of her, and she dropped the glasses again as a heavy weight fell upon her back and half stunned her. Vaguely, she was aware that the hat had been taken away from her. A moment later, as her senses came back into focus, she realized she was being raised into the air. Old Man was holding her in the crook of his arm, supporting part of her weight on his bulging belly.

"My glasses. Please, my glasses. I need them."

"You won't be needin em for a while. But don't worry about em. I got em in my pants pocket. Old Man's takin care a you."

His arm tightened around her so she cried out with pain.

Hoarsely, he said, "You was sent down by the G'yaga to get that hat, wasn't you? Well, it din't work cause The Old Guy's stridin the sky tonight, and he's protectin his own."

Dorothy bit her lip to keep from telling him that she had wanted to destroy the hat because she hoped that that act would also destroy the guilt of having made it in the first place. But she couldn't tell him that. If he knew she had made a false hat, he would kill her in his rage.

"No. Not again," she said. "Please. Don't. I'll scream. They'll come after you. They'll take you to the State Hospital and lock you up for life. I swear I'll scream."

"Who'll hear you? Only The Old Guy, and he'd get a kick out a seein you in this fix cause you're a Falser and you took the stuffin right out a my hat and me with your Falser Magic. But I'm gettin back what's mine and his, the same way you took it from me. The door swings both ways."

He stopped walking and lowered her to a pile of wet leaves.

"Here we are. The forest like it was in the old days. Don't worry. Old Man'll protect you from the cave bear and the bull a the woods. But who'll protect you from Old Man, huh?"

Lightning exploded so near that for a second they were blinded and speechless. Then Paley shouted, "The Old Guy's whoopin it up tonight, just like he used to do! Blood and murder and wickedness're ridin the howlin night air!"

He pounded his immense chest with his huge fist.

"Let The Old Guy and The Old Woman fight it out tonight. They ain't goin to stop us. Dor'thy. Not unless that hairy old god in the clouds is going to fry me with his lightnin, jealous a me cause I'm havin what he kin't."

Lightning rammed against the ground from the charged skies, and lightning leaped up to the clouds from the charged earth. The rain fell harder than before, as if it were being shot out of a great pipe from a mountain river and pouring directly over them. But for some time the flashes did not come close to the cottonwoods. Then, one ripped apart the night beside them, deafened and stunned them.

And Dorothy, looking over Old Man's shoulder, thought she would die of fright because there was a ghost standing over them. It was tall and white, and its shroud flapped in the wind, and its arms were raised in a gesture like a curse.

But it was a knife that it held in its hand.

Then, the fire that rose like a cross behind the figure was gone, and night rushed back in.

Dorothy screamed. Old Man grunted, as if something had knocked the breath from him.

He rose to his knees, gasped something unintelligible, and slowly got to his feet. He turned his back to Dorothy so he could face the thing in white. Lightning flashed again. Once more Dorothy screamed, for she saw the knife sticking out of his back.

Then the white figure had rushed toward Old Man. But instead of attacking him, it dropped to its knees and tried to kiss his hand and babbled for forgiveness.

No ghost. No man. Deena, in her white terrycloth robe.

"I did it because I love you!" screamed Deena.

Old Man, swaying back and forth, was silent.

"I went back to the shanty for a knife, and I came here because I knew what you'd be doing, and I didn't want Dorothy's life ruined because of you, and I hated you, and I wanted to kill you. But I don't really hate you."

Slowly, Paley reached behind him and gripped the handle of the knife. Lightning made everything white around him, and by its brief glare the women saw him jerk the blade free of his flesh.

Dorothy moaned, "It's terrible, terrible. All my fault, all my fault."

She groped through the mud until her fingers came across the Old Man's jeans and its backpocket, which held her glasses. She put the glasses on, only to find that she could not see anything because of the darkness. Then, and not until then, she became concerned about locating her own clothes. On her hands and knees she searched through the wet leaves and grass. She was about to give up and go back to Old Man when another lightning flash showed the heap to her left. Giving a cry of joy, she began to crawl to it.

But another stroke of lightning showed her something else. She screamed and tried to stand up but instead slipped and fell forward on her face.

Old Man, knife in hand, was walking slowly toward her.

"Don't try to run away!" he bellowed. "You'll never get away! The Old Guy'll light thins up for me so you kin't sneak away in the dark. Besides, your white skin shines in the night, like a rotten toadstool. You're done for. You snatched away my hat so you could get me out here defenseless, and then Deena could stab me in the back. You and her are Falser witches, I know damn well!"

"What do you think you're doing?" asked Dorothy. She tried to rise again but could not. It was as if the mud had fingers around her ankles and knees.

"The Old Guy's howlin for the blood a G'yaga wimmen. And he's gonna get all the blood he wants. It's only fair. Deena put the knife in me, and The Old Woman got some a my blood to drink. Now it's your turn to give The Old Guy some a yours."

"Don't!" screamed Deena. "Don't! Dorothy had nothing to do with it! And you can't blame me, after what you were doing to her!"

"She'd done everythin to me. I'm gonna make the last sacrifice to Old Guy. Then they kin do what they want to me. I don't care. I'll have had one moment a bein a real Real Folker."

Deena and Dorothy both screamed. In the next second, lightning broke the darkness around them. Dorothy saw Deena hurl herself on Old Man's back and carry him downward. Then, night again.

There was a groan. Then, another blast of light. Old Man was on his knees, bent almost double but not bent so far Dorothy could not see the handle of the knife that was in his chest.

"Oh, Christ!" wailed Deena. "When I pushed him, he must have fallen on the knife. I heard the bone in his chest break. Now he's dying!"

Paley moaned. "Yeah, you done it now, you sure paid me back, din't you? Paid me back for my takin the monkey off a your back and supportin you all these years."

"Oh, Old Man," sobbed Deena, "I didn't mean to do it. I was just trying to save Dorothy and save you from yourself. Please! Isn't there anything I can do for you?"

"Sure you kin. Stuff up the two big holes in my back and chest. My blood, my breath, my real soul's flowin out a me. Guy In the Sky, what a way to die! Kilt by a crazy woman!"

"Keep quiet," said Dorothy. "Save your strength. Deena, you run to the service station. It'll still be open. Call a doctor."

"Don't go, Deena," he said. "It's too late. I'm hangin onto my soul by its big toe now; in a minute I'll have to let go, and it'll jump out a me like a beagle after a rabbit.

"Dor'thy, Dor'thy, was it the wickedness a The Old Woman put you up to this? I must a meant something to you . . . under the flowers . . . maybe it's better . . . I felt like a god, then . . . not what I really am . . . a crazy old junkman . . . a alley man. . . . Just think a it . . . fifty thousand years behint me . . . older'n Adam and Eve by far . . . now, this. . . ."

Deena began weeping. He lifted his hand, and she seized it.

"Let loose," he said faintly. "I was gonna knock hell outta you for blubberin . . . just like a Falser bitch . . . kill me . . . then cry . . . you never did 'preciate me . . . like Dorothy. . . ."

"His hand's getting cold," murmured Deena.

"Deena, bury that damn hat with me . . . least you kin do. . . . Hey, Deena, who you goin to for help when you hear that monkey chitterin outside the door, huh? Who . . . ?"

Suddenly, before Dorothy and Deena could push him back down, he sat up. At the same time, lightning hammered into the earth nearby and it showed them his eyes, looking past them out into the night.

He spoke, and his voice was stronger, as if life had drained back into him through the holes in his flesh.

"Old Guy's given me a good send-off. Lightnin and thunder. The works. Nothin cheap about him, huh? Why not? He knows this is the end a the trail for me. The last a his worshipers . . . last a the Paleys. . . ."

He sank back and spoke no more.

My Sister's Brother

1960

THE SIXTH NIGHT on Mars, Lane wept.

He sobbed loudly while tears ran down his cheeks. He smacked his right fist into the palm of his left hand until the flesh burned. He howled with loneliness. He swore the most obscene and blasphemous oaths he knew.

After a while, he quit weeping. He dried his eyes, downed a shot of Scotch, and felt much better.

He wasn't ashamed because he had bawled like a woman. After all, there had been a Man who had not been ashamed to weep. He could dissolve in tears the grinding stones within; he was the reed that bent before the wind, not the oak that toppled, roots and all.

Now, the weight and the ache in his breast gone, feeling almost cheerful, he made his scheduled report over the transceiver to the circum-Martian vessel five hundred and eight miles overhead. Then he did what men must do any place in the universe. Afterward, he lay down in the bunk and opened the one personal book he had been allowed to bring along, an anthology of the world's greatest poetry.

He read here and there, running, pausing for only a line or two, then completing in his head the thousand-times murmured lines. Here and there he read, like a bee tasting the best of the nectar. . . .

It is the voice of my beloved that knocketh, saying,
Open to me, my sister, my love, my dove,
    my undefiled . . .

We have a little sister,
And she hath no breasts;
What shall we do for our sister
In the day when she shall be spoken for?

Yea, though I walk through the valley of the shadow of
    death,
I will fear no evil for Thou art with me . . .

Come live with me and be my love
And we shall all the pleasures prove . . .

It lies not in our power to love or hate
For will in us is over-ruled by fate . . .

With thee conversing, I forget all time,
All seasons, and their change, all please alike . . .

He read on about love and man and woman until he had almost forgotten his troubles. His lids drooped; the book fell from his hand. But he roused himself, climbed out of the bunk, got down on his knees, and prayed that he be forgiven and that his blasphemy and despair be understood. And he prayed that his four lost comrades be found safe and sound. Then he climbed back into the bunk and fell asleep.

At dawn he woke reluctantly to the alarm clock's ringing. Nevertheless, he did not fall back into sleep but rose, turned on the transceiver, filled a cup with water and instant, and dropped in a heat pill. Just as he finished the coffee, he heard Captain Stroyansky's voice from the 'ceiver. Stroyansky spoke with barely a trace of Slavic accent.

"Cardigan Lane? You awake?"

"More or less. How are you?"

"If we weren't worried about all of you down there, we'd be fine."

"I know. Well, what are your orders?"

"There is only one thing to do, Lane. You must go look for the others. Otherwise, you cannot get back up to us. It takes at least two more men to pilot the rocket."

"Theoretically, one man can pilot the beast," replied Lane. "But it's uncertain. However, that doesn't matter. I'm leaving at once to look for the others. I'd do that even if you ordered otherwise."

Stroyansky chuckled. Then he barked like a seal. "The success of the expedition is more important than the fate of four men. Theoretically, anyway. But if I were in your shoes, and I'm glad I'm not, I would do the same. So, good luck, Lane."

"Thanks," said Lane. "I'll need more than luck. I'll also need God's help. I suppose He's here, even if the place does look God forsaken."

He looked through the transparent double plastic walls of the dome.

"The wind's blowing about twenty-five miles an hour. The dust is covering the tractor tracks. I have to get going before they're covered up entirely. My supplies are all packed; I've enough food, air, and water to last me six days. It makes a big package, the air tanks and the sleeping tent bulk large. It's over a hundred Earth pounds, but here only about forty. I'm also taking a rope, a knife, a pickax, a flare pistol, half a dozen flares. And a walkie-talkie.

"It should take me two days to walk the thirty miles to the spot where the tracs last reported. Two days to look around. Two days to get back."

"You be back in five days!" shouted Stroyansky. "That's an order! It shouldn't take you more than one day to scout around. Don't take chances. Five days!"

And then, in a softer voice, "Good luck, and, if there is a God, may He help you!"

Lane tried to think of things to say, things that might perhaps go down with the *Doctor Livingstone, I presume,* category. But all he could say was, "So long."

Twenty minutes later, he closed behind him the door to the dome's pressure lock. He strapped on the towering pack and began to walk. But when he was about fifty yards from the base, he felt compelled to turn around for one long look at what he might never see again. There, on the yellow-red felsite plain, stood the pressurized bubble that was to have been the home of the five men for a year. Nearby squatted the glider that had brought them down, its enormous wings spreading far, its skids covered with the forever-blowing dust.

Straight ahead of him was the rocket, standing on its fins, pointing toward the blue-black sky, glittering in the Martian sun, shining with promise of power, escape from Mars, and return to the orbital ship. It had come down to the surface of Mars on the back of the glider in a hundred-and-twenty-mile an hour landing. After it had dropped the two six-ton caterpillar tractors it carried, it had been pulled off the glider and tilted on end by winches pulled by those very tractors. Now it waited for him and for the other four men.

"I'll be back," he murmured to it. "And if I have to, I'll take you up by myself."

He began to walk, following the broad double tracks left by the tank. The tracks were faint, for they were two days old, and the blowing silicate dust had almost filled them. The tracks made by the first tank, which had left three days ago, were completely hidden.

The trail led northwest. It left the three-mile wide plain between two hills of naked rock and entered the quarter-mile corridor between two rows of vegetation. The rows ran straight and parallel from horizon to horizon, for miles behind him and miles ahead.

Lane, on the ground and close to one row, saw it for what it was. Its foundation was an endless three-foot high tube, most of whose bulk, like an iceberg's, lay buried in the ground. The curving sides were covered with blue-green lichenoids that grew on every rock or projection. From the spine of the tube, separated at regular intervals, grew the trunks of plants. The trunks were smooth shiny blue-green pillars two feet thick and six feet high. Out of their tops spread radially many pencil-thin branches, like bats' fingers. Between the fingers stretched a blue-green membrane, the single tremendous leaf of the umbrella tree.

When Lane had first seen them from the glider as it hurtled over them, he had thought they looked like an army of giant hands uplifted to catch the sun. Giant they were, for each rib-supported leaf measured fifty feet across. And hands they were, hands to beg for and catch the rare gold of the tiny sun. During the day, the ribs on the side nearest the moving sun dipped toward the ground, and the furthest ribs tilted upward. Obviously, the daylong maneuver was designed to expose the complete area of the membrane to the light, to allow not an inch to remain in shadow.

It was to be expected that strange forms of plant life would be found here. But structures built by animal life were not expected. Especially when they were so large and covered an eighth of the planet.

These structures were the tubes from which rose the trunks of the umbrella trees. Lane had tried to drill through the rocklike side of the tube. So hard was it, it had blunted one drill and had done a second no good before he had chipped off a small piece. Contented for the moment with that, he had taken it to the dome, there to examine it under a microscope. After an amazed look, he had whistled. Embedded in the cementlike mass were plant cells. Some were partially destroyed; some, whole.

Further tests had shown him that the substance was composed of cellulose, a ligninlike stuff, various nucleic acids, and unknown materials.

He had reported his discovery and also his conjecture to the orbital ship. Some form of animal life had, at some time, chewed up and partially digested wood and then had regurgitated it as a cement. The tubes had been fashioned from the cement.

The following day he intended to go back to the tube and blast a hole in it. But two of the men had set out in a tractor on a field exploration. Lane, as radio operator for that day, had stayed in the dome. He was to keep in contact with the two, who were to report to him every fifteen minutes.

The tank had been gone about two hours and must have been about thirty miles away, when it had failed to report. Two hours later, the other tank, carrying two men, had followed the prints of the first party. They had gone about thirty miles from base and were maintaining continuous radio contact with Lane.

"There's a slight obstacle ahead," Greenberg had said. "It's a tube coming out at right angles from the one we've been parallcl-ing. It has no plants growing from it. Not much of a rise, not much of a drop on the other side, either. We'll make it easy."

Then he had yelled.

That was all.

Now, the day after, Lane was on foot, following the fading trail. Behind him lay the base camp, close to the junction of the two *canali* known as Avernus and Tartarus. He was between two of the rows of vegetation which formed Tartarus, and he was traveling northeastward, toward the Sirenum Mare, the so-called Siren Sea. The Mare, he supposed, would be a much broader group of tree-bearing tubes.

He walked steadily while the sun rose higher and the air grew warmer. He had long ago turned off his suit-heater. This was summer and close to the equator. At noon the temperature would be around seventy degrees Fahrenheit.

But at dusk, when the temperature had plunged through the dry air to zero, Lane was in his sleeping tent. It looked like a cocoon, being sausage-shaped and not much larger than his body. It was inflated so he could remove his helmet and breathe while he warmed himself from the battery-operated heater and ate and drank. The tent was also very flexible; it changed its cocoon shape to a triangle while Lane sat on a folding chair from which hung a plastic bag and did that which every man must do.

During the daytime he did not have to enter the sleeping tent for this. His suit was ingeniously contrived so he could unflap the rear section and expose the necessary area without losing air or pressure from the rest of his suit. Naturally, there was no thought of tempting the teeth of the Martian night. Sixty seconds at midnight were enough to get a severe frostbite where one sat down.

Lane slept until half an hour after dawn, ate, deflated the tent, folded it, stowed it, the battery, heater, food-box, and folding chair into his pack, threw away the plastic sack, shouldered the pack, and resumed his walk.

By noon the tracks faded out completely. It made little difference, for there was only one route the tanks could have taken. That was the corridor between the tubes and the trees.

Now he saw what the two tanks had reported. The trees on his right began to look dead. The trunks and leaves were brown, and the ribs drooped.

He began walking faster, his heart beating hard. An hour passed, and still the line of dead trees stretched as far as he could see.

"It must be about here," he said out loud to himself.

Then he stopped. Ahead was an obstacle.

It was the tube of which Greenberg had spoken, the one that ran at right angles to the other two and joined them.

Lane looked at it and thought that he could still hear Greenberg's despairing cry.

That thought seemed to turn a valve in him so that the immense pressure of loneliness, which he had succeeded in holding back until then, flooded in. The blue-black of the sky became the blackness and infinity of space itself, and he was a speck of flesh in an immensity as large as Earth's land area, a speck that knew no more of this world than a newborn baby knows of his.

Tiny and helpless, like a baby. . . .

No, he murmured to himself, not a baby. Tiny, yes. Helpless, no. Baby, no. I am a man, a man, an Earthman. . . .

Earthman: Cardigan Lane. Citizen of the U.S.A. Born in Hawaii, the fiftieth state. Of mingled German, Dutch, Chinese, Japanese, Negro, Cherokee, Polynesian, Portuguese, Russian-Jewish, Irish, Scotch, Norwegian, Finnish, Czech, English, and Welsh ancestry. Thirty-one years old. Five foot six. One hundred and sixty pounds. Brown-haired. Blue-eyed. Hawkfeatured, M.D. and Ph.D. Married. Childless. Methodist. Sociable mesomorphic mesovert. Radio ham. Dog breeder. Deer hunter. Skin diver. Writer of first-rate but far from great poetry. All contained in his skin and his pressure suit, plus a love of companionship and life, an intense curiosity, and a courage. And now very much afraid of losing everything except his loneliness.

For some time he stood like a statue before the three-foot high wall of the tube. Finally, he shook his head violently, shook off his fear like a dog shaking off water. Lightly, despite the towering pack on his back, he leaped up onto the top of the tube and looked on the other side, though there was nothing he had not seen before jumping.

The view before him differed from the one behind in only one respect. This was the number of small plants that covered the ground. Or rather, he thought, after taking a second look, he had never seen these plants this size before. They were foot-high replicas of the huge umbrella trees that sprouted from the tubes. And they were not scattered at random, as might have been expected if they had grown from seeds blown by the wind. Instead, they grew in regular rows, the edges of the plants in one row separated from the other by about two feet.

His heart beat even faster. Such spacing must mean they were planted by intelligent life. Yet intelligent life seemed very improbable, given the Martian environment.

Possibly some natural condition might have caused the seeming artificiality of this garden. He would have to investigate.

Always with caution, though. So much depended on him: the lives of the four men, the success of the expedition. If this one failed, it might be the last. Many people on Earth were groaning loudly because of the cost of Space Arm and crying wildly for results that would mean money and power.

The field, or garden, extended for about three hundred yards. At its far end there was another tube at right angles to the two parallel ones. And at this point the giant umbrella plants regained their living and shining blue-green color.

The whole setup looked to Lane very much like a sunken garden. The square formation of the high tubes kept out the wind and most of the felsite flakes. The walls held the heat within the square.

Lane searched the top of the tube for bare spots where the metal plates of the caterpillar tractors' treads would have scraped off the lichenoids. He found none but was not surprised. The lichenoids grew phenomenally fast under the summertime sun.

He looked down at the ground on the garden side of the tube, where the tractors had presumably descended. Here there were no signs of the tractors' passage, for the little umbrellas grew up to within two feet of the edge of the tube, and they were uncrushed. Nor did he find any tracks at the ends of the tube where it joined the parallel rows.

He paused to think about his next step and was surprised to find himself breathing hard. A quick check of his air gauge showed him that the trouble wasn't an almost empty tank. No, it was the apprehension, the feeling of eeriness, of something *wrong*, that was causing his heart to beat so fast, to demand more oxygen.

Where could two tractors and four men have gone? And what could have caused them to disappear?

Could they have been attacked by some form of intelligent life? If that had happened, the unknown creatures had either carried off the six-ton tanks, or driven them away, or else forced the men to drive them off.

Where? How? By whom?

The hairs on the back of his neck stood up.

"Here is where it must have happened," he muttered to himself. "The first tank reported seeing this tube barring its way and said it would report again in another ten minutes. That was the last I heard from it. The second was cut off just as it was on top of the tube. Now, what happened? There are no cities on the surface of Mars, and no indications of underground civilization. The orbital ship would have seen openings to such a place through its telescope. . . ."

He yelled so loudly that he was deafened as his voice bounced off the confines of his helmet. Then he fell silent, watching the line of basketball-size blue globes rise from the soil at the far end of the garden and swiftly soar into the sky.

He threw back his head until the back of it was stopped by the helmet and watched the rising globes as they left the ground, swelling until they seemed to be hundreds of feet across. Suddenly, like a soap bubble, the topmost one disappeared. The second in line, having reached the height of the first, also popped. And the others followed.

They were transparent. He could see some white cirrus clouds through the blue of the bubbles.

Lane did not move but watched the steady string of globes spurt from the soil. Though startled, he did not forget his training. He noted that the globes, besides being semitransparent, rose at a right angle to the ground and did not drift with the wind. He counted them and got to forty-nine when they ceased appearing.

He waited for fifteen minutes. When it looked as if nothing more would happen, he decided that he must investigate the spot where the globes seemed to have popped out of the ground. Taking a deep breath, he bent his knees and jumped out into the garden. He landed lightly about twelve feet out from the edge of the tube and between two rows of plants.

For a second he did not know what was happening, though he realized that something was wrong. Then he whirled around. Or tried to do so. One foot came up, but the other sank deeper.

He took one step forward, and the forward foot also disappeared into the thin stuff beneath the red-yellow dust. By now the other foot was too deep in to be pulled out.

Then he was hip-deep and grabbing at the stems of the plants to both sides of him. They uprooted easily, coming out of the soil, one clenched in each hand.

He dropped them and threw himself backward in the hope he could free his legs and lie stretched out on the jellylike stuff. Perhaps, if his body presented enough of an area, he could keep from sinking. And, after a while, he might be able to work his way to the ground near the tube. There, he hoped, it would be firm.

His violent effort succeeded. His legs came up out of the sticky semiliquid. He lay spread-eagled on his back and looked up at the sky through the transparent dome of his helmet. The sun was to his left; when he turned his head inside the helmet he could see the sun sliding down the arc from the zenith. It was descending at a slightly slower pace than on Earth, for Mars's day was about forty minutes longer. He hoped that, if he couldn't regain solid ground, he could remain suspended until evening fell. By then this quagmire would be frozen enough for him to rise and walk up on it. Provided that he got up before he himself was frozen fast.

Meanwhile, he would follow the approved method of saving oneself when trapped in quicksand. He would roll over quickly, once, and then spread-eagle himself again. By repeating this maneuver, he might eventually reach that bare strip of soil at the tube.

The pack on his back prevented him from rolling. The straps on his shoulders would have to be loosened.

He did so, and at the same time felt his legs sinking. Their weight was pulling them under, whereas the air tanks in the pack, the air tanks strapped to his chest, and the bubble of his helmet gave buoyancy to the upper part of his body.

He turned over on his side, grabbed the pack, and pulled himself up on it. The pack, of course, went under. But his legs were free, though slimy with liquid and caked with dust. And he was standing on top of the narrow island of the pack.

The thick jelly rose up to his ankles while he considered two courses of action.

He could squat on the pack and hope that it would not sink too far before it was stopped by the permanently frozen layer that must exist. . . .

How far? He had gone down hip-deep and felt nothing firm beneath his feet. And . . . He groaned. The tractors! Now he knew what had happened to them. They had gone over the tube and down into the garden, never suspecting that the solid-seeming surface covered this quagmire. And down they had plunged, and it had been Greenberg's horrified realization of what lay beneath the dust that had made him cry out, and then the stuff had closed over the tank and its antenna, and the transmitter, of course, had been cut off.

He must give up his second choice because it did not exist. To get to the bare strip of soil at the tube would be useless. It would be as unfirm as the rest of the garden. It was at that point that the tanks must have fallen in.

Another thought came to him: that the tanks must have disturbed the orderly arrangement of the little umbrellas close to the tube. Yet there was no sign of such a happening. Therefore, somebody must have rescued the plants and set them up again.

That meant that somebody might come along in time to rescue him.

Or to kill him, he thought.

In either event, his problem would be solved.

Meanwhile, he knew it was no use to make a jump from the pack to the strip at the tube. The only thing to do was to stay on top of the pack and hope it didn't sink too deeply.

However, the pack did sink. The jelly rose swiftly to his knees, then his rate of descent began slowing. He prayed, not for a miracle but only that the buoyancy of the pack plus the tank on his chest would keep him from going completely under.

Before he had finished praying, he had stopped sinking. The sticky stuff had risen no higher than his breast and had left his arms free.

He gasped with relief but did not feel overwhelmed with joy. In less than four hours the air in his tank would be exhausted. Unless he could get another tank from the pack, he was done for.

He pushed down hard on the pack and threw his arms up in the air and back in the hope his legs would rise again and he could spread-eagle. If he could do that, then the pack, relieved of his weight, might rise to the surface. And he could get another tank from it.

But his legs, impeded by the stickiness, did not rise far enough, and his body, shooting off in reaction to the kick, moved a little distance from the pack. It was just far enough so that when the legs inevitably sank again, they found no platform on which to be supported. Now he had to depend entirely on the lift of his air tank.

It did not give him enough to hold him at his former level; this time he sank until his arms and shoulders were nearly under, and only his helmet stuck out.

He was helpless.

Several years from now the second expedition, if any, would perhaps see the sun glinting off his helmet and would find his body stuck like a fly in glue.

If that does happen, he thought, I will at least have been of some use; my death will warn them of this trap. But I doubt if they'll find me. I think that Somebody or Something will have removed me and hidden me.

Then, feeling an inrush of despair, he closed his eyes and murmured some of the words he had read that last night in the base, though he knew them so well it did not matter whether he had read them recently or not.

Yea, though I walk through the valley of the shadow of death, I will fear no evil; for Thou art with me.

Repeating that didn't lift the burden of hopelessness. He felt absolutely alone, deserted by everybody, even by his Creator. Such was the desolation of Mars.

But when he opened his eyes, he knew he was not alone. He saw a Martian.

A hole had appeared in the wall of the tube to his left. It was a round section about four feet across, and it had sunk in as if it were a plug being pulled inward, as indeed it was.

A moment later a head popped out of the hole. The size of a Georgia watermelon, it was shaped like a football and was as pink as a baby's bottom. Its two eyes were as large as coffee cups and each was equipped with two vertical lids. It opened its two parrotlike beaks, ran out a very long tubular tongue, withdrew the tongue, and snapped the beak shut. Then it scuttled out from the hole to reveal a body also shaped like a football and only three times as large as its head. The pinkish body was supported three feet from the ground on ten spindly spidery legs, five on each side. Its legs ended in broad round pads on which it ran across the jelly-mire surface, sinking only slightly. Behind it streamed at least fifty others.

These picked up the little plants that Lane had upset in his struggles and licked them clean with narrow round tongues that shot out at least two feet. They also seemed to communicate by touching their tongues, as insects do with antennae.

As he was in the space between two rows, he was not involved in the setting up of the dislodged plants. Several of them ran their tongues over his helmet, but these were the only ones that paid him any attention. It was then that he began to stop dreading that they might attack him with their powerful-looking beaks. Now he broke into a sweat at the idea that they might ignore him completely.

That was just what they did. After gently embedding the thin roots of the plantlets in the sticky stuff, they raced off toward the hole in the tube.

Lane, overwhelmed with despair, shouted after them, though he knew they couldn't hear him through his helmet and the thin air even if they had hearing organs.

"Don't leave me here to die!"

Nevertheless, that was what they were doing. The last one leaped through the hole, and the entrance stared at him like the round black eye of Death itself.

He struggled furiously to lift himself from the mire, not caring that he was only exhausting himself.

Abruptly, he stopped fighting and stared at the hole.

A figure had crawled out of it, a figure in a pressure-suit.

Now he shouted with joy. Whether the figure was Martian or not, it was built like a member of *Homo sapiens*. It could be presumed to be intelligent and therefore curious.

He was not disappointed. The suited being stood up on two hemispheres of shiny red metal and began walking toward him in a sliding fashion. Reaching him, it handed him the end of a plastic rope it was carrying under its arm.

He almost dropped it. His rescuer's suit was transparent. It was enough of a shock to see clearly the details of the creature's body, but the sight of the two heads within the helmet caused him to turn pale.

The Martian slidewalked to the tube from which Lane had leaped. It jumped lightly from the two bowls on which it had stood, landed on the three-foot high top of the tube, and began hauling Lane out from the mess. He came out slowly but steadily and soon was scooting forward, gripping the rope. When he reached the foot of the tube, he was hauled on up until he could get his feet in the two bowls. It was easy to jump from them to a place beside the biped.

It unstrapped two more bowls from its back, gave them to Lane, then lowered itself on the two in the garden. Lane followed it across the mire.

Entering the hole, he found himself in a chamber so low he had to crouch. Evidently, it had been constructed by the dekapeds and not by his companion for it, too, had to bend its back and knees.

Lane was pushed to one side by some dekapeds. They picked up the thick plug, made of the same gray stuff as the tube walls, and sealed the entrance with it. Then they shot out of their mouths strand after strand of gray spiderwebby stuff to seal the plug.

The biped motioned Lane to follow, and it slid down a tunnel which plunged into the earth at a forty-five degree angle. It illuminated the passage with a flashlight which it took from its belt. They came into a large chamber which contained all of the fifty dekapeds. These were waiting motionless. The biped, as if sensing Lane's curiosity, pulled off its glove and held it before several small vents in the wall. Lane removed his glove and felt warm air flowing from the holes.

Evidently this was a pressure chamber, built by the ten-legged things. But such evidence of intelligent engineering did not mean that these things had the individual intelligence of a man. It could mean group intelligence such as Terrestrial insects possess.

After a while, the chamber was filled with air. Another plug was pulled; Lane followed the dekapeds and his rescuer up another forty-five degree tunnel. He estimated that he would find himself inside the tube from which the biped had first come. He was right. He crawled through another hole into it.

And a pair of beaks clicked as they bit down on his helmet!

Automatically, he shoved at the thing, and under the force of his blow the dekaped lost its bite and went rolling on the floor, a bundle of thrashing legs.

Lane did not worry about having hurt it. It did not weigh much, but its body must be tough to be able to plunge without damage from the heavy air inside the tube into the almost-stratospheric conditions outside.

However, he did reach for the knife at his belt. But the biped put its hand on his arm and shook one of its heads.

Later, he was to find out that the seeming bite must have been an accident. Always—with one exception—the leggers were to ignore him.

He was also to find that he was lucky. The leggers had come out to inspect their garden because, through some unknown method of detection, they knew that the plantlets had been disturbed. The biped normally would not have accompanied them. However, today, its curiosity aroused because the leggers had gone out three times in three days, it had decided to investigate.

The biped turned out its flashlight and motioned to Lane to follow. Awkwardly, he obeyed. There was light, but it was dim, a twilight. Its source was the many creatures that hung from the ceiling of the tube. These were three feet long and six inches thick, cylindrical, pinkish-skinned, and eyeless. A dozen frondlike limbs waved continuously, and their motion kept air circulating in the tunnel.

Their cold firefly glow came from two globular pulsing organs which hung from both sides of the round loose-lipped mouth at the free end of the creature. Slime drooled from the mouth, and dripped onto the floor or into a narrow channel which ran along the lowest part of the sloping floor. Water ran in the six-inch deep channel, the first native water he had seen. The water picked up the slime and carried it a little way before it was gulped up by an animal that lay on the bottom of the channel.

Lane's eyes adjusted to the dimness until he could make out the water-dweller. It was torpedo-shaped and without eyes or fins. It had two openings in its body; one obviously sucked in water, the other expelled it.

He saw at once what this meant. The water at the North Pole melted in the summertime and flowed into the far end of the tube system. Helped by gravity and by the pumping action of the line of animals in the channel, the water was passed from the edge of the Pole to the equator.

Leggers ran by him on mysterious errands. Several, however, halted beneath some of the downhanging organisms. They reared up on their hind five legs and their tongues shot out and into the open mouths by the glowing balls. At once, the fireworm—as Lane termed it—its cilia waving wildly, stretched itself to twice its former length. Its mouth met the beak of the legger, and there was an exchange of stuff between their mouths.

Impatiently, the biped tugged at Lane's arm. He followed it down the tube. Soon they entered a section where pale roots came down out of holes in the ceiling and spread along the curving walls, gripping them, then becoming a network of many thread-thin rootlets that crept across the floor and into the water of the channel.

Here and there a dekaped chewed at a root and then hurried off to offer a piece to the mouths of the fireworms.

After walking for several minutes, the biped stepped across the stream. It then began walking as closely as possible to the wall, meanwhile looking apprehensively at the other side of the tunnel, where they had been walking.

Lane also looked but could see nothing at which to be alarmed. There was a large opening at the base of the wall which evidently led into a tunnel. This tunnel, he presumed, ran underground into a room or rooms, for many leggers dashed in and out of it. And about a dozen, larger than average, paced back and forth like sentries before the hole.

When they had gone about fifty yards past the opening, the biped relaxed. After it had led Lane along for ten minutes, it stopped. Its naked hand touched the wall. He became aware that the hand was small and delicately shaped, like a woman's.

A section of the wall swung out. The biped turned and bent down to crawl into the hole, presenting buttocks and legs femininely rounded, well shaped. It was then that he began thinking of it as a female. Yet the hips, though padded with fatty tissue, were not broad. The bones were not widely separated to make room to carry a child. Despite their curving, the hips were relatively as narrow as a man's.

Behind them, the plug swung shut. The biped did not turn on her flashlight, for there was illumination at the end of the tunnel. The floor and walls were not of the hard gray stuff nor of packed earth. They seemed vitrified, as if glassed by heat.

She was waiting for him when he slid off a three-foot high ledge into a large room. For a minute he was blinded by the strong light. After his eyes adjusted, he searched for the source of light but could not find it. He did observe that there were no shadows in the room.

The biped took off her helmet and suit and hung them in a closet. The door slid open as she approached and closed when she walked away.

She signaled that he could remove his suit. He did not hesitate. Though the air might be poisonous, he had no choice. His tank would soon be empty. Moreover, it seemed likely that the atmosphere contained enough oxygen. Even then he had grasped the idea that the leaves of the umbrella plants, which grew out of the top of the tubes, absorbed sunlight and traces of carbon dioxide. Inside the tunnels, the roots drew up water from the channel and absorbed the great quantity of carbon dioxide released by the dekapeds. Energy of sunlight converted gas and liquid into glucose and oxygen, which were given off in the tunnels.

Even here, in this deep chamber which lay beneath and to one side of the tube, a thick root penetrated the ceiling and spread its thin white web over the walls. He stood directly beneath the fleshy growth as he removed his helmet and took his first breath of

Martian air. Immediately afterward, he jumped. Something wet had dropped on his forehead. Looking up, he saw that the root was excreting liquid from a large pore. He wiped the drop off with his finger and tasted it. It was sticky and sweet.

Well, he thought, the tree must normally drop sugar in water. But it seemed to be doing so abnormally fast, because another drop was forming.

Then it came to him that perhaps this was so because it was getting dark outside and therefore cold. The umbrella trees might be pumping the water in their trunks into the warm tunnels. Thus, during the bitter subzero night, they'd avoid freezing and swelling up and cracking wide open.

It seemed a reasonable theory.

He looked around. The place was half living quarters, half biological laboratory. There were beds and tables and chairs and several unidentifiable articles. One was a large black metal box in a corner. From it, at regular intervals, issued a stream of tiny blue bubbles. They rose to the ceiling, growing larger as they did so. On reaching the ceiling they did not stop or burst but simply penetrated the vitrification as if it did not exist.

Lane now knew the origin of the blue globes he had seen appear from the surface of the garden. But their purpose was still obscure.

He wasn't given much time to watch the globes. The biped took a large green ceramic bowl from a cupboard and set it on a table. Lane eyed her curiously, wondering what she was going to do. By now he had seen that the second head belonged to an entirely separate creature. Its slim four-foot length of pinkish skin was coiled about her neck and torso; its tiny flat-faced head turned toward Lane; its snaky light blue eyes glittered. Suddenly, its mouth opened and revealed toothless gums, and its bright red tongue, mammalian, not at all reptilian, thrust out at him.

The biped, paying no attention to the worm's actions, lifted it from her. Gently, cooing a few words in a soft many-voweled language, she placed it in the bowl. It settled inside and looped around the curve, like a snake in a pit.

The biped took a pitcher from the top of a box of red plastic. Though the box was not connected to any visible power source, it seemed to be a stove. The pitcher contained warm water which she poured into the bowl, half filling it. Under the shower, the worm closed its eyes as if it were purring soundless ecstasy.

Then the biped did something that alarmed Lane.

She leaned over the bowl and vomited into it.

He stepped toward her. Forgetting the fact that she couldn't understand him, he said, "Are you sick?"

She revealed human-looking teeth in a smile meant to reassure him, and she walked away from the bowl. He looked at the worm, which had its head dipped into the mess. Suddenly, he felt sick, for he was sure that it was feeding off the mixture. And he was equally certain that she fed the worm regularly with regurgitated food.

It didn't cancel his disgust to reflect that he shouldn't react to her as he would to a Terrestrial. He knew that she was totally alien and that it was inevitable that some of her ways would repel, perhaps even shock him. Rationally, he knew this. But if his brain told him to understand and forgive, his belly said to loathe and reject.

His aversion was not much lessened by a close scrutiny of her as she took a shower in a cubicle set in the wall. She was about five feet tall and slim as a woman should be slim, with delicate bones beneath rounded flesh. Her legs were human; in nylons and high heels they would have been exciting—other things being equal. However, if the shoes had been toeless, her feet would have caused much comment. They had four toes.

Her long beautiful hands had five fingers. These seemed nailless, like the toes, though a closer examination later showed him they did bear rudimentary nails.

She stepped from the cubicle and began toweling herself, though not before she motioned to him to remove his suit and also to shower. He stared intently back at her until she laughed a short embarrassed laugh. It was feminine, not at all deep. Then she spoke.

He closed his eyes and was hearing what he had thought he would not hear for years: a woman's voice. Hers was extraordinary: husky and honeyed at the same time.

But when he opened his eyes, he saw her for what she was. No woman. No man. What? It? No. The impulse to think *her, she,* was too strong.

This, despite her lack of mammaries. She had a chest, but no nipples, rudimentary or otherwise. Her chest was a man's, muscled under the layer of fat which subtly curved to give the impression that beneath it . . . budding breasts?

No, not this creature. She would never suckle her young. She did not even bear them alive, if she *did* bear. Her belly was smooth, undimpled with a navel.

Smooth also was the region between her legs, hairless, unbroken, as innocent of organ as if she were a nymph painted for some Victorian children's book.

It was that sexless joining of the legs that was so horrible. Like the white belly of a frog, thought Lane, shuddering.

At the same time, his curiosity became even stronger. How did this thing mate and reproduce?

Again she laughed and smiled with fleshy pale-red humanly everted lips and wrinkled a short, slightly uptilted nose and ran her hand through thick straight red-gold fur. It was fur, not hair, and it had a slightly oily sheen, like a water-dwelling animal's.

The face itself, though strange, could have passed for human, but only passed. Her cheekbones were very high and protruded upward in an unhuman fashion. Her eyes were dark blue and quite human. This meant nothing. So were an octopus's eyes.

She walked to another closet, and as she went away from him he saw again that though the hips were curved like a woman's they did not sway with the pelvic displacement of the human female.

The door swung momentarily open, revealed the carcasses of several dekapeds, minus their legs, hanging on hooks. She removed one, placed it on a metal table, and out of the cupboard took a saw and several knives and began cutting.

Because he was eager to see the anatomy of the dekaped, he approached the table. She waved him to the shower. Lane removed his suit. When he came to the knife and ax he hesitated, but, afraid she might think him distrustful, he hung up the belt containing his weapons beside the suit. However, he did not take off his clothes because he was determined to view the inner organs of the animal. Later, he would shower.

The legger was not an insect, despite its spidery appearance. Not in the Terrestrial sense, certainly. Neither was it a vertebrate. Its smooth hairless skin was an animal's, as lightly pigmented as a blond Swede's. But, though it had an endoskeleton, it had no backbone. Instead, the body bones formed a round cage. Its thin ribs radiated from a cartilaginous collar which adjoined the back of the head. The ribs curved outward, then in, almost meeting at the posterior. Inside the cage were ventral lung sacs, a relatively large heart, and liverlike and kidneylike organs. Three arteries, instead of the mammalian two, left the heart. He couldn't be sure with such a hurried examination, but it looked as if the dorsal aorta, like some Terrestrial reptiles, carried both pure and impure blood.

There were other things to note. The most extraordinary was that, as far as he could discern, the legger had no digestive system. It seemed to lack both intestines and anus unless you would define as an intestine a sac which ran straight through from the throat halfway into the body. Further, there was nothing he could identify as reproductive organs, though this did not mean that it did not possess them. The creature's long tubular tongue, cut open by the biped, exposed a canal running down the length of tongue from its open tip to the bladder at its base. Apparently these formed part of the excretory system.

Lane wondered what enabled the legger to stand the great pressure differences between the interior of the tube and the Martian surface. At the same time he realized that this ability was no more wonderful than the biological mechanism which gave whales and seals the power to endure without harm the enormous pressures a half mile below the sea's surface.

The biped looked at him with round and very pretty blue eyes, laughed, and then reached into the chopped open skull and brought out the tiny brain.

"*Hauaimi,*" she said slowly. She pointed to her head, repeated, "*Hauaimi,*" and then indicated his head. "*Hauaimi.*"

Echoing her, he pointed at his own head. "*Hauaimi*. Brain."

"Brain," she said, and she laughed again.

She proceeded to call out the organs of the legger which corresponded to hers. Thus, the preparations for the meal passed swiftly as he proceeded from the carcass to other objects in the room. By the time she had fried the meat and boiled strips of the membranous leaf of the umbrella plant, and also added from cans various exotic foods, she had exchanged at least forty words with him. An hour later, he could remember twenty.

There was one thing yet to learn. He pointed to himself and said, "Lane."

Then he pointed to her and gave her a questioning look.

"Mahrseeya," she said.

"Martia?" he repeated. She corrected him, but he was so struck by the resemblance that always afterward he called her that. After a while, she would give up trying to teach him the exact pronunciation.

Martia washed her hands and poured him a bowlful of water. He used the soap and towel she handed him, then walked to the table where she stood waiting. On it was a bowl of thick soup, a plate of fried brains, a salad of boiled leaves and some unidentifiable vegetables, a plate of ribs with thick dark legger meat, hard-boiled eggs, and little loaves of bread.

Martia gestured for him to sit down. Evidently her code did not allow her to sit down before her guest did. He ignored his chair, went behind her, put his hand on her shoulder, pressed down, and with the other hand slid her chair under her. She turned her head to smile up at him. Her fur slid away to reveal one lobeless pointed ear. He scarcely noticed it, for he was too intent on the half-repulsive, half heart-quickening sensation he got when he touched her skin. It had not been the skin itself that caused that, for she was soft and warm as a young girl. It had been the *idea* of touching her.

Part of that, he thought as he seated himself, came from her nakedness. Not because it revealed her sex but because it revealed her lack of it. No breasts, no nipples, no navel, no pubic fold or projection. The absence of these seemed wrong, very wrong, unsettling. It was a shameful thing that she had nothing of which to be ashamed.

That's a queer thought, he said to himself. And for no reason, he became warm in the face.

Martia, unnoticing, poured from a tall bottle a glassful of dark wine. He tasted it. It was exquisite, no better than the best Earth had to offer but as good.

Martia took one of the loaves, broke it into two pieces, and handed him one. Holding the glass of wine in one hand and the bread in the other, she bowed her head, closed her eyes, and began chanting.

He stared at her. This was a prayer, a grace-saying. Was it the prelude to a sort of communion, one so like Earth's it was startling?

Yet, if it were, he needn't be surprised. Flesh and blood, bread and wine: the symbolism was simple, logical, and might even be universal.

However, it was possible that he was creating parallels that did not exist. She might be enacting a ritual whose origin and meaning were like nothing of which he had ever dreamed.

If so, what she did next was equally capable of misinterpretation. She nibbled at the bread, sipped the wine, and then plainly invited him to do the same. He did so. Martia took a third and empty cup, spat a piece of wine-moistened bread into the cup, and indicated that he was to imitate her.

After he did, he felt his stomach draw in on itself. For she mixed the stuff from their mouths with her finger and then offered it to him. Evidently, he was to put the finger in his mouth and eat from it.

So the action was both physical and metaphysical. The bread and the wine were the flesh and blood of whatever divinity she worshiped. More, she, being imbued with the body and the spirit of the god, now wanted to mingle hers and that of the god's with his.

What I eat of the god's, I become. What you eat of me, you become. What I eat of you, I become. Now we three are become one.

Lane, far from being repelled by the concept, was excited. He knew that there were probably many Christians who would have refused to share in the communion because the ritual did not have the same origins or conform to theirs. They might even have thought that by sharing they were subscribing to an alien god. Such an idea Lane considered to be not only narrow-minded and inflexible, but illogical, uncharitable, and ridiculous. There could be but one Creator; what names the creature gave to the Creator did not matter.

Lane believed sincerely in a personal god, one who took note of him as an individual. He also believed that mankind needed redeeming and that a redeemer had been sent to Earth. And if other worlds needed redeeming, then they too would have gotten or would get a redeemer. He went perhaps further than most of his fellow religionists, for he actually made an attempt to practice love for mankind. This had given him somewhat of a reputation as a fanatic among his acquaintances and friends. However, he had been restrained enough not to make himself too much of a nuisance, and his genuine warmheartedness had made him welcome in spite of his eccentricity.

Six years before, he had been an agnostic. His first trip into space had converted him. The overwhelming experience had made him realize shatteringly what an insignificant being he was, how awe-inspiringly complicated and immense was the universe, and how much he needed a framework within which to be and to become.

The strangest feature about his conversion, he thought afterward, was that one of his companions on that maiden trip had been a devout believer who, on returning to Earth, had renounced his own sect and faith and become a complete atheist.

He thought of this as he took her proffered finger in his mouth and sucked the paste off it.

Then obeying her gestures, he dipped his own finger into the bowl and put it between her lips.

She closed her eyes and gently mouthed the finger. When he began to withdraw it, he was stopped by her hand on his wrist. He did not insist on taking the finger out, for he wanted to avoid offending her. Perhaps a long time interval was part of the rite.

But her expression seemed so eager and at the same time so ecstatic, like a hungry baby just given the nipple, that he felt uneasy. After a minute, seeing no indication on her part that she meant to quit, he slowly but firmly pulled the finger loose. She opened her eyes and sighed, but she made no comment. Instead, she began serving his supper.

The hot thick soup was delicious and invigorating. Its texture was somewhat like the plankton soup that was becoming popular on hungry Earth, but it had no fishy flavor. The brown bread reminded him of rye. The legger meat was like wild rabbit, though it was sweeter and had an unidentifiable tang. He took only one bite of the leaf salad and then frantically poured wine down his throat to wash away the burn. Tears came to his eyes, and he coughed until she spoke to him in an alarmed tone. He smiled back at her but refused to touch the salad again. The wine not only cooled his mouth, it filled his veins with singing. He told himself he should take no more. Nevertheless, he finished his second cup before he remembered his resolve to be temperate.

By then it was too late. The strong liquor went straight to his head; he felt dizzy and wanted to laugh. The events of the day, his near-escape from death, the reaction to knowing his comrades were dead, his realization of his present situation, the tension caused by his encounters with the dekapeds, and his unsatisfied curiosity about Martia's origins and the location of others of her kind, all these combined to produce in him a half-stupor, half-exuberance.

He rose from the table and offered to help Martia with the dishes. She shook her head and put the dishes in a washer. In the meantime, he decided that he needed to wash off the sweat, stickiness, and body odor left by two days of travel. On opening the door to the shower cubicle, he found that there wasn't room enough to hang his clothes in it. So, uninhibited by fatigue and wine, also mindful that Martia, after all, was *not* a female, he removed his clothes.

Martia watched him, and her eyes became wider with each garment shed. Finally, she gasped and stepped back and turned pale.

"It's not that bad," he growled, wondering what had caused her reaction. "After all, some of the things I've seen around here aren't too easy to swallow."

She pointed with a trembling finger and asked him something in a shaky voice.

Perhaps it was his imagination, but he could swear she used the same inflection as would an English speaker.

"Are you sick? Are the growths malignant?"

He had no words with which to explain, nor did he intend to illustrate function through action. Instead, he closed the door of the cubicle after him and pressed the plate that turned on the water. The heat of the shower and the feel of the soap, of grime and sweat being washed away, soothed him somewhat, so that he could think about matters he had been too rushed to consider.

First, he would have to learn Martia's language or teach her his. Probably both would happen at the same time. Of one thing he was sure. That was that her intentions toward him were, at least at present, peaceful. When she had shared communion with him, she had been sincere. He did not get the impression that it was part of her cultural training to share bread and wine with a person she intended to kill.

Feeling better, though still tired and a little drunk, he left the cubicle. Reluctantly, he reached for his dirty shorts. Then he smiled. They had been cleaned while he was in the shower. Martia, however, paid no attention to his smile of pleased surprise but, grim-faced, she motioned to him to lie down on the bed and sleep. Instead of lying down herself, however, she picked up a bucket and began crawling up the tunnel. He decided to follow her, and, when she saw him, she only shrugged her shoulders.

On emerging into the tube, Martia turned on her flashlight. The tunnel was in absolute darkness. Her beam playing on the ceiling, showed that the glowworms had turned out their lights. There were no leggers in sight.

She pointed the light at the channel so he could see that the jetfish were still taking in and expelling water. Before she could turn the beam aside, he put his hand on her wrist and with his other hand lifted a fish from the channel. He had to pull it loose with an effort, which was explained when he turned the torpedo--shaped creature over and saw the column of flesh hanging from its belly. Now he knew why the reaction of the propelled water did not shoot them backward. The ventral-foot acted as a suction pad to hold them to the floor of the channel.

Somewhat impatiently, Martia pulled away from him and began walking swiftly back up the tunnel. He followed her until she came to the opening in the wall which had earlier made her so apprehensive. Crouching, she entered the opening, but before she had gone far she had to move a tangled heap of leggers to one side. These were the large great-beaked ones he had seen guarding the entrance. Now they were asleep at the post.

If so, he reasoned, then the thing they guarded against must also be asleep.

What about Martia? How did she fit into their picture? Perhaps she didn't fit into their picture at all. She was absolutely alien, something for which their instinctual intelligence was not prepared and which, therefore, they ignored. That would explain why they had paid no attention to him when he was mired in the garden.

Yet there must be an exception to that rule. Certainly Martia had not wanted to attract the sentinels' notice the first time she had passed the entrance.

A moment later he found out why. They stepped into a huge chamber which was at least two hundred feet square. It was as dark as the tube, but during the walking period it must have been very bright because the ceiling was jammed with glowworms.

Martia's flash raced around the chamber, showing him the piles of sleeping leggers. Then, suddenly, it stopped. He took one look, and his heart raced, and the hairs on the back of his neck rose.

Before him was a worm three feet high and twenty feet long.

Without thinking, he grabbed hold of Martia to keep her from coming closer to it. But even as he touched her, he dropped his hand. She must know what she was doing.

Martia pointed the flash at her own face and smiled as if to tell him not to be alarmed. And she touched his arm with a shyly affectionate gesture.

For a moment, he didn't know why. Then it came to him that she was glad because he had been thinking of her welfare. Moreover, her reaction showed she had recovered from her shock at seeing him unclothed.

He turned from her to examine the monster. It lay on the floor, asleep, its great eyes closed behind vertical slits. It had a huge head, football-shaped like those of the little leggers around it. Its mouth was big, but the beaks were very small, horny warts on its lips. The body, however, was that of a caterpillar worm's, minus the hair. Ten little useless legs stuck out of its side, too short even to reach the floor. Its side bulged as if pumped full of gas.

Martia walked past the monster and paused by its posterior. Here she lifted up a fold of skin. Beneath it was a pile of a dozen leathery-skinned eggs, held together by a sticky secretion.

"Now I've got it," muttered Lane. "Of course. The egg-laying queen. She specializes in reproduction. That is why the others have no reproductive organs, or else they're so rudimentary I couldn't detect them. The leggers are animals, all right, but in some things they resemble Terrestrial insects.

"Still, that doesn't explain the absence also of a digestive system."

Martia put the eggs in her bucket and started to leave the room. He stopped her and indicated he wanted to look around some more. She shrugged and began to lead him around. Both had to be careful not to step on the dekapeds, which lay everywhere.

They came to an open bin made of the same gray stuff as the walls. Its interior held many shelves, on which lay hundreds of eggs. Strands of the spiderwebby stuff kept the eggs from rolling off.

Nearby was another bin that held water. At its bottom lay more eggs. Above them minnow-sized torpedo shapes flitted about in the water.

Lane's eyes widened at this. The fish were not members of another genus but were the larvae of the leggers. And they could be set in the channel not only to earn their keep by pumping water which came down from the North Pole but to grow until they were ready to metamorphose into the adult stage.

However, Martia showed him another bin which made him partially revise his first theory. This bin was dry, and the eggs were laid on the floor. Martia picked one up, cut its tough skin open with her knife, and emptied its contents into one hand.

Now his eyes did get wide. This creature had a tiny cylindrical body, a suction pad at one end, a round mouth at the other, and two globular organs hanging by the mouth. A young glowworm.

Martia looked at him to see if he comprehended. Lane held out his hands and hunched his shoulders with an I-don't-get-it air. Beckoning, she walked to another bin to show him more eggs. Some had been ripped from within, and the little fellows whose hard beaks had done it were staggering around weakly on ten legs.

Energetically, Martia went through a series of charades. Watching her, he began to understand.

The embryos that remained in the egg until they fully developed went through three main metamorphoses: the jetfish stage, the glowworm stage, and finally the baby dekaped stage. If the eggs were torn open by the adult nurses in one of the first two stages, the embryo remained fixed in that form, though it did grow larger.

What about the queen? he asked her by pointing to the monstrously egg-swollen body.

For answer, Martia picked up one of the newly-hatched. It kicked its many legs but did not otherwise protest, being, like all its kind, mute. Martia turned it upside down and indicated a slight crease in its posterior. Then she showed him the same spot on one of the sleeping adults. The adult's rear was smooth, innocent of the crease.

Martia made eating gestures. He nodded. The creatures were

born with rudimentary sexual organs, but these never developed. In fact, they atrophied completely unless the young were given a special diet, in which case they matured into egg-layers.

But the picture wasn't complete. If you had females, you had to have males. It was doubtful if such highly developed animals were self-fertilizing or reproduced parthenogenetically.

Then he remembered Martia and began doubting. She gave no evidence of reproductive organs. Could her kind be self-reproducing? Or was she a martin, her natural fulfillment diverted by diet?

It didn't seem likely, but he couldn't be sure that such things were not possible in her scheme of Nature.

Lane wanted to satisfy his curiosity. Ignoring her desire to get out of the chamber, he examined each of the five baby dekapeds. All were potential females.

Suddenly Martia, who had been gravely watching him, smiled and took his hand, and led him to the rear of the room. Here, as they approached another structure, he smelled a strong odor which reminded him of clorox.

Closer to the structure, he saw that it was not a bin but a hemispherical cage. Its bars were of the hard gray stuff, and they curved up from the floor to meet at the central point. There was no door. Evidently the cage had been built around the thing in it, and its occupant must remain until he died.

Martia soon showed him why this thing was not allowed freedom. It—he—was sleeping, but Martia reached through the bars and struck it on the head with her fist. The thing did not respond until it had been hit five more times. Then, slowly, it opened its sidewise lids to reveal great staring eyes, bright as fresh arterial blood.

Martia threw one of the eggs at the thing's head. Its beak opened swiftly, the egg disappeared, the beak closed, and there was a noisy gulp.

Food brought it to life. It sprang up on its ten long legs, clacked its beak, and lunged against the bars again and again.

Though in no danger, Martia shrank back before the killer's

lust in the scarlet eyes. Lane could understand her reaction. It was a giant, at least two feet higher than the sentinels. Its back was on a level with Martia's head; its beaks could have taken her head in between them.

Lane walked around the cage to get a good look at its posterior. Puzzled, he made another circuit without seeing anything of maleness about it except its wild fury, like that of a stallion locked in a barn during mating season. Except for its size, red eyes, and a cloaca, it looked like one of the guards.

He tried to communicate to Martia his puzzlement. By now, she seemed to anticipate his desires. She went through another series of pantomimes, some of which were so energetic and comical that he had to smile.

First, she showed him two eggs on a nearby ledge. These were larger than the others and were speckled with red spots. Supposedly, they held male embryos.

Then she showed him what would happen if the adult male got loose. Making a face which was designed to be ferocious but only amused him, clicking her teeth and clawing with her hands, she imitated the male running amok. He would kill everybody in sight. Everybody, the whole colony, queen, workers, guards, larvae, eggs, bite off their heads, mangle them, eat them all up, all, all. And out of the slaughterhouse he would charge into the tube and kill every legger he met, devour the jetfish, drag down the glowworms from the ceiling, rip them apart, eat them, eat the roots of the trees. Kill, kill, kill, eat, eat, eat!

That was all very well, sighed Lane. But how did . . . ?

Martia indicated that, once a day, the workers rolled, literally rolled the queen across the room to the cage. There they arranged her so that she presented her posterior some few inches from the bars and the enraged male. And the male, though he wanted to do nothing but get his beak into her flesh and tear her apart, was not master of himself. Nature took over; his will was betrayed by his nervous system.

Lane nodded to show he understood. In his mind was a picture of the legger that had been butchered. It had had one sac at the internal end of the tongue. Probably the male had two, one to hold excretory matter, the other to hold seminal fluid.

Suddenly Martia froze, her hands held out before her. She had laid the flashlight on the floor so she could act freely; the beam splashed on her paling skin.

"What is it?" said Lane, stepping toward her.

Martia retreated, holding out her hands before her. She looked horrified.

"I'm not going to harm you," he said. However, he stopped so she could see he didn't mean to get any closer to her.

What was bothering her? Nothing was stirring in the chamber itself besides the male, and he was behind her.

Then she was pointing, first at him and then at the raging dekaped. Seeing this unmistakable signal of identification, he comprehended. She had perceived that he, like the thing in the cage, was male, and now she perceived structure and function in him.

What he didn't understand was why that should make her so frightened of him. Repelled, yes. Her body, its seeming lack of sex, had given him a feeling of distaste bordering on nausea. It was only natural that she should react similarly to his body. However, she had seemed to have gotten over her first shock.

Why this unexpected change, this horror of him?

Behind him, the beak of the male clicked as it lunged against the bars.

The click echoed in his mind.

Of course, the monster's lust to kill!

Until she had met him, she had known only one male creature. That was the caged thing. Now, suddenly, she had equated him with the monster. A male was a killer.

Desperately, because he was afraid that she was about to run in panic out of the room, he made signs that he was not like this monster; he shook his head no, no, no. He wasn't, he wasn't, he wasn't!

Martia, watching him intently, began to relax. Her skin regained its pinkish hue. Her eyes became their normal size. She even managed a strained smile.

To get her mind off the subject, he indicated that he would like to know why the queen and her consort had digestive systems, though the workers did not. For answer, she reached up into the downhanging mouth of the worm suspended from the ceiling. Her hand, withdrawn, was covered with secretion. After smelling her fist, she gave it to him to sniff also. He took it, ignoring her slight and probably involuntary flinching when she felt his touch.

The stuff had an odor such as you would expect from pre-digested food.

Martia then went to another worm. The two light organs of this one were not colored red, like the others, but had a greenish tint. Martia tickled its tongue with her finger and held out her cupped hands. Liquid trickled into the cup.

Lane smelled the stuff. No odor. When he drank the liquid, he discovered it to be a thick sugar water.

Martia pantomimed that the glowworms acted as the digestive systems for the workers. They also stored food away for them. The workers derived part of their energy from the glucose excreted by the roots of the trees. The proteins and vegetable matter in their diet originated from the eggs and from the leaves of the umbrella plant. Strips of the tough membranous leaf were brought into the tubes by harvesting parties which ventured forth in the daytime. The worms partially digested the eggs, dead leggers, and leaves and gave it back in the form of a soup. The soup, like the glucose, was swallowed by the workers and passed through the walls of their throats or into the long straight sac which connected the throat to the larger blood vessels. The waste products were excreted through the skin or emptied through the canal in the tongue.

Lane nodded and then walked out of the room. Seemingly relieved, Martia followed him. When they had crawled back into her quarters, she put the eggs in a refrigerator and poured two glasses of wine. She dipped her finger in both, then touched the finger to her lips and to his. Lightly, he touched the tip with his tongue. This, he gathered, was one more ritual, perhaps a bedtime one, which affirmed that they were at one and at peace. It might be that it had an even deeper meaning, but if so, it escaped him.

Martia checked on the safety and comfort of the worm in the bowl. By now it had eaten all its food. She removed the worm, washed it, washed the bowl, half filled it with warm sugar water, placed it on the table by the bed, and put the creature back in. Then she lay down on the bed and closed her eyes. She did not cover herself and apparently did not expect him to expect a cover.

Lane, tired though he was, could not rest. Like a tiger in its cage, he paced back and forth. He could not keep out of his mind the enigma of Martia nor the problem of getting back to base and eventually to the orbital ship. Earth must know what had happened.

After half an hour of this, Martia sat up. She looked steadily at him as if trying to discover the cause of his sleeplessness. Then, apparently sensing what was wrong, she rose and opened a cabinet hanging down from the wall. Inside were a number of books.

Lane said, "Ah, maybe I'll get some information now!" and he leafed through them all. Wild with eagerness, he chose three and piled them on the bed before sitting down to peruse them.

Naturally he could not read the texts, but the three had many illustrations and photographs. The first volume seemed to be a child's world history.

Lane looked at the first few pictures. Then he said, hoarsely, "My God, you're no more Martian than I am!"

Martia, startled by the wonder and urgency in his voice, came over to his bed and sat down by him. She watched while he turned the pages over until he reached a certain photo. Unexpectedly, she buried her face in her hands, and her body shook with deep sobs.

Lane was surprised. He wasn't sure why she was in such grief. The photo was an aerial view of a city on her home planet—or some planet on which her people lived. Perhaps it was the city in which she had—somehow—been born.

It wasn't long, however, before her sorrow began to stir a response in him. Without any warning he, too, was weeping.

Now he knew. It was loneliness, appalling loneliness, of the kind he had known when he had received no more word from the men in the tanks and he had believed himself the only human being on the face of this world.

After a while, the tears dried. He felt better and wished she would also be relieved. Apparently she perceived his sympathy, for she smiled at him through her tears. And in an irresistible gust of rapport and affection she kissed his hand and then stuck two of his fingers in her mouth. This, he thought, must be her way of expressing friendship. Or perhaps it was gratitude for his presence. Or just sheer joy. In any event, he thought, her society must have a high oral orientation.

"Poor Martia," he murmured. "It must be a terrible thing to have to turn to one as alien and weird as I must seem. Especially to one who, a little while ago, you weren't sure wasn't going to eat you up."

He removed his fingers but, seeing her rejected look, he impulsively took hers in his mouth.

Strangely, this caused another burst of weeping. However, he quickly saw that it was happy weeping. After it was over, she laughed softly, as if pleased.

Lane took a towel and wiped her eyes and held it over her nose while she blew.

Now, strengthened, she was able to point out certain illustrations and by signs give him clues to what they meant.

This child's book started with an account of the dawn of life on her planet. The planet revolved around a star that, according to a simplified map, was in the center of the Galaxy.

Life had begun there much as it had on Earth. It had developed in its early stages on somewhat the same lines. But there were some rather disturbing pictures of primitive fish life. Lane wasn't sure of his interpretation, however, for these took much for granted.

They did show plainly that evolution there had picked out biological mechanisms with which to advance different from those on Earth.

Fascinated, he traced the passage from fish to amphibian to reptile to warm-blooded but non-mammalian creature to an upright ground-dwelling apelike creature to beings like Martia.

Then the pictures depicted various aspects of this being's prehistoric life. Later, the invention of agriculture, working of metals, and so on.

The history of civilization was a series of pictures whose meaning he could seldom grasp. One thing was unlike Earth's history. There was a relative absence of warfare. The Rameseses, Genghis Khans, Attilas, Caesars, Hitlers, seemed to be missing.

But there was more, much more. Technology advanced much as it had on Earth, despite a lack of stimulation from war. Perhaps, he thought, it had started sooner than on his planet. He got the impression that Martia's people had evolved to their present state much earlier than *Homo sapiens*.

Whether that was true or not, they now surpassed man. They could travel almost as fast as light, perhaps faster, and had mastered interstellar travel.

It was then that Martia pointed to a page which bore several photographs of Earth, obviously taken at various distances by a spaceship.

Behind them an artist had drawn a shadowy figure, half-ape, half-dragon.

"Earth means this to you?" Lane said. *"Danger? Do not touch?"*

He looked for other photos of Earth. There were many pages dealing with other planets but only one of his home. That was enough.

"Why are you keeping us under distant surveillance?" said Lane. "You're so far ahead of us that, technologically speaking, we're Australian aborigines. What're you afraid of?"

Martia stood up, facing him. Suddenly, viciously, she snarled and clicked her teeth and hooked her hands into claws.

He felt a chill. This was the same pantomime she had used when demonstrating the mindless kill-craziness of the caged male legger.

He bowed his head. "I can't really blame you. You're absolutely correct. If you contacted us, we'd steal your secrets. And then, look out! We'd infest all of space!"

He paused, bit his lip, and said, "Yet we're showing some signs of progress. There's not been a war or a revolution for fifteen years; the UN has been settling problems that would once have resulted in a world war; Russia and the U.S. are still armed but are not nearly as close to conflict as they were when I was born. Perhaps . . . ?

"Do you know, I bet you've never seen an Earthman in the flesh before. Perhaps you've never seen a picture of one, or if you did, they were clothed. There are no photos of Earth people in these books. Maybe you knew we were male and female, but that didn't mean much until you saw me taking a shower. And the suddenly revealed parallel between the male dekaped and myself horrified you. And you realized that this was the only thing in the world that you had for companionship. Almost as if I'd been shipwrecked on an island and found the other inhabitant was a tiger.

"But that doesn't explain what you are doing here, alone, living in these tubes among the indigenous Martians. Oh, how I wish I could talk to you!

"*With thee conversing,*" he said, remembering those lines he had read the last night in the base.

She smiled at him, and he said, "Well, at least you're getting over your scare. I'm not such a bad fellow, after all, heh?"

She smiled again and went to a cabinet and from it took paper and pen. With them, she made one simple sketch after another. Watching her agile pen, he began to see what had happened.

Her people had had a base for a long time—a long long time— on the side of the Moon the Terrestrials could not see. But when rockets from Earth had first penetrated into space, her people had obliterated all evidences of the base. A new one had been set up on Mars.

Then, as it became apparent that a Terrestrial expedition would be sent to Mars, that base had been destroyed and another one set up on Ganymede.

However, five scientists had remained behind in these simple quarters to complete their studies of the dekapeds. Though Martia's people had studied these creatures for some time, they still had not found out how their bodies could endure the differences between tube pressure and that in the open air. The four believed that they were breathing hot on the neck of this secret and had gotten permission to stay until just before the Earthmen landed.

Martia actually was a native, in the sense that she had been born and raised here. She had been seven years here, she indicated, showing a sketch of Mars in its orbit around the sun and then holding up seven fingers.

That made her about fourteen Earth years old, Lane estimated. Perhaps these people reached maturity a little faster than his. That is, if she were mature. It was difficult to tell.

Horror twisted her face and widened her eyes as she showed him what had happened the night before they were to leave for Ganymede.

The sleeping party had been attacked by an uncaged male legger.

It was rare that a male got loose. But he occasionally managed to escape. When he did, he destroyed the entire colony, all life in the tube wherever he went. He even ate the roots of the trees so that they died, and oxygen ceased to flow into that section of the tunnel.

There was only one way a forewarned colony could fight a rogue male—a dangerous method. That was to release their own male. They selected the few who would stay behind and sacrifice their lives to dissolve the bars with an acid secretion from their bodies while the others fled. The queen, unable to move, also died. But enough of her eggs were taken to produce another queen and another consort elsewhere.

Meanwhile, it was hoped that the males would kill each other or that the victor would be so crippled that he could be finished off by the soldiers.

Lane nodded. The only natural enemy of the dekapeds was an escaped male. Left unchecked, they would soon crowd the tubes and exhaust food and air. Unkind as it seemed, the escape of a male now and then was the only thing that saved the Martians from starvation and perhaps extinction.

However that might be, the rogue had been no blessing in

disguise for Martia's people. Three had been killed in their sleep before the other two awoke. One had thrown herself at the beast and shouted to Martia to escape.

Almost insane with fear, Martia had nevertheless not allowed panic to send her running. Instead, she had dived for a cabinet to get a weapon.

—A weapon, thought Lane. I'll have to find out about that.

Martia acted out what had happened. She had gotten the cabinet door open and reached in for the weapon when she felt the beak of the rogue fastening on her leg. Despite the shock, for the beak cut deeply into the blood vessels and muscles, she managed to press the end of the weapon against the male's body. The weapon did its work, for the male dropped on the floor. Unfortunately, the beaks did not relax but held their terrible grip on her thigh, just above the knee.

Here Lane tried to interrupt so he could get a description of what the weapon looked like and of the principle of its operation. Martia, however, ignored his request. Seemingly, she did not understand his question, but he was sure that she did not care to reply. He was not entirely trusted, which was understandable. How could he blame her? She would be a fool to be at ease with such an unknown quantity as himself. That is, if he were unknown. After all, though she did not know him well personally, she knew the kind of people from whom he came and what could be expected from them. It was surprising that she had not left him to die in the garden, and it was amazing that she had shared that communion of bread and wine with him.

Perhaps, he thought, it is because she was so lonely and any company was better than nothing. Or it might be that he acted on a higher ethical plane than most Earthmen and she could not endure the idea of leaving a fellow sentient being to die, even if she thought him a bloodthirsty savage.

Or she might have other plans for him, such as taking him prisoner.

Martia continued her story. She had fainted and some time later had awakened. The male was beginning to stir, so she had killed him this time.

One more item of information, thought Lane. The weapon is capable of inflicting degrees of damage.

Then, though she kept passing out, she had dragged herself to the medicine chest and treated herself. Within two days she was up and hobbling around, and the scars were beginning to fade.

They must be far ahead of us in everything, he thought. According to her, some of her muscles had been cut. Yet they grew together in a day.

Martia indicated that the repair of her body had required an enormous amount of food during the healing. Most of her time had been spent in eating and sleeping. Reconstruction, even if it took place at a normal accelerated rate, still required the same amount of energy.

By then the bodies of the male and of her companions were stinking with decay. She had to force herself to cut them up and dispose of them in the garbage burner.

Tears welled in her eyes as she recounted this, and she sobbed.

Lane wanted to ask her why she had not buried them, but he reconsidered. Though it might not be the custom among her kind to bury the dead, it was more probable that she wanted to destroy all evidence of their existence before Earthmen came to Mars.

Using signs, he asked her how the male had gotten into the room despite the gate across the tunnel. She indicated that the gate was ordinarily closed only when the dekapeds were awake or when her companions and she were sleeping. But it had been the turn of one of their number to collect eggs in the queen's chamber. As she reconstructed it, the rogue had appeared at that time and killed the scientist there. Then, after ravening among the still-sleeping colony, it had gone down the tube and there had seen the light shining from the open tunnel. The rest of the story he knew.

Why, he pantomimed, why didn't the escaped male sleep when all his fellows did? The one in the cage evidently slept at the same time as his companions. And the queen's guards also slept in the belief they were safe from attack.

Not so, replied Martia. A male who had gotten out of a cage knew no law but fatigue. When he had exhausted himself in his eating and killing, he lay down to sleep. But it did not matter if it was the regular time for it or not. When he was rested, he raged through the tubes and did not stop until he was again too tired to move.

So then, thought Lane, that explains the area of dead umbrella plants on top of the tube by the garden. Another colony moved into the devastated area, built the garden on the outside, and planted the young umbrellas.

He wondered why neither he nor the others of his group had seen the dekapeds outside during their six days on Mars. There must be at least one pressure chamber and outlet for each colony, and there should be at least fifteen colonies in the tubes between this point and that near his base. Perhaps the answer was that the leaf-croppers only ventured out occasionally. Now that he remembered it, neither he nor anyone else had noticed any holes on the leaves. That meant that the trees must have been cropped some time ago and were now ready for another harvesting. If the expedition had only waited several days before sending out men in tracs, it might have seen the dekapeds and investigated. And the story would have been different.

There were other questions he had for her. What about the vessel that was to take them to Ganymede? Was there one hidden on the outside, or was one to be sent to pick them up? If one was to be sent, how would the Ganymedan base be contacted? Radio? Or some—to him—inconceivable method?

The blue globes! he thought. Could they be means of transmitting messages?

He did not know or think further about them because fatigue overwhelmed him, and he fell asleep. His last memory was that of Martia leaning over him and smiling at him.

When he awoke reluctantly, his muscles ached, and his mouth was as dry as the Martian desert. He rose in time to see Martia drop out of the tunnel, a bucket of eggs in her hand. Seeing this, he groaned. That meant she had gone into the nursery again, and that he had slept the clock around.

He stumbled up and into the shower cubicle. Coming out much

refreshed, he found breakfast hot on the table. Martia conducted the communion rite, and then they ate. He missed his coffee. The hot soup was good but did not make a satisfactory substitute. There was a bowl of mixed cereal and fruit, both of which came out of a can. It must have had a high energy content, for it made him wide awake.

Afterward, he did some setting-up exercises while she did the dishes. Though he kept his body busy, he was thinking of things unconnected with what he was doing.

What was to be his next move?

His duty demanded that he return to the base and report. What news he would send to the orbital ship! The story would flash from the ship back to Earth. The whole planet would be in an uproar.

There was one objection to his plan to take Martia back with him.

She would not want to go.

Halfway in a deep knee bend, he stopped. What a fool he was! He had been too tired and confused to see it. But if she had revealed that the base of her people was on Ganymede, she did not expect him to take the information back to his transmitter. It would be foolish on her part to tell him unless she were absolutely certain that he would be able to communicate with no one.

That must mean that a vessel was on its way and would arrive soon. And it would not only take her but him. If he was to be killed, he would be dead now.

Lane had not been chosen to be a member of the first Mars expedition because he lacked decision. Five minutes later, he had made up his mind. His duty was clear. Therefore, he would carry it out, even if it violated his personal feelings toward Martia and caused her injury.

First, he'd bind her. Then he would pack up their two pressure suits, the books, and any tools small enough to carry so they might later be examined on Earth. He would make her march ahead of him through the tube until they came to the point opposite his base. There they would don their suits and go to the dome. And as soon as possible the two would rise on the rocket to the orbital ship. This step was the most hazardous, for it was extremely difficult for one man to pilot the rocket. Theoretically, it could be done. It had to be done.

Lane tightened his jaw and forced his muscles to quit quivering. The thought of violating Martia's hospitality upset him. Still, she had treated him so well for a purpose not altogether altruistic. For all he knew, she was plotting against him.

There was a rope in one of the cabinets, the same flexible rope with which she had pulled him from the mire. He opened the door of the cabinet and removed it. Martia stood in the middle of the room and watched him while she stroked the head of the blue-eyed worm coiled about her shoulders. He hoped she would stay there until he got close. Obviously, she carried no weapon on her nor indeed anything except the pet. Since she had removed her suit, she had worn nothing.

Seeing him approaching her, she spoke to him in an alarmed tone. It didn't take much sensitivity to know that she was asking him what he intended to do with the rope. He tried to smile reassuringly at her and failed. This was making him sick.

A moment later, he was violently sick. Martia had spoken loudly one word, and it was as if it had struck him in the pit of his stomach. Nausea gripped him, his mouth began salivating, and it was only by dropping the rope and running into the shower that he avoided making a mess on the floor.

Ten minutes later, he felt thoroughly cleaned out. But when he tried to walk to the bed, his legs threatened to give way. Martia had to support him.

Inwardly, he cursed. To have a sudden reaction to the strange food at such a crucial moment! Luck was not on his side.

That is, if it was chance. There had been something so strange and forceful about the manner in which she pronounced that word. Was it possible that she had set up in him—hypnotically or otherwise—a reflex to that word? It would, under the conditions, be a weapon more powerful than a gun.

He wasn't sure, but it did seem strange that his body had

accepted the alien food until that moment. Hypnotism did not really seem to be the answer. How could it be so easily used on him since he did not know more than twenty words of her language?

Language? Words? They weren't necessary. If she had given him a hypnotic drug in his food, and then had awakened him during his sleep, she could have dramatized how he was to react if she wanted him to do so. She could have given him the key word, then have allowed him to go to sleep again.

He knew enough hypnotism to know that that was possible. Whether his suspicions were true or not, it was a fact that he had laid flat on his back. However, the day was not wasted. He learned twenty more words, and she drew many more sketches for him. He found out that when he had jumped into the mire of the garden he had literally fallen into the soup. The substance in which the young umbrella trees had been planted was a zoogloea, a glutinous mass of one-celled vegetables and somewhat larger anaerobic animal life that fed on the vegetables. The heat from the jam-packed water-swollen bodies kept the garden soil warm and prevented the tender plants from freezing even during the forty degrees below zero Fahrenheit of the midsummer nights.

After the trees were transplanted into the roof of the tube to replace the dead adults, the zoogloea would be taken piecemeal back to the tube and dumped into the channel. Here the jetfish would strain out part and eat part as they pumped water from the polar end of the tube to the equatorial end.

Toward the end of the day, he tried some of the zoogloea soup and managed to keep it down. A little later, he ate some cereal.

Martia insisted on spooning the food for him. There was something so feminine and tender about her solicitude that he could not protest.

"Martia," he said, "I may be wrong. There can be good will and rapport between our two kinds. Look at us. Why, if you were a real woman, I'd be in love with you.

"Of course, you may have made me sick in the first place. But if you did, it was a matter of expediency, not malice. And now you are taking care of me, your enemy. Love thy enemy. Not because you have been told you should but because you do."

She, of course, did not understand him. However, she replied in her own tongue, and it seemed to him that her voice had the same sense of sympático.

As he fell asleep, he was thinking that perhaps Martia and he would be the two ambassadors to bring their people together in peace. After all, both of them were highly civilized, essentially pacifistic, and devoutly religious. There was such a thing as the brotherhood, not only of man, but of all sentient beings throughout the cosmos, and . . .

Pressure on his bladder woke him up. He opened his eyes. The ceiling and walls expanded and contracted. His wristwatch was distorted. Only by extreme effort could he focus his eyes enough to straighten the arms on his watch. The piece, designed to measure the slightly longer Martian day, indicated midnight.

Groggily, he rose. He felt sure that he must have been drugged and that he would still be sleeping if the bladder pain hadn't been so sharp. If ony he could take something to counteract the drug, he could carry out his plans now. But first he had to get to the toilet.

To do so, he had to pass close to Martia's bed. She did not move but lay on her back, her arms flung out and hanging over the sides of the bed, her mouth open wide.

He looked away, for it seemed indecent to watch when she was in such a position.

But something caught his eye—a movement, a flash of light like a gleaming jewel in her mouth.

He bent over her, looked, and recoiled in horror.

A head rose from between her teeth.

He raised his hand to snatch at the thing but froze in the posture as he recognized the tiny pouting round mouth and little blue eyes. It was the worm.

At first, he thought Martia was dead. The thing was not coiled in her mouth. Its body disappeared into her throat.

Then he saw her chest was rising easily and that she seemed to be in no difficulty.

Forcing himself to come close to the worm, though his stomach muscles writhed and his neck muscles quivered, he put his hand close to its lips.

Warm air touched his fingers, and he heard a faint whistling.

Martia was breathing through it!

Hoarsely, he said, "God!" and he shook her shoulder. He did not want to touch the worm because he was afraid that it might do something to injure her. In that moment of shock he had forgotten that he had an advantage over her, which he should use.

Martia's lids opened; her large gray-blue eyes stared blankly.

"Take it easy," he said soothingly.

She shuddered. Her lids closed, her neck arched back, and her face contorted.

He could not tell if the grimace was caused by pain or something else.

"What is this—this monster?" he said. "Symbiote? Parasite?"

He thought of vampires, of worms creeping into one's sleeping body and there sucking blood.

Suddenly, she sat up and held out her arms to him. He seized her hands, saying, "What is it?"

Martia pulled him toward her, at the same time lifting her face to his.

Out of her open mouth shot the worm, its head pointed toward his face, its little lips formed into an O.

It was reflex, the reflex of fear that made Lane drop her hands and spring back. He had not wanted to do that, but he could not help himself.

Abruptly, Martia came wide awake. The worm flopped its full length from her mouth and fell into a heap between her legs. There it thrashed for a moment before coiling itself like a snake, its head resting on Martia's thigh, its eyes turned upward to Lane.

There was no doubt about it. Martia looked disappointed, frustrated.

Lane's knees, already weak, gave way. However, he managed to continue to his destination. When he came out, he walked as far as Martia's bed, where he had to sit down. His heart was thudding against his ribs, and he was panting hard.

He sat behind her, for he did not want to be where the worm could touch him.

Martia made motions for him to go back to his bed and they would all sleep. Evidently, he thought, she found nothing alarming in the incident.

But he knew he could not rest until he had some kind of explanation. He handed her paper and pen from the bedside table and then gestured fiercely. Martia shrugged and began sketching while Lane watched over her shoulder. By the time she had used up five sheets of paper, she had communicated her message.

His eyes were wide, and he was even paler.

So—Martia *was* a female. Female at least in the sense that she carried eggs—and, at times, young—within her.

And there was the so-called worm. So called? What could he call it? It could not be designated under one category. It was many things in one. It was a larva. It was a phallus. It was also her offspring, of her flesh and blood.

But not of her genes. It was not descended from her.

She had given birth to it, yet she was not its mother. She was neither one of its mothers.

The dizziness and confusion he felt was not caused altogether by his sickness. Things were coming too fast. He was thinking furiously, trying to get this new information clear, but his thoughts kept going back and forth, getting nowhere.

"There's no reason to get upset," he told himself. "After all, the splitting of animals into two sexes is only one of the ways of reproduction tried on Earth. On Martia's planet Nature—God—has fashioned another method for the higher animals. And only He knows how many other designs for reproduction He has fashioned on how many other worlds."

Nevertheless, he was upset.

This worm, no, this larva, this embryo outside its egg and its secondary mother . . . well, call it, once and for all, larva, because it did metamorphose later.

This particular larva was doomed to stay in its present form until it died of old age.

Unless Martia found another adult of the Eeltau.

And unless she and this other adult felt affection for each other.

Then, according to the sketch she'd drawn, Martia and her friend, or lover, would lie down or sit together. They would, as lovers do on Earth, speak to each other in endearing, flattering, and exciting terms. They would caress and kiss much as Terrestrial man and woman do, though on Earth it was not considered complimentary to call one's lover Big Mouth.

Then, unlike the Terran custom, a third would enter the union to form a highly desired and indeed indispensable and eternal triangle.

The larva, blindly, brainlessly obeying its instincts, aroused by mutual fondling by the two, would descend tail first into the throat of one of the two Eeltau. Inside the body of the lover a fleshy valve would open to admit the slim body of the larva. Its open tip would touch the ovary of the host. The larva, like an electric eel, would release a tiny current. The hostess would go into an ecstasy, its nerves stimulate electrochemically. The ovary would release an egg no larger than a pencil dot. It would disappear into the open tip of the larva's tail, there to begin a journey up a canal toward the center of its body, urged on by the contraction of muscle and whipping of cilia.

Then the larva slid out of the first hostess's mouth and went tail first into the other, there to repeat the process. Sometimes the larva garnered eggs, sometimes not, depending upon whether the ovary had a fully developed one to release.

When the process was successful, the two eggs moved toward each other but did not quite meet.

Not yet.

There must be other eggs collected in the dark incubator of the larva, collected by pairs, though not necessarily from the same couple of donors.

These would number anywhere from twenty to forty pairs.

Then, one day, the mysterious chemistry of the cells would tell the larva's body that it had gathered enough eggs.

A hormone was released, the metamorphosis begun. The larva swelled enormously, and the mother, seeing this, placed it tenderly in a warm place and fed it plenty of predigested food and sugar water.

Before the eyes of its mother, the larva then grew shorter and wider. Its tail contracted; its cartilaginous vertebrae, widely separated in its larval stage, shifted closer to each other and hardened, a skeleton formed, ribs, shoulders. Legs and arms budded and grew and took humanoid shape. Six months passed, and there lay in its crib something resembling a baby of *Homo sapiens*.

From then until its fourteenth year, the Eeltau grew and developed much as its Terran counterpart.

Adulthood, however, initiated more strange changes. Hormone released hormone until the first pair of gametes, dormant these fourteen years, moved together.

The two fused, the chromatin of one uniting with the chromatin of the other. Out of the two—a single creature, wormlike, four inches long, was released into the stomach of its hostess.

Then, nausea. Vomiting. And so, comparatively painlessly, the bringing forth of a genetically new being.

It was this worm that would be both fetus and phallus and would give ecstasy and draw into its own body the eggs of loving adults and would metamorphose and become infant, child, and adult.

And so on and so on.

He rose and shakily walked to his own bed. There he sat down, his head bowed, while he muttered to himself.

"Let's see now. Martia gave birth to, brought forth, or up, this larva. But the larva actually doesn't have any of Martia's genes. Martia was iust the hostess for it

"However, if Martia has a lover, she will, by means of this worm, pass on her heritable qualities. This worm will become an adult and bring forth, or up, Martia's child."

He raised his hands in despair.

"How do the Eeltau reckon ancestry? How keep track of their relatives? Or do they care? Wouldn't it be easier to consider your foster mother, your hostess, your real mother? As, in the sense of having borne you, she is?

"And what kind of sexual code do these people have? It can't, I would think, be much like ours. Nor is there any reason why it should be.

"But who is responsible for raising the larva and child? Its pseudo-mother? Or does the lover share in the duties? And what about property and inheritance laws? And, and . . ."

Helplessly, he looked at Martia.

Fondly stroking the head of the larva, she returned his stare.

Lane shook his head.

"I was wrong. Eeltau and Terran couldn't meet on a friendly basis. My people would react to yours as to disgusting vermin. Their deepest prejudices would be aroused, their strongest taboos would be violated. They could not learn to live with you or consider you even faintly human.

"And as far as that goes, could you live with us? Wasn't the sight of me naked a shock? Is that reaction a part of why you don't make contact with us?"

Martia put the larva down and stood up and walked over to him and kissed the tips of his fingers. Lane, though he had to fight against visibly flinching, took her fingers and kissed them. Softly, he said to her, "Yet . . . individuals could learn to respect each other, to have affection for each other. And masses are made of individuals."

He lay back on the bed. The grogginess, pushed aside for a while by excitement, was coming back. He couldn't fight off sleep much longer.

"Fine noble talk," he murmured. "But it means nothing.

Eeltau don't think they should deal with us. And we are, un-knowingly, pushing out toward them. What will happen when we are ready to make the interstellar jump? War? Or will they be afraid to let us advance even to that point and destroy us before then? After all, one cobalt bomb . . ."

He looked again at Martia, at the not-quite-human yet beauti-ful face, the smooth skin of the chest, abdomen, and loins, inno-cent of nipple, navel, or labia. From far off she had come, from a possibly terrifying place across terrifying distances. About her, however, there was little that was terrifying and much that was warm, generous, companionable, attractive.

As if they had waited for some key to turn, and the key had been turned, the lines he had read before falling asleep the last night in the base came again to him.

> *It is the voice of my beloved that knocketh, saying,*
> *Open to me, my sister, my love, my dove,*
> *   my undefiled . . .*

> *We have a little sister,*
> *And she hath no breasts:*
> *What shall we do for our sister*
> *In the day when she shall be spoken for?*

> *With thee conversing, I forget all time,*
> *All seasons, and their change, all please alike.*

"*With thee conversing,*" he said aloud. He turned over so his back was to her, and he pounded his fist against the bed.

"Oh dear God, why couldn't it be so?"

A long time he lay there, his face pressed into the mattress. Something had happened; the overpowering fatigue was gone; his body had drawn strength from some reservoir. Realizing this, he sat up and beckoned to Martia, smiling at the same time.

She rose slowly and started to walk to him, but he signaled that she should bring the larva with her. At first, she looked puzzled. Then her expression cleared, to be replaced by understanding. Smiling delightedly, she walked to him, and though he knew it must be a trick of his imagination, it seemed to him that she swayed her hips as a woman would.

She halted in front of him and then stooped to kiss him full on the lips. Her eyes were closed.

He hesitated for a fraction of a second. She—no, it, he told himself—looked so trusting, so loving, so womanly, that he could not do it.

"For Earth!" he said fiercely and brought the edge of his palm hard against the side of her neck.

She crumpled forward against him, her face sliding into his chest. Lane caught her under the armpits and laid her facedown on the bed. The larva, which had fallen from her hand onto the floor, was writhing about as if hurt. Lane picked it up by its tail and, in a frenzy that owed its violence to the fear he might not be able to do it, snapped it like a whip. There was a crack as the head smashed into the floor and blood spurted from its eyes and mouth. Lane placed his heel on the head and stepped down until there was a flat mess beneath his foot.

Then, quickly, before she could come to her senses and speak any words that would render him sick and weak, he ran to a cabinet. Snatching a narrow towel out ot it, he ran back and gagged her. After that he tied her hands behind her back with the rope.

"Now, you bitch!" he panted. "We'll see who comes out ahead! You would do that with me, would you! You deserve this; your monster deserves to die!"

Furiously he began packing. In fifteen mintues he had the suits, helmets, tanks, and food rolled into two bundles. He searched for the weapon she had talked about and found something that might conceivably be it. It had a butt that fitted to his hand, a dial that might be a rheostat for controlling degrees of intensity of whatever it shot, and a bulb at the end. The bulb, he hoped, expelled the stunning and killing energy. Of course, he might be wrong. It could be fashioned for an entirely different purpose.

Martia had regained consciousness. She sat on the edge of the bed, her shoulders hunched, her head drooping, tears running down her cheeks and into the towel around her mouth. Her wide eyes were focused on the smashed worm by her feet.

Roughly, Lane seized her shoulder and pulled her upright. She gazed wildly at him, and he gave her a little shove. He felt sick within him, knowing that he had killed the larva when he did not have to do so and that he was handling her so violently because he was afraid, not of her, but of himself. If he had been disgusted because she had fallen into the trap he set for her, he was so because he, too, beneath his disgust, had wanted to commit that act of love. Commit, he thought, was the right word. It contained criminal implications.

Martia whirled around, almost losing her balance because of her tied hands. Her face worked, and sounds burst from the gag.

"Shut up!" he howled, pushing her again. She went sprawling and only saved herself from falling on her face by dropping on her knees. Once more, he pulled her to her feet, noting as he did so that her knees were skinned. The sight of the blood, instead of softening him, enraged him even more.

"Behave yourself, or you'll get worse!" he snarled.

She gave him one more questioning look, threw back her head, and made a strange strangling sound. Immediately, her face took on a bluish tinge. A second later, she fell heavily on the floor.

Alarmed, he turned her over. She was choking to death.

He tore off the gag and reached into her mouth and grabbed the root of her tongue. It slipped away and he seized it again, only to have it slide away as if it were a live animal that defied him.

Then he had pulled her tongue out of her throat; she had swallowed it in an effort to kill herself.

Lane waited. When he was sure she was going to recover, he replaced the gag around her mouth. Just as he was about to tie the knot at the back of her neck, he stopped. What use would it be to continue this? If allowed to speak, she would say the word that would throw him into retching. If gagged, she would swallow her tongue again.

He could save her only so many times. Eventually, she would succeed in strangling herself.

The one way to solve his problem was the one way he could not take. If her tongue were cut off at the root, she could neither speak nor kill herself. Some men might do it; he could not.

The other way to keep her silent was to kill her.

"I can't do it in cold blood," he said aloud. "So, if you want to die, Martia, then you must do it by committing suicide. That, I can't help. Up you go. I'll get your pack, and we'll leave."

Martia turned blue and sagged to the floor.

"I'll not help you this time!" he shouted, but he found himself frantically trying to undo the knot.

At the same time, he told himself what a fool he was. Of course! The solution was to use her own gun on her. Turn the rheostat to a stunning degree of intensity and knock her out whenever she started to regain consciousness. Such a course would mean he'd have to carry her and her equipment, too, on the thirty-mile walk down the tube to an exit near his base. But he could do it. He'd rig up some sort of travois. He'd do it! Nothing could stop him. And Earth . . .

At that moment, hearing an unfamiliar noise, he looked up. There were two Eeltau in pressure suits standing there, and another crawling out of the tunnel. Each had a bulb-tipped handgun in her hand.

Desperately, Lane snatched at the weapon he carried in his belt. With his left hand he twisted the rheostat on the side of the barrel, hoping that this would turn it on full force. Then he raised the bulb toward the group . . .

He woke flat on his back, clad in his suit, except for the helmet, and strapped to a stretcher. His body was helpless, but he could turn his head. He did so, and saw many Eeltau dismantling the room. The one who had stunned him with her gun before he could fire was standing by him.

She spoke in English that held only a trace of foreign accent. "Settle down, Mr. Lane. You're in for a long ride. You'll be more comfortably situated once we're in our ship."

He opened his mouth to ask her how she knew his name but closed it when he realized she must have read the entries in the log at the base. And it was to be expected that some Eeltau would be trained in Earth languages. For over a century their sentinel spaceships had been tuning in to radio and TV.

It was then that Martia spoke to the captain. Her face was wild and reddened with weeping and marks where she had fallen.

The interpreter said to Lane, "*Mahrseeya* asks you to tell her why you killed her . . . baby. She cannot understand why you thought you had to do so."

"I cannot answer," said Lane. His head felt very light, almost as if it were a balloon expanding. And the room began slowly to turn around.

"I will tell her why," answered the interpreter. "I will tell her that it is the nature of the beast."

"That is not so!" cried Lane. "I am no vicious beast. I did what I did because I had to! I could not accept her love and still remain a man! Not the kind of man . . ."

"*Mahrseeya*," said the interpreter, "will pray that you be forgiven the murder of her child and that you will someday, under our teaching, be unable to do such a thing. She herself, though she is stricken with grief for her dead baby, forgives you. She hopes the time will come when you will regard her as a—sister. She thinks there is some good in you."

Lane clenched his teeth together and bit the end of his tongue until it bled while they put his helmet on. He did not dare to try to talk, for that would have meant he would scream and scream. He felt as if something had been planted in him and had broken its shell and was growing into something like a worm. It was eating him, and what would happen before it devoured all of him he did not know.

T HE BIOLOGISTS WAS showing the distinguished visitor through the zoo and laboratory.

"Our budget," he said, "is too limited to re-create all known extinct species. So we bring to life only the higher animals, the beautiful ones that were wantonly exterminated. I'm trying, as it were, to make up for brutality and stupidity. You might say that man struck God in the face every time he wiped out a branch of the animal kingdom."

He paused, and they looked across the moats and the force fields. The quagga wheeled and galloped, delight and sun flashing off his flanks. The sea otter poked his humorous whiskers from the water. The gorilla peered from behind bamboo. Passenger pigeons strutted. A rhinoceros trotted like a dainty battleship. With gentle eyes a giraffe looked at them, then resumed eating leaves.

"There's the dodo. Not beautiful but very droll. And very helpless. Come, I'll show you the re-creation itself."

In the great building, they passed between rows of tall and wide tanks. They could see clearly through the windows and the jelly within.

"Those are African Elephant embryos," said the biologist. "We plan to grow a large herd and then release them on the new government preserve."

"You positively radiate," said the distinguished visitor. "You really love the animals, don't you?"

"I love all life."

"Tell me," said the visitor, "where do you get the data for recreation?"

"Mostly, skeletons and skins from the ancient museums. Excavated books and films that we succeeded in restoring and then translating. Ah, see those huge eggs? The chicks of the giant moa are growing within them. There, almost ready to be taken from the tank, are tiger cubs. They'll be dangerous when grown but will be confined to the preserve."

The visitor stopped before the last of the tanks.

"Just one?" he said. "What is it?"

"Poor little thing," said the biologist, now sad. "It will be so alone. But I shall give it all the love I have."

"Is it so dangerous?" said the visitor. "Worse than elephants, tigers, and bears?"

"I had to get special permission to grow this one," said the biologist. His voice quavered.

The visitor stepped sharply back from the tank. He said, "Then it must be . . . But you wouldn't dare!"

The biologist nodded.

"Yes. It's a man."